This book should be returned to any branch of the
Lancashire County Library on or before the date

NMo

2 6 MAR 2016

1 7 NOV 2016

- 5 JUN 2018

1 3 JUL 2018

1 5 OCT 2018

2 5 OCT 2018

1 0 SEP 2019

Lancashire County Library
Bowran Street
Preston PR1 2UX

Lancashire
County Council

www.lancashire.gov.uk/libraries

THE VISITORS
Patrick O'Keeffe

BLOOMSBURY

LONDON · NEW DELHI · NEW YORK · SYDNEY

First published in Great Britain 2014

Copyright © 2014 by Patrick O'Keeffe

Bloomsbury Circus is an imprint of Bloomsbury Publishing Plc
50 Bedford Square
London
WC1B 3DP

www.bloomsbury.com

Bloomsbury is a trademark of Bloomsbury Publishing Plc

Bloomsbury Publishing, London, New Delhi, New York and Sydney

A CIP catalogue record for this book is available from the British Library

ISBN 978 1 4088 5080 0

10 9 8 7 6 5 4 3 2 1

Printed and bound in Great Britain by CPI Group (UK) Ltd, Croydon CR0 4YY

To Tom and Kathy Zeller

Part One

Seven years ago, near the end of July 2000, was the first time he appeared at the screen door. Two weeks earlier I passed him on a sidewalk three streets over, and the week before, he was sitting beside the homeless on their bench outside the post office, and two nights before, I saw him on Main Street. A street festival was ending. I was out for a walk. He was staring into a brimming trash can, and his face was close to its mouth.

That one-room flat on West Washington Street was an overhauled garage that jutted out the back of an old brick house. There were three bigger apartments in front, but I had my own door. Outside it was a small yard, evergreens at the back, maples on both sides, and during the summer months I kept my door open and the screen door hooked until bedtime.

It was around ten. Wednesday night. The window above the futon bed was open, and I heard footsteps on the gravel. I was sitting in the armchair, the music was on, and I stood quickly, turned it down, and glanced about for anything unsightly. Then I stood at the screen door and switched the outside light on.

—An old lady lying in the middle of your street, he said.

He was lanky, about four inches taller than me, and somewhere in his fifties. A few top teeth were gone. His face was speckled and sunburned, and he wore a baseball cap. I knew enough about the game to know that the team with the feathers is the Cleveland Indians.

I stepped back from the screen door.

—In the middle of the street, he said.

He pressed his hands flat against the screen. The frame creaked. A moth spun around his cap.

—In front of your building, he said.

Then he turned and ran.

A few minutes later I was standing under the maple whose roots had cracked the sidewalk. He was a few feet away. No old woman was lying in the street.

—So, right there, man, I said, and nodded at the street.

—Seen her, man. Coming back from the park, he said.

Before me two new Hondas were parked, like every other night. Across the street shades and curtains were drawn and porches were dark.

—Wearing white sneakers and a bathrobe, he said. —Got down and asked if she was okay. Said she needed to get up or a car would smash her. Old lady's eyes were closed. She said nothing.

I didn't say a word, nor look at him, when I crossed the street to the other footpath and looked up and down, with my back to him and the street. An elderly woman lived in a white two-story near the corner. In the evenings she sat on her porch, on a white plastic chair with a red cushion. She rested her feet on an old wooden soda crate and watched the street traffic and the fit young couples strolling the sidewalk, pushing their baby or two in pricey strollers. I walked down the footpath and crossed over, but right before I reached her house I was stalled by a dark stream shining across the footpath and vanishing down a gully. I thought that stream was blood red, though seconds later I was standing in the clearest water and listening to the seductive hiss of a sprinkler.

Earlier I'd smoked weed. And I was drinking red wine. The weed I got from a young mother at the bakery where I worked five or six mornings a week. My shift ended around noon, and when classes were in session, I drove to my apartment, washed, changed clothes, and walked to campus. That car was a rusted-out blue two-door Toyota

Tercel hatchback. It had a FREE TIBET sticker on the back bumper. I'd purchased the car very cheaply from a thirty-four-year-old graduate student whose parents had bought him a new one as a lure to finish the dissertation he'd been working on for eight years. Before the Tercel, I had a 1972 Chevrolet Camaro. My friend Brendan and I drove it from Boston to this university town in Michigan.

The old woman's house was in darkness. In her yard, like in others, were a few election posters. Her white plastic chair shone in the light from a streetlamp. The cushion was gone, but the crate was there. On the walk back, I knelt and looked underneath a few cars and petted one of the neighborhood cats. I was feeling good. Weed and wine, of course, a warm July night, maples in full leaf, the trill of the cicadas, and I dallied, hoping the stranger would have vanished, but there I was, standing in the street before him, staring up at the sunburned face lit by a streetlight. His shirt was buttoned to the neck. The sleeves covered his hands, and the unbuttoned cuffs flopped like Beethoven's. A shabby-looking backpack rested upon his left foot.

—Old lady, she was right there, he said.

He pointed to the street. I half-turned from him.

—I don't doubt that she was, I said.

—Looked in the front of your building, but no light, so walked down the driveway and saw your light back there.

I turned to him. He buttoned his cuffs and undid his neck button. I didn't say that one of the couples in front was hiking through Thailand for the summer and the other was on vacation, in a monastery, in Japan.

—You don't believe me, man, he said.

—Yes, I do, man, I said.

—She was lying there, he said.

—I know very well she was, I said.

—You don't believe me, man—

—I don't care if you believe me or not, man, I said. —I'll make you some coffee.

—Coffee's good, he immediately said.

I stepped onto the short graveled driveway. He picked up the backpack, hooked it over his left shoulder, and followed me.

—Not too late for you, he said.

—I don't have to work in the morning, I said.

He asked the time. I told him. I asked his name.

—Walter, he said.

I turned and shook his hand.

—James, I said, and he shook my hand.

—Thanks, man, he said.

—It's fine, man, I said.

I pointed to one of the three chairs and asked him to sit. I turned the music back up, started the coffee then poured myself some wine, and when I sat in the armchair, I pushed books aside on the small table to make room for the glass. I inquired if cheap South American wine was to his liking. He said no. And so I offered him a cigarette.

—Grateful, he said.

I lit one, passed him one and the lighter, and asked if he'd like some toast.

—Grateful, he said.

I dropped the bread in the toaster and pulled a saucer from the pile in the sink, wiped it clean, handed it to him, and told him to use it as an ashtray. The smell of brewing coffee filled that small room. Smoke clouded the lampshades. At the ceiling layers of smoke shifted like lazy ocean waves.

I asked him where he was from. Florida. I asked if his parents were from there. Mom from Greenville. Dad from Rockford, Illinois. I told him I'd never been to Florida, but I think I'd passed signs for Rockford once. I was with a friend, I said, we were driving to Chicago, we'd lost our way, but then beyond the trees and the buildings the beautiful lake appeared.

—It rose up and flashed like a monster, I added.

He told me that when he was eight his mom moved to Chicago, but

he stayed on in Florida with his aunt. Then his mom moved to Flag-
staff, Arizona. I told him that ever since I was a kid, I had dreamed of
visiting the desert and the mountains, though when I did a few years
ago, they looked so familiar, maybe because I'd seen them so much on
television and in movies. And I asked where his parents were now.

—Passed on, he said.

I buttered his toast and took a plate from the sink and washed it. I
laid the plate of toast and the coffee on the floor beside him. I was
blinking into the fridge when I asked if he needed milk.

—Not necessary, man, he said.

Which was good to hear. The fridge was empty except for two
sticks of butter and an empty water jug.

He held the plate underneath his chin and took tiny bites. We didn't
talk for fifteen or twenty minutes. I changed the music, sat down,
picked up a book from the table, and read sentences, a few being all I
could manage. And so I stood and added wine to the glass, crossed the
room to the screen door and lit another cigarette, blew smoke into the
dark, and hummed along to the music. I flicked the outside light on.
The moths appeared. I flicked the light off. When he was done eating I
sat back down.

He smelled like dry rotting wood. And the shirt he wore was faded
blue, Western-style, Sears or Levi's from the sixties or seventies, with
that fine stitching around the collar and the chest pockets. I had two
like them. Una Lyons got them in a hand-me-down shop, on Francis
Street in Dublin. It was my seventeenth or eighteenth birthday. She and
I said the shirts looked ugly, but we also said they were cool.

He sipped the coffee and gazed about that room: the two low bookcases the previous tenant had left, the futon bed that was my own, the
desk I had bought from a fellow graduate student in English who'd
enrolled in law school in another state, and on the small rug between
us, a stack of used books with dog-eared pages.

He told me he read the newspaper every day in the library. I said I
read the Sunday newspaper, but I listened to music more than I read,

which wasn't good for my studies, which were moving at a snail's pace, but I told him the university paid me something for teaching writing to first-year students, and I had a job at a bakery.

And he told me he didn't have any way to listen to music outside of the library, though when he was alone in the park he'd recollect a song, block out the world, and fully hear the song in his head. He liked the Grateful Dead and Jimi Hendrix. I said I liked them, too, but that blocking out the world was a bit of a task. He shrugged and asked what books I'd read when I was a kid. I said there were a few I took out of the school library more than once, but the one I borrowed the most was *Robinson Crusoe*.

—It ends in a slapdash way, Friday is a lie, but then there was nothing like it, I said.

He yawned and rested his head on the back of the chair. He folded his arms and slowly stretched his legs. Above him a cobweb dangled from the low ceiling. I asked if he'd like another cigarette. He didn't reply, and it worried me that he might fall asleep, but then he startled me by jerking up his right hand and slowly massaging his jaw. He said he'd slept on concrete the night before. I asked why he didn't sleep in the shelter out on Huron. He said the people there made him crazy, and he sat upright and stared at me.

—You're not from here, man. How do you end up here, man?

I stood and switched the music off.

—Hear! Hear, man! I said, and laughed. —I ended up here the way you ended up at my screen door over an hour ago. Or I ended up here with the friend I drove to Chicago with. A good few years ago, we arrived from Boston, but my friend went back home. He got tired of it. Homesick, I suppose. But I wanted to stay. I like it here fine.

And so I told him I once lived on the next street over, that I lived there for a time with the woman who showed me the desert. I think I told him her name was Sarah, and I definitely told him she wrote her dissertation on urban gangs, and that she and I put the kibosh on things a while back.

—She wanted to move back west. The west, where she was from, I said.

I was staring down at the pile in the sink.

I drained the wine bottle and sat down.

—Wine and pot, man. Both should be illegal, I said. —But that woman hasn't left my head all night.

—Woman out west, he said.

—She's never in the head, I said. —The one you saw lying in the street. I should have called the police, but who wants to invite the cops—

—She just got up and went on home. Folks change their minds, he said.

—Indeed, they do, very wise, I said.

He took his cap off and ran his fingers through his graying, stubborn hair.

—Told the truth, man, he said.

He fixed the cap back on.

—I don't doubt you, man, I said. —An old woman lives down the street, that's all, but I've never really spoken to her and I don't see her that much.

2

Around noon the next day, I opened out the door and hooked the screen. I sat in the chair, drank coffee, and picked up a book. Five minutes later I stood in the doorway and shook out the rug and the cushion he'd sat on. I turned my face away from the dust and shouted at the squirrels. The traffic along Huron murmured in the evergreens. I dropped the rug into place, put the stack of books on it, swept the floor, emptied the ashtray, and while I was doing all that, I kept seeing the old woman lying in the dark street in her bathrobe. And I was seeing cars tearing down the street. Then his burned face at the screen door. But he was lying. I felt sure of it.

An hour later I was standing on the sidewalk in front of her house. The chair and crate were still there. Vines circled her porch railings. Their white blossoms resembled crushed trumpets, and lazy bees floated around them. I stepped onto her bottom step, and it took me five minutes to get the balls to mount the other steps, cross the porch, and knock on her door. The second time, I knocked louder. And before I left her porch to walk down the driveway, I lifted the flap and looked into her empty mailbox. In the middle of the backyard were two rusted iron chairs underneath a weeping willow. At the back were the same patchy evergreens that grew behind my place. Cardinals and blue jays screeched at two swinging, empty feeders. I went up the flagstone path that led to her screened-in porch, which was cluttered with magazines and newspapers, and had a big metal office desk covered with stacks of paperback books. I stood back and stared up at two windows. The one on the right was open and a yellow curtain was blowing out, like a fan was going inside. I shouted hello into the air a few times. On my way back up the driveway, I found a fifty-dollar bill. I shoved it into my arse pocket. A few minutes later I was wandering the aisles of the supermarket. And at the liquor store I bought a big bottle of Chilean wine, cigarettes, and a six-pack of American beer.

Around half-eight that evening, the light in the room turned gloomy, and the leaves rattled in the trees. I'd heard on the radio that a storm was imminent, and so I switched on the lamps, shut both windows, walked onto the sidewalk, and stood in the shade of the maple. Across the way a young couple I knew jumped out of their porch seats and darted indoors. When the rain arrived I was standing at the screen door, watching it pour over the ledge above the doorway, and when I got tired of that I put in a CD, stood at the sink, rolled my sleeves up. With the pissing rain, the running water, and the music, I didn't hear his feet on the gravel, and I don't know if he ever knocked, or how long he stood there and looked in. His lankiness against the screen startled me, but I crossed the room, switched the outside light on, unhooked the screen door, and asked him to come out of the rain that dripped from his flattened hair and green windbreaker, which had a faded logo on the left breast, the sort American football coaches wore in the seventies, I think. He stood inside the door, glanced away from me, and asked if I minded him stopping by. I said if I did I wouldn't have invited him in, and I inquired as to why he was not wearing the baseball cap.

—Never wear it when it's raining, he said.

In a lighthearted way I inquired if he'd come across any old ladies lying in the street. He was easing the backpack off of his shoulder and didn't answer. I gathered up socks and underpants from the chair and flung them into the closet. On the way to the toilet to get him a towel, I told him to sit in the chair.

He draped the towel over his head like a boxer or a basketball player and began to dry his hair. When he was done the towel lay around his shoulders like a prayer shawl. I asked if he wanted to take the windbreaker off. No. Then I asked if he'd like to take the shoes off. No again, if it was okay with me. I told him I didn't give a fuck, that I'd asked only for the sake of politeness. He wore tattered dress shoes, the same ones he had on the night before. The soles looked sturdy. There was a lace in one row of eyelets.

When I handed him a cigarette, the lighter, the washed saucer, he said he was in the library earlier, and a guy who works there made him leave, and so he went to the park, lay under the trees, and slept. The rain on the leaves woke him, and he remembered he'd left his shirt in the library, but that guy would have thrown it out. I was filling the coffeepot and said that losing things was a nuisance. I dropped the bread into the toaster and inquired if he liked marmalade. He said that was cool and I said something about golden oranges ripening in the Florida sun, warm blue water, and gorgeous, lazy sunbathers in Miami.

—And if it's milk you want, I have it, I said.

—Don't need it, he said.

The lights blinked off then on. Music stalled, the toaster popped. We watched the screen door, and he was still watching it when I put the coffee and the plate on the floor beside him. He began to eat like he'd done the night before. I lifted out a CD and put in another. I took a beer from the fridge. The rain had stopped and I stood on the futon bed and opened the window to the slow drip from the gutter, that gamey smell of wet summer streets, trees, and mown grass. Fireflies floated out of the grass in the yard next door. I turned back to him. With eyes downcast, he placed the plate on the floor and said he needed a favor. I said to go ahead, and I got off of the bed and sat in the armchair.

In the next couple of days, he needed a drive about ten or fifteen miles outside of town to visit an aunt of his. If I drove him he'd find his own way back. I sipped the beer and asked how many miles did he say it was, but I'd heard. He told me the distance again, and I asked what day it was he'd like to go. Four days from now, Monday, if it was cool with me, sorry to ask. He pulled the towel from around his shoulders and pressed it to his eyes. I said no worries; stop by on Monday, around one. And I also said that I thought the aunt lived in Florida. He said this aunt was his father's sister. She was old. He never knew her. I said no more about her, but I asked if he minded whether I brought a friend with me.

—Her name is Zoë, I said. —She lives in the neighborhood, and we arranged to get together next week. A student, a teacher at times, the boyfriend in medical school, in Austin. She's dark-haired, funny, and smart as a whip, a bit impatient, exactly my type.

He said it was cool with him. I asked how he intended to get back to town, and he said his aunt might pay for a cab. Or he'd walk or hitch. I said if I drove him there I'd drive him back. I'd do the job right. He said he was grateful. I said a drive in the country with Zoë and him would be an adventure. Then I picked up the beer and asked if he should put on dry clothes, because if he got sick we would not be going anywhere.

On my way to the closet to fetch him another towel I hummed along to the music, and I'd shut the closet door when those shirts came into my head. I opened the door, reached in back, and pulled the shirts from their hangers. One had a blue boxy pattern that in my head was red. The blue in the other was lighter than I'd recalled. I handed him the towel and the shirts, said I was heading outside, and if the shirts didn't suit him, he could give them to the shelter or to Saint Mary's. I never liked the shirts, I told him, though it looked like they'd fit him. He stood, then laid the shirts and the towel on the chair and picked up the backpack and unzipped it. I turned, flicked on the light, and opened the screen door. A few slow lines of rain dripped over the doorway ledge. Moths danced around the naked bulb, which was spotted with the shit and remains of other insects.

A branch ripped down by wind lay in the middle of the street. The very green leaves shone in the streetlight. I lit a cigarette and picked the branch up and threw it onto the yard opposite. Rainwater flowed loud and hard in the gully. The smell rose from the sewer. I waited for a fast

car with a dodgy muffler, a blinking pizza sign on its roof, to pass before I crossed back over and stood underneath the maple. A young
woman jogged up the middle of the street. She wore a pink baseball
cap and black skimpy shorts. A breeze shook the wet leaves. Raindrops
fell onto my head. The smell of the sewer faded. I flicked the cigarette
into the gutter and heard the jogger's sharp breath and her sneakers
striking the wet street. I wished her a good night.

—Hi, she said.

I stood on the footpath and stared up at the old woman's door before I quietly mounted her steps and crossed her porch then stood at
her window. The curtain was drawn. The house was in darkness.
When I was stealing back across her porch I saw the pair of sneakers
behind the footrest, and I picked one up by the lace, headed down the
steps, and held the sneaker under the beam of a streetlamp. I did think
it was white when I'd picked it up, but I wanted to make sure. I put the
sneaker back where I'd found it. Then I was staring down her pitch-
dark driveway. About ten feet from me, a set of eyes shone very low to
the ground. I thought for a second she was lying there—but it was an
opossum or a skunk. They foraged around the trash cans and rambled
freely through my backyard, their too many young ones trailing
behind. The shining eyes moved a few feet before vanishing. The traffic
hissed on Huron. Headlights shot through the darkened evergreens.

I opened the screen door to him standing by the chair. The backpack
was on. He had changed into a shapeless polo. The gray hair was slicked
back. A few stiff wisps sprang over his forehead. In the low lamplight his
cheekbones looked purple and his darkened eyes looked weary. The
music had stopped, and he did not look at me when I said the night was
fine but for raindrops falling from the leaves. He said he'd hung the
towels in the bathroom. I said there were no worries regarding towels.

—Grateful for the shirts, he said.

—You're welcome, man, I said.

He buttoned the windbreaker to the neck. I shoved open the screen
door. He stepped outside. When the door clicked shut I hooked it with-

out looking down. He stepped onto the grass at the edge of the light. A moth spun around his head. He coughed and the moth tumbled into the dark. Then he pulled the pack higher on his back, turned sideways, and stared up the driveway.

—Something I need to say, man, he said. —Should have said it last night, but it didn't seem right because of the old lady.

—Tell Zoë and me in the car, man. It'll give us things to talk about.

—Have to tell you now, man, when no one's around.

—You're not in some kind of trouble, I said.

—No, he said.

—That's good to hear, man, I suppose, I said.

—Know someone you know, he said.

—You do. Someone in town? At the university?

—Not here, man. Before here. You know Kevin Lyons.

I waited a minute or so.

—There must be a ton of men in this country with that name, I then said.

—Needs and wants you to go see him, he said.

—I can't afford to go to the fucking corner, I said.

—He's paying for it—

—That's very generous of him, but you have the wrong man—

—No, man, he said. —Talks like you. Your dad and his dad were best buddies. Two brothers. Twins, I guess. Sister in Scotland, somewhere over there—

—Our dads were best friends, I said after a while. —And the sister, she lives in London, the last I heard, and she just so happened to buy me those ugly shirts I gave you. Isn't that quite the coincidence, Mister Mysterious Walter. But I should be better at throwing shit away.

—Grateful for the shirts. Needs you to go see him, he said.

—I'm not going anywhere. I don't know him. I ran into him once in Boston—

—Said he saw you there twice, he said.

—Whatever. I forget, man. It was a while ago—

—Said you never went to his wedding. Just saying what he said to say, man—

—You seem to know more about me than I do, man, I said.

I went to the table and picked up the beer. I came back and lit a cigarette and blew the smoke through the screen.

—So you work for Mr. Lyons, I said.

—Done work for him. Need to deal with this bird—

—That's an odd one. What sort of bird—

—A whippoorwill, man—

—Oh, like in that song, I said.

—Makes him crazy. Can't sleep at night over it. Asked me to deal with it—

—Well, poor Mr. Lyons, I said.

—You still taking me to see my aunt, he said.

—I should have nothing to do with you, but Zoë would enjoy that trip, I said. —I know she would. And so would I.

—Grateful, man, he said.

He stepped out of the light. His feet crunched the gravel. I pressed my face against the screen, swiped a cobweb from my lips, and asked loudly for him to come back.

—I'm here, man, he said, though I could not see him.

—The old woman, that was a lie, man, I said.

—She was there, man. Didn't plan on knocking on your door last night—

—You said she wore white sneakers.

—Don't remember, man. An old lady—

—What about karma, man? What the fuck about that?

—Lying in the street before this house, man—

—Lyons paid you for this nonsense, didn't he? I said.

—Just doing like he asked. That's all, man. Grateful, he said.

—No one can make me go anywhere, man, I said.

—Needs and wants you to go see him, he said.

3

Michael Lyons was the father. Nora was the mother. They had four children. Kevin was the eldest, Una was a year younger, and the twins, Seamus and Tommy, were four or five years younger than Una. Michael once worked in the copper mines in Gortdrum, but when I was growing up he built indoor toilets, milking parlors, and pump houses—things people were then building. One summer he dug a well, built a pump house, and installed an immersion heater for my family.

My father and Michael were best friends, although my father was at least twelve years older than his friend, who was around my mother's age. Michael had a round, handsome face, thick, wavy dark hair, and large dark eyes. He wore a trilby hat to Mass. A little feather with flashy colors was tucked inside the band. He was the only man at Mass who wore a trilby. The others wore cloth caps.

Lyons's white cottage was about three miles from our house. It was the third one on the right, if you turn left at the Creamery Cross, which is still called the Creamery Cross, even though the creamery was shut down the year after Michael built the pump house, and before I left for the States the creamery yard was already overgrown with weeds and grass, the three buildings were skeletons, and the casting was gone from the two roadside pumps. The windows in the creamery buildings were smashed inside a week after the shutting. Boys walking home from National school dropped their schoolbags in the middle of the road and held rousing stone-throwing contests. My brother Stephen was one of those boys, and so was Seamus Lyons.

Behind Lyons's cottage was Michael's shed. I was once inside it. It was a spring evening, and I was with my father—a few months before Michael built the pump house. Against the back wall of the shed a red bus seat was tucked underneath a plywood desk. Above the desk, tools were arranged on hooks. Beside them hung two framed photographs of the Limerick hurling team. The photos were cut from Sunday newspapers. On a shelf next to the tools was a row of notebooks—copybooks, we called them. In National school we used them. Their pages had blue horizontal lines, and my father bought them at O'Shea's grocery and post office, which was on the right of the cross, directly across from the creamery entrance. O'Shea's shut about six months after the creamery did.

A number was written in red ink on the wood beneath each notebook, and I gripped the back of the red bus seat, stood tiptoe, plucked one out, laid it on the desk, and opened it. Michael turned from chatting with my father, and he smiled and said what was written in the copybook were records of his jobs, which were of no interest to a boy of my age. I told him I was sorry and shut the notebook.

If I saw anything written in it I don't recall it, in that I don't recall a column of building items with prices in an opposite column, nor do I recall reading sentences that sounded like a voice that spoke only to itself. But I well recall my father's red face, his outstretched hand, his shaking finger pointing at the shed doorway, when he bluntly ordered me to go outside and not dare come back into the shed again. And I well recall Michael staring at the side of my father's face as my father reprimanded me, and that Michael's own face looked tormented then. I had turned from my father's face to Michael's, and when my father was done, Michael turned to me, and he smiled again, and politely asked that I put the copybook back where I'd found it. And so I gripped the bus seat, stood tiptoe, scrutinized the tiny red numbers, and slid that notebook back.

—An attentive boy, Michael said.

—I'm not too sure about that, my father said.

—Your sister's godson. Tess's, Michael said.

Two years before this, Auntie Tess had died in Dublin. She was a nurse, the younger of my father's two sisters. She never married. No one in the family attended her funeral, in Dublin. Not even Auntie Hannah, who was too decrepit to leave the City Home in Limerick.

—Him all right, my father said.

And he dropped the match onto the floor and stamped on it.

—Looks a bit like her in the face, all right, Michael said.

And he stared down at the match.

I stood on the cobblestone path. Kevin was kicking a football very hard against the side wall of the cottage. Nora opened the window and shouted at her son to go and kick the ball someplace else. To have some sort of decency and not kick the blasted ball so close to her shrubs. Then she shut the window. The ball spun past me and skinned my right ankle. Kevin ran up the path after the ball. He elbowed me off the path and shoved his mouth up to my ear.

—You must think now you're it, he said.

And then he kicked the ball around the shed.

I was eleven. He was fifteen or sixteen, and as tall as the men in the shed. And he'd never noticed me before. Not once had he said a word.

I stepped back onto the path, stared in at the men, and wiped my ear with the corner of my shirt. On the other side of the cottage, the leaves on the silver birches sparkled in the fading daylight. Kevin was now kicking the ball against the back wall of the shed. The men were talking. The well and the pump house. The date to start. Sometime in June or it might have to be July. Take two months at the most. Maybe more depending on the weather. Never know. Then the other jobs Michael had done and the ones he was doing and then what it was like down in the copper mines. Frightfully dark down there. Never seen anything like that dark. What the dead wake up to. What we all will wake up to some fine day. Then the talk turned to last Saturday's horse races. Who was home first. Who was placed. And who made no appearance. A hand slapping the plywood desk followed by Michael's bold laugh. The kitchen window in the cottage glowed. Nora's shadow came and went on the windowpane. Her hand moved above her eyes. Their supper was ready. But Nora did not call the men. She knew that men in the shed meant business. I had stepped closer to the shed doorway. At my feet the cobblestones looked pale like eggs. And the ball went on striking the back wall. The rhythm and the power never once diminished. And not once a pause in the men's talk. And if the noise of the ball agitated them, they didn't show it. Their heads bowed, hands deep in pockets, their feet apart. The ashtray on the plywood desk brimmed with burned-out Sweet Aftons. On the back of Sweet Afton boxes were two lines by Robert Burns that I then loved to read.

Flow gently, Sweet Afton, among thy green braes,
Flow gently, I'll sing thee a song in thy praise.

Anyway, Michael's spotless shed was tidier than any house I had ever been inside, tidier than the house I grew up in, where my mother and my sisters faithfully scrubbed, swept, tidied, dusted, cooked, twice a day scalded milking churns, milked cows, fed calves, hens, chickens, ducks, turkeys, pigs, dogs, and agitated at whoever happened to be near their brooms, mops, wooden spoons, dusters, the underclothes they scoured, soaked, then washed, their worn-down scrubbing brushes, their battered pots of boiling water, their daily bread dough, and their constantly employed frying pan.

But I heard my father tell my mother in our kitchen that Michael never let any of his children inside that shed. And I heard him tell her that the only adults Michael let in were the ones he was doing jobs for. And they were let in only once.

My father visited Michael. They sauntered up and down the road. Or they crossed the ditch opposite Lyons's cottage and walked through the fields and meadows. And Michael visited our house. He appeared on Saturday mornings and sat in the chair across the range from my father and told him dirty jokes. In those jokes *hole* rhymed with *pole*, and once *hole* with *coal*.

My mother did not like Michael telling those jokes. She didn't want anyone in her house hearing about holes and poles, and every time Michael left, she complained bitterly to her husband that he'd let no one else get away with such vulgarity. Her husband had one response: He demanded that the television be turned on so that he could watch the horse races. His wife always obeyed—though at the same time, my mother was fond of Michael, and her way of handling his vulgarity was to pray for him. One saint she prayed to was Saint Francis, whose picture sat atop the television. A huge crucifix hung from his neck. His right hand rested on a massive sheepdog, and birds swam in his dazzling halo. At his naked feet a bowl of milk that a cat and a rat sipped from. And not even once did my mother show her disapproval to Michael's face. Not her. Not my dead mother. She smiled and bowed when she lifted the teapot from the range to fill Michael's and my father's tea mugs, and she smiled and bowed when she added sugar and milk then stirred each mug with a teaspoon she kept in her apron pocket.

I longed to hear Michael's jokes, the sharp rhymes, and his daring laugh at the punch lines, when he gripped his knees and his greasy John Garfield curl toppled down his forehead, and then his fingers shooting up, hastily fixing that clump back into place. During the telling of those jokes, my father sucked his lips in, his forehead was long and wrinkled, and at the punch lines, a smile flared at the corners of his mouth. It flared for seconds only—a smile so quick that you're still not sure you ever saw it, like something shining brightly and rapidly falling down a country sky on a dark night.

Michael died the spring after he built the pump house. A male neighbor told us about the death. The neighbor's name is gone, but I recall the rap of his knuckles on our opened door. It was a Saturday morning, in August, between nine and ten. We were eating breakfast. My oldest brother, Anthony, had just arrived back from the creamery.

My father was sitting in his chair and reading the newspaper Anthony had brought from O'Shea's, and while my father read, his hand darted from behind the paper, and his finger, broken the year he worked on building sites in London, tipped the cigarette ash onto the blackened top of the white range.

Anthony sat at one end of the kitchen table. I sat at the other. Stephen, the youngest, sat next to me. The hood of the red secondhand Massey Ferguson 35 crammed the kitchen window. A fly buzzed around the marmalade jar. A knife was sticking out of the jar. Hannah, my youngest sister, was washing dishes. Tess, the second eldest, was cutting bread at the table. My mother was frying eggs. She pressed the spatula down hard on each egg and shouted at me and my brothers to stop complaining, because even if the undercooked or overcooked egg was not to our liking, any sort of egg was better than no egg.

Seconds before the knuckles touched the door, the two sheepdogs barked in a way that warns you a stranger has entered the yard, and at the knock my mother dropped the spatula, ran her hand through her black hair, quickly retied her apron, then dashed down the short hall to greet the neighbor, and before she led him in she shouted at the dogs to pipe down, and when he was in she invited him to sit in the chair across the range from my father, the chair Michael sat in. But the neighbor didn't sit. He stood close enough to me that I smelled cowshit and old sweat, and he shoved his dirty balled-up cap from one hand to the other and bit down on his bottom lip, his cheeks reddening and his eyes shifting from the floor to my father and then to my mother, who stood by him with her arms folded. Her eyes had that look that said this man was not bearing good news.

—Hello, God bless, he eventually said. —Lovely weather. Hello to all the lads. But sorry to have to stop in but, at such a frightfully bad time of the day but, and sorry to have to be the one with the news, but God rest him Michael Lyons died at the table this morning. Didn't even get to finish his mug of tea. Didn't even open the boiled egg. Nora in an awful state. Mercury in the blood. Picked that up in Gortdrum all them years back. Still in the system. So they're saying anyways.

Every pew in the church was full at Michael's funeral Mass. We knelt halfway up the church. Hannah was beside me; Tess was next to her, then my father and my brothers. My mother knelt behind me. Kevin was first up the aisle. All I recall is a sports coat flapping open. Next came Nora. Michael's older brother, Big Roger, had his arm around her back, his hand clutching her left side, her dress was ruffled around his fingers, and her head looked snug in Roger's armpit. She pressed a balled-up paper hankie to her mouth, and the black veil she wore looked like the one my mother was wearing. The twins were next. They wore dark suits, wrinkled white shirts, and bow ties. Una was last. She walked slowly, chin up. The dark raincoat reached her knees. Her tights were black and a velvet band held her long hair back from her forehead. After she passed I hopped up, stared, and my mother jabbed her fingers into my right arse cheek. I turned to her. Through the veil the solemn eyes declaring: Kneel down, don't bring attention to yourself, know your place, don't disgrace us, don't disgrace me.

I don't remember seeing Una again for five years. The news was that she was a bit distant, she'd her father's eye, and she'd secured a place in the civil service, which was the sort of job bright young women and men aspired to.

In January 1984, I moved to Dublin. Una had been living there about two years. My mother often chatted with Nora after Sunday Mass, and in one of my mother's letters was Una's address, and my mother wrote that I should visit Una; the mothers agreed it would be grand for us to see someone from home. In another letter, my mother asked that when I did visit Una to let on nothing about the you-know-what. This you-know-what concerned Big Roger and Nora. Big Roger began visiting Nora not too long after Michael died. People saw Big Roger's car coming and going and they saw Big Roger walking in and out of the cottage. In another letter, my mother said that Roger Lyons's car was stationed in a brazen manner outside you-know-who's cottage. By "brazen manner" she meant the car was parked in front.

Una's flat was in a three-story shabby Georgian house on Drumcondra Road, next to the canal bridge, Binns Bridge. I lived off Drumcondra Road farther down, on Botanic Avenue, and one Sunday afternoon, in late July, I put on my black drainpipe pants and a shirt I'd bought in a shop on Talbot Street the week before and headed up the high and wide footpath, with the grassy slope and the old trees to my left, and the B&B with the shamrock sign on the pole to my right, and pushed open her small iron gate with my hip. A messy hedge spilled over the crumbling left pier. The yard was one gray cement slab. I walked across it, pressed her bell, shoved my hands back into my pockets, then took one hand out and fiddled with my pants zipper. The peeling gray paint on her door looked like the main door to my own flat. I counted three full minutes, and was turning to leave when I heard the harsh turning of locks. The door opened a bit, her face appeared. I stared at the door then the cement slab. There was perfume, the brand I never knew, the scent I can't describe, but also in the hall was the smell of yesterday's boiled cabbage, a smell you came across then only in flats where country people lived.

She opened the door all the way. Her hair was short at the back and her fringe was gelled and spiked above the forehead. My own hair looked something like this. She wore a white short-sleeved blouse with a frilly collar, two strings dangling from the neck, and a tight wine-colored skirt. I said my name and something about my mother saying that I should visit, that Una's mother said the same thing to my mother. By then I was staring at her pale and lovely made-up face.

—I only live down the road from you, like a twenty-minute walk, I said.

—I know who you are. You'll have a cup of tea, Jimmy, she said. She smiled.

—I don't want to be a bother, Una, it being a Sunday and all that—

—You're not a bother. Can't you come up?

—I will, if you like, I said.

Her flat was on the second floor. Two high windows faced Drumcondra Road. Emulsion white bare walls. Below the window opposite the door was a small sink, a single cabinet to the left of it, a hot plate and a short counter below it. The floor there was covered in blue and white tiles that were stained with large splotches of brown paint that to this day make me think of a clown's face. Under the other window was a dressed single bed. A stack of women's magazines on it, three pairs of shoes underneath it, a lamp and a few novels on the small bedside table. On a low shelf between the two windows were more books and a small black-and-white television with lopsided rabbit ears. Behind the door, a round table and two chairs. She told me to sit in one of the chairs, and she went and filled a kettle.

She brought the tea things over on a tray, unloaded them, took the tray back, opened the cabinet, and returned with a plate of ginger biscuits. She sat in the other chair and said that she didn't remember seeing my face on the school bus, and that she sat on the bottom deck. I said I sat on the top, and she would have left by the time I started, and that my first year was Kevin's last year, and she said she did remember seeing Tess on the bus and in the convent schoolyard, but they had different friends, and so they hardly ever spoke, and she then asked if I went to the convent or the tech. I said I went to the tech for a few years, and she said I was lucky to go there, because the nuns and brothers were pure savages. I said I had heard all about that from Tess, but the technical school had its share of savages, and there were no brothers or nuns there. She stirred the teapot, asked if I liked Dublin.

—I like making my own money, I said.

—So glad to be out on my own, she said.

—The same here, I said.

—Do you go down home often?

—Heading down there soon for a week's holiday to help out with the hay, I said.

—The train on Friday afternoon is the fastest. The bus is cheaper, but it takes you all over the country, she said.

She poured my tea, then her own, and she told me to help myself to the ginger biscuits. She picked one up herself, nibbled at it, and then put it back on the edge of the plate. She said when she first arrived in Dublin she cried herself to sleep every night.

—It was so hard, because of the noise from the cars and the buses and the people coming out of the pubs late and their shouting and laughing and fighting outside the chipper up the street. And I missed my room at home so much. I missed waking up and looking out the window at the silver birches.

She was looking at me when she said she didn't cry now, and her pale hands trembled when she said, —I suppose you heard the news about my mother and my uncle Roger.

—Not a word, I said.

—You have. Don't lie, she said. —They all have. You know as well as I do what they're like.

—No, I haven't, I said.

I scooted my chair away from the table and shoved my hands into my pockets. From the footpath the shrill voices and laughter of children who lived in the Corporation flats on the canal bank. Young Dublin men walked past: *You wouldn't ride her. Yous was afraid to ride her. Yous was bleedin' afraid.*

She looked toward the window that the bed was next to.

—My uncle Roger is going to marry my mother, she said, and folded her arms. —That's the latest news from my house.

I looked at her, then out that window. What she told me was a shock, but more shocking was that she would tell it. We're from people who told nothing. And she didn't stop there.

—Big Roger started visiting our house after Daddy died, she said. —He hadn't talked to my father in years because Roger had inherited my grandfather's farm and house, and that's a big farm, so I saw little of Roger till Daddy died. Then I saw Roger all the time, and seeing

Roger was the main reason I made sure to get good marks in the exams and get the place in the civil service. You see, Roger would walk into our house without knocking, like he was Daddy, but Daddy'd let us know he was on the way. He would sing or whistle on the path, but Roger would walk in without a scrap of manners and sit in Daddy's chair, and my mother would order me about. And I obeyed her. I had to. After I made his dinner I made him his tea—I boiled him his spuds and peeled them and served them to him, with all that salt and butter he likes so much, and I picked up his plate and served him his dessert. Big Roger with all the land got fine and healthy after Daddy died. He kept saying to my mother, Fine land, and lots of it. Not a wet spot on it. Fine big house with enough rooms for these children and more like them. Rooms I never venture into, he'd kept saying. So you see, Jimmy—

—Jim's what I like now, I said.

—So you see, Jim, Roger got a brand-new life, he did, but the worst of all was him visiting in summertime. He'd come in from the meadow, no shirt on him, and he'd sit in Daddy's chair and the sweat trickled down his chest and his pig belly and the hayseed were stuck to his blond chest hair. It was terrible to have to look at him, sitting like a king in Daddy's chair, like that was his to sit in—and I had to serve him. And I'd smell the sweat from him when I served him. I'd hold my breath, but my mother made me, my mother who would barely leave the house for months after the funeral, only to go to Mass, who wore black and cried morning, noon, and night, and then the black was wrapped up in plastic and put into the back of the wardrobe. Good meat was bought from the shop, not bacon, but beefsteak. Rhubarb tarts were baked. Custard was made every evening, because Roger liked all that. My mother and I fought like cats and dogs over the way she'd gawk in the mirror when she knew Roger was on his way, she screaming at me that I didn't understand, but I understood well enough. She was spending more time before the mirror than I did, and this from a woman who drummed it into me that any woman who spent too much time looking in a mirror is no better than a prostitute. My brothers, they ignored it. They went outside and kicked the football around, and I could hear them outside, kicking their ball and laughing, and the two of us screaming inside, so you see, Jim, I'm happy to be far away from all that—

I asked how the twins were, but I asked only because I wanted her to keep staring out the window, arms folded, the blouse strings dangling.

—The twins will go to London, she said. —In a year or two they will. They have jobs lined up in hotels. My mother's older sister is in London. Her son is high up in the hotels.

I knew that Kevin had been living in Dublin for a while, so I inquired how he was.

—I don't see that much of him, she said. —He works for this landlord, who's also a property developer. Kevin has his own eye on a few old tenements he wants to buy—but by the way, how did you get the job in the bar? Any sort of a job is hard to come by these days.

—My father's second cousin, I said. —He's high up in the union.

The second cousin grew up on a farm near where my father grew up on the hill with Aunt Hannah and Aunt Tess. He left for Dublin around the age I was at this time. My father wrote him a letter about a job for me, and a few weeks later, my father was sitting in his chair by the range. He had his glasses on; the newspaper was folded at his feet, and he was reading a letter the postman had just delivered. It was a Tuesday afternoon, in early December, and I was shoving wood into the range. I'd cut the wood on a sawhorse I'd built at the end of the house. My father told me to leave that fire alone, take a gawk at this. He raised the letter and turned it toward me. Held it open like a scroll. His dirty fingernails pierced the top and bottom of it. His hands and the letter shook.

These two sentences you recall: Put him on the afternoon train to

Dublin in the next three or four weeks. I will meet the young fellow on the platform at Heuston.

I was sixteen that March I'd quit the technical school. I don't remember the day it happened, but I well remember how much I despised school. They all made that easy, right from day one in National school. And my parents were fine with me quitting; they forever needed a hand on the farm, and they themselves had stopped school early. Had to help out at home. Help out on the land. School to them was a sort of long holiday from the life of real work that lay ahead, and so they found endless farm jobs for me. But I wasn't good at farmwork. And I didn't like being around my father. I didn't like his grunts, his grating breath, his daily legion of orders, but when my father ordered you to do something, you did it.

After you'd read that letter your father told you to hand him the calendar. You crossed the kitchen and took it from the nail above the television. Your sisters and brothers weren't in the kitchen, but your mother was. When you walked in with the wood cradled to your chest she was washing the dishes or cleaning. She wasn't baking bread, because you'd remember it. And when you handed your father the calendar they were talking about the farm jobs you needed to finish. How long those jobs might take. Your father had the calendar opened on his lap. Your mother was standing at the sink with her arms folded. The way she often stood. The way you recall her. And you were watching out that sink window at the faraway Galtee Mountains when your father chose a day in January. He wrote his cousin back that evening, and the moment he licked the letter shut you went and stood before him and asked if you might be the one to post the letter and your father said yes then handed it to you.

The week before I left, I took the bus into Limerick to say good-bye to Aunt Hannah in the City Home. Your mother said Aunt Hannah would give you money. I sat on a chair beside my aunt's bed and happened to mention how sad it was I'd never get to know Aunt Tess in

Dublin. Aunt Hannah gripped my wrist. Her eyes rolled toward me. The eyes narrowed.

—Jimmy, she said. —Didn't your aunt Tess fling herself under one of them city buses across the street from the Garden of Remembrance, and that was that for her. I can tell you that now, Jimmy, she added. —You'll never live here again, but my sister, God knows, she was haywire. None of us knew what was going on inside her head at all, she kept things to herself, and your father and myself were more than glad that she did, like you have to keep what I'm telling you to yourself, but my sister did that woeful thing to us, did that to her own family, your father and mother know every bit of it, they knew about it the time it happened, but your aunt Tess, Jimmy, was the odd one, but every family has the misfortune of having one of them, and only one if they're lucky.

Aunt Hannah let my wrist go. Her eyes were all tears. I looked from them to the low city buildings outside the window. I imagined myself sitting on a train to Dublin. All their tears and their farm jobs and their sordid secrets were falling behind me. Then Auntie Hannah shoved her hand under the blanket. I looked down. The hand scampered about like a rat. When it came out it pressed a fifty-quid note into my opened hand.

The morning I left, my mother cried when she packed my bag. I put my arms around her and kissed her. I squeezed her hands and said I would write a letter home every week. Cross my heart and hope to die. The bag was brown, with a glossy finish. A woman's bag, with long, cushioned handles. Aunt Tess's, which arrived in our house by way of Aunt Hannah. Some of my dead aunt's things were sent to her sister. My mother pinned a Sacred Heart medal on the inside of the bag. She said the medal would forever protect me. Someone I was friendly with for a short time when I first moved to Dublin stole the bag.

My mother had washed two of my father's blue Sunday shirts. They hung drying on the bar above the range that morning. Steam flowed around them, like steam on summer days rising from an American city grate. My mother clutched the shirts. Not dry enough yet, Jimmy, but they'll be fine and dry in time for the train, Jimmy. Then she spent a long time ironing them. She steered the hissing iron into every corner. Her teardrops fell onto the shirts and the iron went back and forth over each teardrop until they all vanished. And I never once wore those shirts. With my first paycheck, I bought my own. Nor did I see my mother neatly fold the shirts and place them in my dead aunt's bag. I didn't because I was saying good-bye to Stephen and Anthony. I don't remember that at all, but I do remember standing with Tess at the side of the house. We stood where I chopped and cut the wood and stared at the mountains, whose peaks were capped in snow, and my shoes sank into the thick patch of snow-covered sawdust.

—Stop crying, Tess, I pleaded. —Come to the train station with me. You promised last night you would. You gave your word, Tess—

—I can't go, Jimmy. Hannah is going. I can't—

—You promised me. Wipe your face, Tess. I want you to be the last person I see out the train window—

—I can't, Jimmy. I don't want you to go at all, but I know you have to—

—You'll be gone soon, Tess, gone in a few months. But you promised!

—I know I did, Jimmy, but I don't want any of us to go. I never ever wanted this day to come, never, Jimmy—

—But I'm so glad this day is here, Tess, I'm so glad—

She then ran around the back of the house. I ran after her and stood and held the barbed wire that she had slipped under, and I called after her to come back, but Tess was running in the snowy field. She ran around the cows. Her red hair and purple coat were flying around her.

My father's cousin, Eddie, met me off the train and took me to the pub I was to work in. He introduced me to the owner, and the two older men I'd work with, who were going to train me. They were countrymen. They'd worked in the bar for forty years; they each shook hands with me, and told me to start the next morning. One of them said the apprenticeship was three years. I thanked them and said I'd see them in the morning. The cousin next drove me to a grocery on Lower Drumcondra Road. He told me to buy what food I needed and not to forget the fifty-pence pieces for the meter.

My father gave me twenty pounds. We were standing on the platform at Limerick Junction. Hannah was holding the sleeve of my jumper. I don't recall what my father said when he handed me the money. He probably said, Good luck to you now. And he would have warned me to not forget to send the money back when I was on my feet, and he would have warned me not to forget to write to my mother when I arrived at the digs that evening and to post the letter tomorrow, because my mother would be anxious to hear from me. His reddened hand with the purple veins dipped into the coat pocket. With her free hand Hannah was pointing at the train. She was saying how much she'd like to take the train to Dublin with me. She'd take it and then take the next one back home. Then his fist came out and he slipped me the note. It was folded up in a small square. His sharp nails touched my palms and the corners of the square were sharp. I didn't look but shoved the money down my left pants pocket. But I did look the moment I found a seat on the train. I flattened the note out on my left knee then lifted my face and waved and smiled through the window at Hannah, who was waving and smiling too. Her brown hair was tangled. She wore the bright red cardigan that my mother's friend in England had posted, and seeing Hannah by herself on that platform made me mad all over again at Tess—but him waiting till the last moment to do that. The platform empty except for the three of us. My father turned from us and lit a Sweet Afton. Hannah tugged at my sleeve. Coleman Daly, the train guard, sauntered up, orange flag in hand, and said that if I didn't get on, it would leave without me. Then he asked Hannah which of the two Dwyer girls she was. Hannah said her name. Coleman said she was a lovely girl, and one fine day she'd make a handsome man like her father frightfully happy. Hannah giggled, and Coleman looked at his watch and said that the train was going to boot it in the next three minutes. Hannah tugged harder on my sleeve. I was staring at the faces on the train. My father and Coleman were talking about last Saturday's horse races. I turned from the train faces. Coleman shoved the flag into his back pocket, clapped his hands, and said it was a fierce cold day for a journey. Hannah piped up and said it was a lovely day to take the train. The smile appeared at the corner of my father's mouth. I picked up the bag. The cushioned handles felt warm. Coleman was saying to my father that he fancied two, maybe even three horses in two or three races next Saturday. He was going to put a few pounds on a few of them. Coleman mentioned the horses' names, and my father said to Coleman he couldn't put a foot wrong there. I stepped closer to the train. Hannah gasped when I pushed her hand away.

The Sunday afternoon in late July when I first visited Una's flat, that day in January already felt like years ago. And you never stood on the train platform with your sister and your father—but bright sunlight lit the snowy fields. Cattle crowded around troughs filled with silage and hay, and the pale, stern winter faces on the train stared out. And I was ashamed. Ashamed of my father. I could not see myself then. Could not see what I was or who I wasn't—but ashamed of the cowshit underneath his nails, the ragged everyday coat and cap, and the hand slipping into the pocket at the last moment, for all those pale and stern winter faces to see. He taking his sweet time. He punishing you. That's what he was doing—but it's only now I know he knew that what I wanted was to get on the train and put him and home and all of them behind me for good.

The cousin next drove me to that flat on Botanic Avenue. He had secured it for me. The landlord was a close friend. A tiny second-floor flat that I immediately liked, a twenty-five-minute walk to my job. That tiny flat with the tiny fridge, a hot plate with two rings, the table and two chairs facing the only window. The shared shower and toilet on my floor. The black coin-box phone at the bottom of the stairs. Large water stains on two walls and the smell of mold. That window looked out onto a slate roof that was covered with fat green moss. Pressed against the edge of the roof were the tops of evergreens.

My father's cousin and I sat on the edge of the single bed and smoked his cigarettes. He stared at the floor between his opened legs, fidgeted with his thinning brown fringe, and warned me to be fair and honest in my dealings with others, and to not ever be late for work, because if I was, or if I misbehaved in any way, it was a mark against him, and a mark against him was a mark against the union, and it nearly killed him and a few others to get the union going. I told him I'd be good, and I reached into my pocket and handed him the money for the flat—I'd counted the notes on the train, counted them about twenty times—and without looking up, he shoved the notes into the sports coat pocket then said my father was a great man, his most favorite cousin, who stood with him at Limerick Junction when he took the train to Dublin all those years ago. The two of them piked hay in the meadows, the women crossed the meadows and the ditches with bottles of tea, ham and tomato sandwiches, tin-can gallons of well water, the best water he ever tasted, no water anyplace in the world like it, not like the filthy city water, you've no idea whatsoever, young fellow, what might be floating in that, and my father and he cycled together to dances and hurling matches, they acted in plays in the school hall, when it came to acting my father was hard to beat. And no one could read the horses like my father. Not one.

He looked up. He offered me another cigarette, held the match out, told me I looked clever enough, I was a fairly all-right-looking young fellow, but I wasn't handsome the way my father was, I must look like the other side, who he didn't know anything about, but I needed to look out for myself, because no one else would, and he reached into the coat pocket where he'd put the money and handed me twenty pounds—I don't know if it was one of the notes I'd given him—and he leaned back and reached into his left pants pocket and handed me ten cigarettes and a box of matches. I took them and thanked him, and he was fidgeting again with his fringe when he said, —Don't forget to tell your father the next time you see him how well we got along, and don't forget to tell him I was mad asking for him, and don't forget to tell him that I was good to his young fellow.

We stood up from the bed and walked down the narrow stairs. We shook hands on the front steps. I can't remember what else we said. The exhaust of his small car made loud farting noises when it took off. And I felt great wonder sitting there by myself on the top step. Men walked past in overcoats, and workmen in anoraks and women hurried past with their plastic shopping bags. A group of teenagers shuffled past. They were laughing and smoking and they had cool haircuts and wore cool city clothes. A barking dog ran down the middle of the street. Someone far up the street shouted the dog's name and cursed. And smoke from the chimneys was mixed in with the fog and was the color of mud in the beams of the streetlamps.

I got up from the step and went upstairs and took the food out of the bag and put it in the fridge. I pushed two fifty-pence pieces into the meter and turned the metal key. The fridge hummed to life. It took me five minutes to open up the stuck window. Cold air filled the room. I pulled out the chair and sat down at the table and opened the box of cigarettes Eddie gave me, lit one, and stared across the fat moss at the evergreens. I felt hungry, but I'd fry some eggs later. I'd need to write that letter to my mother, but that, too, could wait. Strange voices were trapped before the window for seconds. Those voices sounded thrilling. My first night without them, and I didn't feel lonely.

And I never again saw or heard from Eddie. But his part was played. He did what a cousin from home had asked of him.

—I have a close relation for years in the civil service, Una said.

—I like the pub, I said. —People tell you strange things, and they sing. They sing the Dublin songs.

—You'll get tired of all that, Jim. Mark my words, she said. —You like it now because it's new, and you are new to the city. I know Daddy used to visit your house. He was so fond of your father, more than he was of most people, but Daddy visited more than your house. I think he visited houses to let people know he was available if they needed a handyman. It was the country way of doing business.

—I remember him very well, I said.

—I don't think about him like I used to. I'm being honest, she said, and released her arms.

—He was very funny. When he came to the house he told jokes that my mother and father didn't like to hear.

She made a quick knot on the strings, without looking down. She placed her right hand on her hip. —I might go and live in France or Germany. Do you know anyone who's even gone there?

—Not a one, I said.

—I was very good at the French in school, if you don't mind my saying so—

—I don't—

—I was good at the Irish, too, but the nuns lashed the French verbs into me. My mother, mind you, wouldn't like to hear me say that I was going anyplace. So you can't repeat any of this to your mother or it'll go straight back to mine.

—I won't open my mouth to any of them.

She stood and crossed the room. An empty pram was bouncing along the footpath, and before Una reached the window the pram crashed into a lamppost and the children were laughing and screaming. She lowered the window and sat on the sill, her head bent. The light made her hair look more red than black. Her shadow fell along her bed. Then a cloud moved and her shadow vanished.

She came back from the window and picked up the ginger biscuit. She stared at it before putting it back on the edge of the plate. She touched her fingertips together then quickly folded her arms again, holding herself like she were cold, and she gazed down at me, her eyes blinking in a way that made me wonder if she had forgotten I was there. I coughed and covered my mouth. She slowly sat on the edge of the chair, again watching toward that window.

—I used to fill Daddy's flask of tea and make his sandwiches before I got on the bus. I had the flask filled that morning. I had to throw the tea out four days after. It was still sitting there on the table. No one in the house would touch the flask. And Daddy knew people enjoyed his company. He could get a rise out of the stiffest of them.

—He did out of my father and mother, I said.

—That was Daddy's way, she went on. —Get a rise out of them. You know he spent a half-hour before the mirror every morning, combing his hair, before going out to shovel concrete and fix things for people, many of them who never paid him, like the big farmers, the ones who could. But his work shirts and his pants had to be ironed. He demanded that. Every morning he'd ask me if he looked grand. He'd ask me when I handed him that flask of tea and the two sandwiches. I told him that he did look grand. Vain, that's what Daddy was, but I liked that in him.

—He was on my mind, when I was walking up Drumcondra Road earlier, I said. —He was a fine builder. I heard it said many times at the creamery—

—A laborer is what he was, she said.

She looked at me. I looked away. Bus brakes screeched then hissed at the lights.

—But I am so happy you came by, she said. —When the bell rang I knew well it was you. My mother had been saying that you would stop by some Sunday, but when the bell rang, I opened the curtain and looked out but could not see who was down there, and then when I was going down the stairs I had that odd feeling I was who I was six or seven years ago. I didn't like the feeling at all, and I sat on the stairs for a while and shut my eyes till it faded. Do you know what I mean, Jim?

—I'm starting to, Una.

—I had to wait for it to pass, she said. —But in my mind when I sat up from the step and went toward the door you looked different than you do. You look nice, and you'll visit me again. I hope you will, but I know I have been talking and telling too much. It's just that they are things you'd understand, being neighbors, being from there, our fathers being such good friends.

—I'll visit you whenever you'd like, Una. I'll ring the bell next Sunday.

—Do so, Jim. Please do. I'll be looking forward to it all week. I'm fine, you know. I'm grand, but I never know what to do with myself on Sundays. During the week I have the work and I am so knackered when I get home that I eat a bite and fall into the bed and stay in it till I have to get up for work the next morning. I look at the telly, but there's nothing much on it. Then on Sundays, I couldn't be bothered with Mass, where everyone around me is a stranger. You are going to write to your mother now and tell her you saw me. Tell her the things we chatted about.

—I don't have to tell her anything, Una. I don't have to tell anyone anything.

—I'd like you didn't say a word, Jim.

—I'll say I never saw you, Una. I'll make something up.

—Do so, Jim. I won't say a word to my mother either. The less they know, the better. And take a few ginger biscuits with you. You didn't even have one.

—I'm grand, I said.

—Oh, take a few, she said. —I brought them out especially for you.

She went to the cabinet, pulled out a plastic bag, and put six or seven biscuits into it. I stood and thanked her when she handed me the bag. She folded her arms and smiled.

It was after three when I left her flat. The sun was shining. I crossed the bridge and walked up Lower Dorset Street. I stepped into a newsagent to buy a Sunday newspaper. I passed the North Circular Road and wandered into a pub between there and Eccles Street. The bartender handed me a Club Orange. I sat underneath a window, in a seat warmed by sunlight. No one sat around me, but a man was sitting on every barstool. They were watching the football match on the television, a dense cloud of cigarette smoke above them. I opened the newspaper but then folded it up.

In front of the pub was a bus stop. I considered taking a bus to the city center to see a film, but I'd seen every film that was showing. Many I'd seen twice. I'd do that, to pass the time, on days off, sit in the cinema all day, and there was nothing like it. You got to see and hear all the things you missed the first time around, and you got to escape the things that were in your head. Or I could buy a record. I had a list of them written down, along with a list of books, but the record shops and Eason's were close to closing. A few friends I knew from the bar trade drank in a pub that was in walking distance. They were either there or in the games arcade next door, playing Space Invaders, pinball, poker, but I wasn't in the mood for them, and game arcades bored me, and like everyone else, they would be watching that match. On my walk home, I'd stop at the Italian chipper and get something to eat. I'd chat with the young dark Italian woman. We didn't understand a word we said to each other, but I enjoyed hearing the sounds of her words, and I enjoyed watching her, and smelling the frying cod and chips. She would not be watching that match.

I stood and went to the bar and ordered another Club Orange. The men's faces transfixed by the game. I watched my reflection in the smoky mirror and wondered how I'd kill the dull minutes and the tedious hours until I'd see Una again next Sunday. There was the letter to write to my mother. (A cancer was growing in my mother then. She would be gone inside sixteen months.) I'd write to her tomorrow night after work. I'd sit at the table, write that I was fine. I hoped everything was fine there. I love my job. I'll be down home soon. I missed everyone. And I did stop by Una's flat after Mass. I rang the bell, but she wasn't there. I might try her again some other Sunday. And I'd fold a twenty-pound note into the crease of the letter. That made my mother happy. She'd write back and say I was a good boy for sending it. God would reward me. And don't forget to drop a line when I did talk to Una.

The country barman was looking up at the television when he handed me the Club Orange. I put the exact change on the counter, thanked him, and sat back in the seat. The sun was gone. The seat had cooled.

You'll get tired of all that. Una was the one to say it. Day in, day out. Polishing mirrors, wiping dust from shelves, sweeping floors, cleaning up spills, stocking shelves, intervening badly in fights, mopping up the vomit and the shit in the jacks, filling endless pints of beer, small ones, vodka and red, vodka and orange, a drop of the cat, young man—but I liked chatting with the locals. They told you things. Their hatred of bosses and foremen. The factories closing. The need for stronger unions. Thatcher is less than a cunt because a cunt is of some use. The young ones and the drugs. The brazenness of robbers and criminals. The redundancy check will last only a few months. The missus and the fucking children wanting every fucking penny of it. Lucky if you get a few fucking pints out of it in the end. You'll have to stand me a few pints, young fellow. You will. When there's nothing left. You will.

The men sitting on the barstools looked like the men I served in the pub. Most lived locally, or they once did, before their families were moved to housing estates beyond the city center, and on Sundays they returned to the old neighborhoods to drink with friends they played in the street with when they were children.

A man I didn't notice when I came in was sitting apart from the others at the very end of the bar. He was not looking at the match. He was reading the newspaper. He made me think of Nathan, who was a regular in my bar, but hadn't visited in a while. Some regulars said Nathan had booked himself into a home. Others said he'd gone to live with relatives. Many said you never know with Nathan. A FOR SALE sign had gone up in Nathan's yard that past week, and someone had gawked in the windows of the house and reported that the rooms were empty.

Nathan visited the bar every evening from four until eight. He sat on the same stool at the end of the counter and read the *Evening Press*.

Men read either the *Evening Press* or the *Evening Herald*. The men
who bet on horses, which was most of them, also read the English tab-
loids: the *Mirror*, the *Sun*, the *News of the World*. Those papers had
the horse-racing form at the back and on page three a color photo of a
young woman whose breasts took up most of the page.

Nathan was in his mid-sixties. He was retired from his desk job at
the post office. He lived down the road from the bar. The wife was
dead. The children were grown and gone. They visited only at Christmas. When Nathan was drunk, he'd tell me how sad it was that he
never saw his children. He'd lament the loss of the wife. He drank
three pints, and between 7:15 and 8:00, he drank two half Jameson's
with water. Regulars said Nathan was a gentleman, because he had
fine manners and he dressed the way you think a gentleman might: a
pressed navy blue shirt buttoned to the neck, matching tie, and a sports
coat, with a handkerchief in the breast pocket. During winter he wore
a hat and a herringbone topcoat.

There is one story Nathan told me many times. He did when I put
the second glass of Jameson's on the counter before him, then wiped
the counter and emptied his ashtray, and he folded the newspaper and
smiled his dazzling denture smile. And I sometimes wonder why this
story he told has stayed. But I also wonder why he never came in to say
good-bye, why he never told me where it was he was going.

The story involved a close friend of his, and this happened when
he and Nathan were in their early twenties. This friend was ex-army.
He was notably handsome, a seducer, who happened to get one of the
women he seduced pregnant, but when the woman told the ex-soldier
she was pregnant, and that he was the father, the ex-soldier called her
a hoor and a liar. She spent months begging and pestering him. He ignored her, went about his business seducing, and I'm not sure if
Nathan ever told me, or I've forgotten, what happened to the pregnant woman. Anyway, the sister of the woman he got pregnant was a
beautiful-looking woman, and she sought him out. She found out
where he lived. The bars he drank in and the bookie shops where he

placed his bets. She went to the bars and sat close to him, and they got to talking. He bought her drinks. She drank the drinks and gave him a fake name. And after a few meetings, she let him take her back to his flat, but she would not let him make love to her. He put bunches of flowers he bought on Moore Street on her doorstep. He took her to the cinema. They walked arm-in-arm and he took her out to eat at good restaurants and paid. He even bought theater tickets. Still she did not allow him to make love to her, and he finally broke down and told her he was madly in love with her. She cried and said she would so make love to him, but only at Glendalough, in County Wicklow, in the meadow above Saint Kevin's Bed. The ex-soldier arranged the trip, and one summer's afternoon they took the bus there, and they sat down in a sunny meadow where they could see The Round Tower. He brought a flask. They sipped from the flask and talked. Eventually they got down to business. Buttons opened. Zippers unzipped. They lay back in the warm grass. The ex-soldier whispered in her ear that no doubt she was the one for him. He was ready to spend the rest of his life with her. He gets her skirt up, she gets his pants and underpants around his knees, and she strokes and strokes him, he shuts his eyes and once again whispers how much he loves her, and while he's whispering, she slips a razor from the waistband of her skirt, and in one rapid swipe she slices his penis off at the base. Then she stands and flings his bloody penis as far as she can toward Saint Kevin's tower, and next she runs off across the meadow, fixing her skirt back into place as she runs, laughing and telling him that she's on her way home to tell her sister that the wrong that was done to her is righted. The ex-soldier lies whimpering and bleeding in the sunny grass.

When Nathan told the story it more or less went that way, but the last time he told it, the week before he vanished, the sister stands over the ex-soldier with her bloody razor, and she does not throw the penis toward the tower, she doesn't even pick up the penis. No. She begs the ex-soldier's forgiveness, says that she wants to marry him, no matter what he is missing, because she is in love with him, too, but her duty to her sister had to be fulfilled.

Nathan laughed every time he told the story. Then a few weeks after he disappeared, I told it to one of the regulars, and when I finished it, I said Nathan used to tell that story to me. The regular smirked and said the story was about Nathan himself. Everyone knows that. I said that couldn't be true. Nathan had children. Nathan was not that kind of a person. Nathan was a gentleman. The regular smirked again and said Nathan was a great man for the women. Got the cushy job in the post office because of his job in the army. Then some woman's pregnant sister beguiled him and chopped your man off. Nathan became remorseful for the wrong he had caused and he ended up marrying this woman whose husband had died from the big C. She had three young children, and she and Nathan raised them. They did a good job. Children did fine. Then a few years ago the wife died, and the longer the wife is dead the more Nathan goes downhill. Eventually goes all the way downhill. All the way back to his old ways. But he didn't only have age against him, of course, he didn't have the equipment. But still he visited the prostitutes. The worst ones you could find. Nathan took to the leather like you'd slip the saddle on a racehorse. Got down on all fours and begged for the whip like the gentleman he was. Very fond of the whip, Nathan was. Had three pensions. The army and the post office and the old age. Spent them on the prostitutes. The rest in here.

The regular smiled and winked.

—We're all gentlemen in here, he said. —Every single one of us. And now, young man, you have it. You have now what everyone else have.

The sun was shining again. It burned the back of my neck. I finished the Club Orange and stood up. I was heading through the bar door when someone scored in the match. Then the boisterous cheers and groans. I turned to look, but I could not see the man who reminded me of Nathan. Some of the men were clapping and laughing.

Others cursed and pounded the bar with their fists, jarring the cloud of cigarette smoke. I envied them in that moment, but then I let the bar door shut. Across the street, the steel curtains on the shop fronts were drawn. I read the graffiti: Damo loves Sandra. Derek likes a fat cock in his tight hole. Brits out! Liverpool rules! What do we get for our trouble and pain? The Six Counties is ours. P.A.Y.E. = pay all you earn. R.I.P. Philo. Then the band posters: The Blades at the Baggot Inn. The Smiths at the SFX. The Wolfe Tones at the Baggot Inn.

I shoved my hands into my pockets and decided to walk the streets close to the canal. Then I'd head to the chipper, buy something to eat, chat with the Italian girl. So I headed back down Dorset Street, crossed the canal bridge, and took a right onto Fitzroy Avenue. Sunshine brightened the red bricks and the windows of the tiny houses. Smells of supper from the houses. Fish and chips. Spice burgers. Bisto gravy. Reheated roasted potatoes. Family voices shot from the houses in spurts like from a machine gun. And I was at the Five Lamps when I remembered I had left the newspaper and Una's biscuits on the seat in the pub. The paper I didn't care about, but the loss of the biscuits made me dismal. She'd put them in the plastic bag then knotted it. And that stupid bartender would have flung them into the rubbish by now.

I stepped into a phone box. Tess was in nursing school in Cork. She'd been there a few months. A long letter had arrived from her two weeks before. I hadn't written her back, although I'd read the letter every night after coming in from work. Tess liked nursing school fine. She was making some friends, though she missed home terribly. Did I miss it the way she did? And Tess couldn't stop thinking about the stories she and I made up. Do you remember, Jimmy, the ones about the teacher and her husband? Do you remember, Jimmy, we made them live in a hovel? There was no light and there was a hole in the roof. The damp smoke flowed up through the hole. And they were starving. They plucked dock leaves and nettles from the fields and boiled them in a pot over the fire. And why was my last letter only a few lines telling nothing? And why hadn't I rang? Tess'd rang my hall phone four or five times. Was I not listening for the ring?

I knew Tess's number by heart, and I fumbled the coins into the slot and picked up the receiver. But the promise to Una came into my head, and I knew if I rang Tess I'd tell her about Roger, the forgotten biscuits, and I'd tell that something had happened to me with Una, that the wait to see her again was killing me. I would because that's the way Tess and I were then, but the something that happened was not to be shared, poked fun of, banished, or changed into something else. And so I hung up the receiver, put the change back in my pocket, and stepped out of the phone box. It was a long walk back to my flat. I couldn't be bothered with the chipper anymore. I wasn't a bit hungry. And I could not wait to lock the door of my flat. Close the curtains. Put a record on, lie on the bed, and see Una again sitting on that windowsill. Her long shadow for less than a minute of your life along a single bed.

4

—How's your life, I said to Zoë.

She was standing on the other side of the screen door.

—Quite fancy, I imagine, compared to your new friend, my dear.

I opened the screen door. Zoë stepped in and we hugged. I took the white tote bag and placed it on the chair Walter had sat on. Zoë looked about.

—The place looks clean, James—

—Some dusting wouldn't be remiss, I said.

—Who cares, my dear, Zoë said.

—I can't think of one person, my dear, I said.

I went to the fridge and filled Zoë a glass of water and said we should stand on the futon bed and watch for Walter. She slipped her sandals off. I was in my socks. We stood on the bed, leaned our elbows on the windowsill, and stared through the screen. I looked at her when I told her the light green summer dress suited her. She thanked me. I turned and lit a cigarette and blew the smoke through the dusty screen.

—I'm so excited to meet your new friend, Zoë said.

—I'm still not sure if he's homeless, I said.

—You said he looks homeless, Zoë said.

—We would say that, I said.

—Then he is probably homeless, my dear, Zoë said.

—He might just be traveling around, my dear—

—He's not a born-again, my dear—

—Not once has he mentioned Jesus, my dear—

I looked at my watch.

—You seem nervous, Zoë said.

—I'm not used to going places, I said.

—We're driving twenty miles. You've gone several places, my dear. Did you discover any more about your neighbor?

—Not beyond the sneakers. She's not been sitting on her porch. The mailbox is empty.

—Someone is picking her mail up. Her family came for her, my dear—

—The truth is there's more to Walter, but I don't want to go into it.

—I want to hear, my dear.

—Not now, my dear—

—Why not now, my dear. It's so much more exciting than writing the proposals my dad sends my way—

—I might tell you later, my dear—

—Might, my dear.

—*Might* is what I said, my dear.

—You don't have to tell me anything, my dear. That's your call. But can I tell you something—

—I love to hear you talk, my dear.

—It's about a trip I once took with my parents, my dear.

—Before they divorced, I said.

—Yes, before then, when I was a kid, my dear. We drove to Maine. It was a trip we had taken several times during the summer. My family owned a cabin on the coast. It was really a house, my dear, but we called it the cabin. There were decks and a huge sitting room downstairs with a big window that looked out onto the ocean. Dad's parents owned the house, and Dad liked it to look rugged. When the families down the beach knocked down their homes to build mansions, Dad was determined not to change, but Mom wanted something different. Mom wanted skylights and wraparound porches. And at the end of this summer it was painted fuchsia.

—An ugly color, if I may say so, I said.

—I agree, my dear. And Dad hated it, too, I know he did, but my parents never discussed it in front of my brother, Luke, and I, but on this one trip I was sitting in the back of the car. I was ten or eleven, surrounded by books, and my parents did not speak during the entire trip. I played games. Luke and I always did, on the trips to Maine. My parents made us play games that increased our verbal skills—

—Like spelling things you saw on the highway?

—Not like that, my dear—

—Like what, then, my dear?

—I forget, my dear. It's not important. Then my first summer home from college I was in Dad's law office in New Haven. He looked great. He was going to a gym five mornings a week. I had a boyfriend in college I liked until we liked other people, but that happened later, my dear. Dad excused himself. He went down the hall to a meeting. I was left sitting in Dad's leather chair. He used to lift me into that chair when I was a little girl, and he'd sit on the chair across the desk, where his clients sat. After he left I opened the top drawer of his desk. I was not snooping. I just slid it open. Wouldn't you do that, my dear?

—In a heartbeat, my dear—

—There was a photograph in there of my dad with a woman. This woman did not look like my mom. This woman, my dear, was more than twenty years younger than my dad. The photo was taken in front of the fuchsia cabin. The woman's shoulders were tanned. Her shoulders I remember, my dear. Swimsuits hung on the porch railing behind them. And Dad's motorcycle was there. The helmets were on the ground. Dad kept this motorcycle in the garage behind the cabin. He spent hours working on it. He loved it. I'd look out my bedroom window in the morning and he would be kneeling before the motorcycle, the little parts in a circle around him, and the radio playing in the garage. He used to take me for rides on the motorcycle. I'd wrap my arms around him. We'd ride along the hard sand. The back roads and the village streets.

—That sounds cool, I said.

—It was very cool, my dear. But of course my dad and this woman were screwing. He had come back from the cabin two weeks before. He went up there once every year in late spring. His long weekend away from work with his old college buddies. They fished. They went to the bars in the village. They drank scotch and smoked my dad's cigars. He kept them in this nice wooden box. I used to think when I was a kid if I opened the box I'd find pistols in there. They probably spent most of their time speculating on real estate and retelling their stories about their college days. Their glorious hijinks. And in the photograph, my dad's striped shirt was opened to his belly button. I was so disgusted. The white hair on his chest. My dad looked like Hugh Hefner with one of his chicks!

Zoë paused. I handed her the water glass. She took two sips. I was watching the corner of the house.

—I ran out of the office and got into my car and drove home, my dear. I forget how I later explained why I left, and a little over a month later, Mom called me in tears to say they were divorcing.

—I know this part, my dear, I said.

—But I didn't tell you, my dear, that this was the summer I thought I was going to be a painter. I'd studied it in an art history class that spring. I'd taken classes in high school and college, so I went to an art colony in South Carolina. And a few days after I arrived was when my mom called. Dad then called me. He called ten times a day for a week, but I never picked up the phone. He left messages, crying, apologizing. He said he loved me, but I let him cry, and I cried when I listened to his messages. My boyfriend came to visit. We hiked the mountains. We drove to the beach. We smoked pot I scored from some dude I met. Another message from Mom said Dad had moved into an apartment. I had told Luke about the photograph. And I never again saw the woman. I have often wondered who she was.

—Maybe they weren't screwing, my dear. They were just hanging out, you know—

—They were screwing, my dear—

—If you think they were, then they were, my dear—

—Dad married my stepmom less than two years later, my dear. And my stepmom mails gifts on my birthday, the Fourth of July, Christmas, Hanukkah, my birthday, of course. And I write my stepmom a card every time she sends a gift. I tell her how the gift was exactly what I wanted, but I've never liked one gift she mailed. In fact, my dear, I've hated every one of them. You will think me very ungrateful, my dear—

—I'm more interested in the cabin and the motorbike, my dear.

—The cabin was sold. Luke and I call it the first victim. The motorcycle was the second. I laugh now, but not then.

—I believe you there, my dear, I said.

—But I looked forward so much to visiting the cabin, my dear. The beautiful house I grew up in was dull compared to it. And I'm sure the new people have torn it down and sold the property. They bought it for that reason, I imagine. I was driving close to there last summer, and wanted to go see it, but I was afraid. I loved the big front room. I read so many books at that window, while my parents ate out in the evening with friends who lived in other summer homes. The light was beautiful in that room. The sky turned this shade of pink over the water every evening. I called it the pink hour. The small boats bobbed on the horizon. But I apologize for going on, James. I just wanted to tell about the car ride. But you must tell me about a journey you went on with your dad.

—Is this one of the games you played in the car—

—It's just something on my mind—

—It sounds to me like a game—

—It's not a game, my dear. We are waiting for your new friend. You begged me to come along. A fun day in the country, you said. And we have not seen each other in a while—

—We haven't, but I think this is something I got myself into—

—A short trip. Stop fretting, my dear—

—I'm not fretting—

—You are, my dear.

—You were mad with your father, I said.

—Back then. But I love Dad. Dad is very kind. Dad is Dad.

Dad is Dad, Zoë repeated—almost sang it, when she stepped off the futon. The fridge door opened. Water poured into a glass. The fridge hummed. A cloud shifted. Sunlight filled the yard. I lit a cigarette. I kept on staring at the corner.

—Sorry, I should have put on some music, Zoë, I turned and said.

—Don't apologize, James. And you don't have to tell me anything—

—I'm beginning to think he's not going to arrive.

Zoë touched my shoulder. She placed the glass on the sill.

—He'll show up, my dear. He wants to see this aunt—

—Who would think the homeless would be so impolite—

—Just tell me your story, my dear—

—Arrive, won't arrive, my dear. I was around the age you were, my dear. My father was buying hay. It was raining when we started out, but then the sun appeared, and we stopped at all the churches we passed. My father did that, when he went on the road. He could not pass a church without going into it and kneeling for a while, and so going anywhere with him took time, because there were many churches. But we were on the road for a while, when we came to an abbey. It was Glenstal Abbey, which I didn't know then. There is a castle next to it and a boarding school for boys. There were trees, stone walls, and trimmed hedges. I had never seen anything so lovely. My father drove in and parked. Flowers—roses, definitely, big bushes of them—but also copper beech trees, crocuses, lilacs, and hedges of rhododendrons, and we walked through a garden where cucumbers and rosemary and parsley were growing, and more flowers. My father knew this place, I think now that he did, but I only think it because I'm telling you. He ordered me not to touch anything in the garden. I obeyed him. I always did. And he reached into his coat pocket and brought out his beads and started praying, mumbling, like in ecstasy, or like a lunatic, depending on your thinking. Maybe he was just praying that he would get the hay at the price he wanted—

—It's a very good reason to pray, my dear, Zoë said.

—I suppose, my dear. But I couldn't pray with the castle rising above the trees and the scent of flowers and herbs. And at this man's house the hay was bought, the deal went down, hay bought at a price that pleased my father, because if it wasn't at that price it wouldn't have been bought, the bottle of Powers brought out, palms spat on then slapped, speculating about the weather and the price of cattle, the lack of jobs, the dreadful politicians, and last Saturday's horse races. The man's wife brought out the whiskey. She served little glasses of it, with a splash of water—she used a teaspoon. She smiled down at me when she put a tall glass of lemonade and a thick slice of sponge cake before me. The table was covered in an oilcloth. Two red geraniums bloomed at my elbow. A gray cat was sleeping on the windowsill outside. I put my hand through the window and petted the cat—

—How beautiful, my dear—

—It was, my dear. Indeed, it was. But on the drive back we stopped at the abbey again. It was darker now, on the ground, but not above the trees, and the place was silent but for the crows cawing in the big trees. My father stood in the same place and took out his beads and prayed. And he warned me again to not touch anything, maybe thanking God now for the price he got, that was all there was to it—

—Good karma, my dear—

—Karma, indeed, my dear. But we drove away from the abbey, and on the drive home he talked about the year he spent in England. He had never talked to me about that before, although I had heard it around the house that he had once worked in England. I was still too young to be curious. And we weren't a family who talked about those sorts of things. His year in England was the year before he met my mother. He was home at Christmas, and he met my mother at a dance and never again went back to work in England.

—You're losing it, my dear, but keep going—

—Thank you, my dear. My mother, she had a small farm. I think her whole life was about waiting to marry and have children. I don't think she imagined much beyond that. That and God were it. She talked to God like I'm talking now to you. Maybe the glass of whiskey caused my father to talk, but he was in a good mood. He told me he liked working on the buildings, the hardiness of it, meeting men from all over. He said the Connemara men were the worst—you are not going to understand any of this, my dear—

—I'm liking your story, my dear. And your new friend has yet to show—

—He won't appear, Zoë—

—Yes, James, he will—

—Well, the Connemara men spoke only Irish, and it was their version of Irish. They were the toughest, you didn't want to get into a fight with them, because you weren't just fighting one of them, you were fighting a tribe, and one Connemara man was more than enough for any man to fight, though the Connemara men were highly valued as laborers. All the building sites wanted them. These men were proud of their strength, and they sold it to whoever wanted it, for the right money, of course, which wasn't much money, just enough for lodgings, food, and pints of beer. And then my father tells me that he never slept that year. After work he just walked the streets of Kilburn and Camden, he never went back to the digs he was staying in, he never went to the pubs, he was so homesick, he said, so he sat on park benches for the hours when he wasn't working, and he slept on the benches and got up the next morning and went off to work, but I have no idea why he told me all of that then. Maybe, like you in your dad's office, you just happen to be there—

—Oh, my dear—

Zoë took a quick sip from the glass.

—And so there I was, my dear, sitting next to my father, not watching him, but having to listen to him, to endure him, and I never liked to look into his face, though his was a handsome face, narrow with strong

jawbones, pale, with tiny red veins that spread out along the cheeks—
you remember things that are of no use, you remember things that are
of no use, he used to say to me—but I listened, I had no other choice
but to listen to him, and I watched the fields and the meadows, the
cows and the houses that drifted past so slowly, and I thought I was
never going to be home and free from that car and him and his voice—

—I imagine that's your new friend at the corner, my dear, wearing
the baseball cap, Zoë said.

Her finger was pressed against the screen. I reached my hand up
and wiped dust from it. The backpack was at his feet. A loose bunch of
flowers lay atop it. The shirt was tight across the shoulders, but it otherwise fitted him.

—Mister Mysterious Walter, my dear—

—And flowers for his aunt, my dear. How sweet is that—

—He stole them from the park, my dear. He's late, and I gave him
that shirt—

—I never imagined you wearing a cowboy shirt, my dear—

—When I was a teenager in Dublin, a girl bought it for me. It was a
bit of a joke—

—Did she buy you a horse, too?

—No horse, my dear, or spurs, in case you are curious.

—Don't be rude to him because he's late.

—I was hoping I'd seen the last of him, my dear—

I was sitting on the edge of the bed and lacing my shoes. Zoë was
pressing the screen door open. The tote bag swung in her other hand.
She tapped the screen with her nails—the bare, skinny arm extended,
the palm flat against the screen.

—Let's not keep him waiting, James. He must be nervous about
seeing someone he hasn't seen in so long.

5

At the end of June, Michael located the well down the paddock from the front of our house. The next week he brought a small JCB and drilled. Two weeks later he dug the foundation for the pump house. In early July, he brought a cement mixer, hitched to the back of his Nissan lorry. Pipes of all shapes and sizes, cement blocks, bags of cement, wood, and heaps of sand and gravel were delivered from the creamery store. We covered them with sheets of plastic against the rain, though that was a summer of sunshine.

When the seven-by-seven foundation was set, Michael and a brick-layer built the walls. Michael plastered the walls himself. I remember walking out our front door, out to turn in cows, or cut wood for the range, and I'd stand in my mother's flower garden and listen to Michael whistling tunes on his ladder, and it wasn't until I moved to Dublin that I heard those tunes again, and there I also heard the words. Songs by Patsy Cline, Cole Porter, Billie Holiday, and Frank Sinatra that the locals sang late on Saturday nights.

That first day, my mother told Michael to be sure to tell Nora the moment he got inside the door that evening to not bother with his lunch. My mother would make his lunch, she had to make lunches for us anyway, and because of the fine weather, there were plenty of toma-toes, scallions, and lettuce. My father grew these beside my mother's flower garden, along with potatoes, onions, parsnips, carrots, straw-berries, and raspberries. Michael sat on a cement block and ate my mother's sandwiches and drank her tea from his white enamel mug.

My father sat with him, unless we were making hay, and if that was the case, Michael helped out.

Two or three days a week, Michael brought Kevin, and they started to stay late in the evening. There was a problem with how the well was lined, a leak, something like that, I forget, but I remember hearing them nailing down the frame of the roof while we milked the cows. After they were milked, my mother and sisters made supper, which Michael and Kevin sometimes stayed for, and after supper my father and Michael smoked Sweet Aftons by the range and drank bottles of stout, while Michael retold his jokes and we watched television, and when this one program we liked to watch was over, my parents told us to go outside, run around, enjoy the fine long evenings, what were we doing indoors anyway, watching that awful American trash, but if we were going to the river we were to be careful, even though the water was low.

High or low in summertime, we went to the river. Oh, how I loved the river so! We'd take our shoes off and stand in the warm mud below the sloping bank and we'd laugh and shove each other and slowly sink into that mud that boiled up to our ankles. Then we waded in and tore out the rushes, ferns, and water lilies, and we swatted the fat bluebottles and the clouds of midges and laid down jam jars and tin cans on the sandy riverbed to catch the tiny fish we called brickeens. We decorated the jars and cans with moss and pebbles from the riverbed and placed them on our bedroom windows. The brickeens survived a few weeks.

Anthony stopped coming to the river with us that summer. He had stopped spending any time with his younger brothers and sisters, and when our parents told us to go outside, Anthony was allowed to cycle up the road to meet the Mahers, who had a record player and two or three K-tel records. The Mahers and Anthony smoked Majors and drank cheap English cider. Rarely had they the money to buy them, so they just shoplifted them. My parents knew nothing about any of this. Or if they did, they pretended they didn't. Rules for boys being way more lenient than rules for girls.

Kevin's interest in coming to the river with us was Tess. She was sixteen. She was beautiful. She knew this. And she rejoiced in Kevin's telling her how nice her red hair looked, how fine she was in her pink skirt, and she sat before the mirror in the girls' room and rolled the hissing curling iron through her hair and carefully brushed on mascara and eye shadow.

—Don't put that stuff on your face, they'll go stone mad, Hannah used to say.

—Let them go stone mad, Tess used to say.

And she'd smile at me in the mirror and I'd smile back at her, and she'd press her face closer to the mirror.

—Tell her not to do it, Jimmy. She'll listen to you, Hannah used to say.

—She won't listen to me, I used to say.

—Don't blame me when they get mad at you, Hannah used to say.

—Don't worry, I won't, Tess used to say.

Then Tess would laugh in the mirror, and when she laughed I did.

—You'll get us all into trouble. That's what you'll do, Hannah used to say.

And she'd tightly fold her arms and sigh and turn her back on Tess and the mirror.

On one of those evenings in early July, Kevin sat on the riverbank. He took off his work boots and socks and rolled his pants legs up to his knees. Tess sat beside him and slipped her sandals off. They had walked hand in hand through the meadow behind the three of us. Hannah and Stephen were bent over, singing into the water.

Bobby Shafto's gone to sea
Silver buckles on his knee
When he comes back he'll marry me
Bobby, Bobby Shafto!

Tess was wearing the pink skirt and the tight gray blouse that had two or three cloth-covered buttons at the neck. The skirt and the blouse, Tess's purple coat, other secondhand clothes, and four pairs of girl's platform shoes had arrived a few weeks before in a parcel from my mother's old National school friend who lived in a neighborhood at the end of the Piccadilly Line in North London.

Kevin and Tess stood whispering in the mud. The three of us were eyeing the fleeting shoals of brickeens. I'd follow one brickeen, pick it out from the rest, but every time it got lost among the others. Stephen and Hannah were shouting with delight that there were more brickeens this evening than ever before. Kevin and Tess left the riverbank and headed toward the small hill a few hundred yards away. I waited ten or fifteen minutes before I told Hannah and Stephen that I needed to piss. They weren't listening; they were too into their brickeens. And so I waded out and strolled up the side of the hill. At the top of it I hid behind one of the hay pikes we had made the week before. Michael and Kevin Lyons had helped. At the bottom of the hill sat Kevin and my sister. Their backs were against a hay pike.

I had seen one porn magazine. They were illegal, but the Mahers had one. One of their Liverpool cousins had sneaked it over on the boat. And one Sunday in May, after second Mass, when I was walking the road home with the Mahers and Anthony, the oldest of the Mahers pulled his jumper up, reached his hand down the back of his pants, pulled the magazine out, opened it up, and shoved it into my face. They laughed. And so did I. It was a glossy photograph of a naked and bony young woman on all fours. A naked man knelt at either end of her. The men were hairy, fat, and older. One had a thick mustache, the kind you imagined a bandit wearing. And it all looked so brutal. The hungry look on the woman's face, the tip of her swollen pink tongue clamped against her bottom lip, the men blissfully stroking themselves, warming up for the real action. But sure enough, I was terribly excited by it. I didn't yet have pubic hair, but I believed that when I did, I'd fit right in, be accepted by Anthony and the Mahers, and go forth with them on their adventures.

Long and thin goes too far in and does not suit the lady
Short and thick does the trick and out pops the baby

I read the story below the photograph. I don't know if the Mahers or Anthony did. They might have got what they wanted by looking. Boys read the *Beano, Hotspur, Batman, Superman,* and *Spider-Man,* when we could get our hands on them. I read those and Andrew Lang's version of the *Odyssey* and the *Iliad,* the Greek myths, the Norse and Irish myths, tales of King Arthur and the Knights of the Round Table, Old and New Testament stories, *The Arabian Nights, Treasure Island, Don Quixote, The Last of the Mohicans, The Adventures of Robin Hood, Lorna Doone, The Swiss Family Robinson,* and *Robinson Crusoe.* Those books were in the National school library, which was a two-door glass cabinet that the teacher unlocked on Friday afternoons—but the story in the porn magazine has also stayed. The man with the bandit mustache told it. He said the woman chewed on the end of his penis like it was a cigar. How could you forget *cigar*? How could you forget *chew*?

Bricks and mortar will not stay,
Will not stay, will not stay,
Bricks and mortar will not stay,
My fair lady.

Kevin and Tess were pure electricity when they skipped along the top then down the side of that small hill. Tess's pink skirt blowing out in a breeze. I was back in the river. I said nothing to Stephen and Hannah about what I had seen. I was learning to be secretive. Then Kevin and Tess were behind me, but I didn't turn. I didn't want to give them any hint that I was in the know. I reached down and flung handfuls of water at Stephen and Hannah. They kept shouting at me that I'd frighten all the brickeens away, but I didn't stop. I laughed. I played the fool. The fool being the next-door neighbor of the secretive. Late evening sunshine on the water and on the two large rocks on the opposite bank. The sweet smell of ripening hay, the laughter and the shouts from my younger brother and sister, and behind me my elder sister and Kevin Lyons giggling.

I'm not sure how it came about. I did think Tess and he were still in the mud behind me, though next their laughter came from up the riverbank, then harsh words from him, clothes being ripped, a scream from Tess, a splash, Tess crying, and the bluebottles before me turning furious.

None of us could swim, and the water between Tess and us was crowded with the stiff rushes and the slimy water lilies and the sharp reeds that would slice your skin open. Columns of wasps skimmed in and out of a mossy hole in the riverbank—but I dashed out of that river, ran along the bank, past the unripened blackberry bush, slapping at the midges, calling my sister's name, who was crying and calling my name. Hannah was also crying and Stephen was crying because Hannah was. Kevin stood on the edge of the riverbank, his arms flat against his side, his head down. I said nothing when I ran around him, down the riverbank, through the soft mud, and into the water, where I grabbed my sister's hands and pulled her to her feet. She would not have drowned. The water was shallow. But you never know. And Tess was otherwise in bits. Stephen and Hannah were by then beside us. Hannah held her sister's right hand while Stephen and I walked Tess out of the river and sat her on the bank. She was crying and gripping the ripped blouse at the neck. The buttons had vanished. I looked up to see Kevin Lyons running at the edge of the meadow. He clutched his boots and socks to his chest. He'd made powerful tracks.

The two men in the kitchen were on their third or fourth bottle of porter. My mother was cleaning up and circling the men like a hawk. Asking what else they needed. They ignored her unless another bottle was called for. Their pale ashes and the burned-out butts of Sweet Aftons scattered across the range top, where a blackened kettle and teapot sat. And then us huddled in the middle of that kitchen. Like we had stepped unwillingly onto a stage. Tess's red hair matted against her cheeks. Broken rushes sticking out of her hair like knitting needles. Like swords stuck in stones. The muddy and wrinkled pink skirt. Tess was still crying and gripping the blouse to her neck. Hannah was still crying. She stood in front. Stephen was on one side of Tess. I was on her other. And the first thing my mother said when she saw us was for us not to drip all over the tiles that she had spent the last hour mopping. And the second thing she said was did she not warn us a million times to be careful when we ventured to the river.

Hannah blurted it out.

—Kevin Lyons shoved Tess into the river and ran away! And because of that all my brickeens escaped!

—What has come over that young fellow at all, Michael turned to my father and said.

—The same thing that's come over these wretches before us, my father looked at his friend and said.

My mother smoothed the front of her apron then stepped between the men and us. She pushed the hair from her face and placed her hands on her hips. Her eyes were on Tess.

—Go down to your room immediately and put on something decent! Fix your hair, and did I not warn you a million times to not plaster that muck on your eyes, how many times! How many! How many!

—I'm sorry! I'm sorry! Tess cried.

—You're not sorry! Not one bit! If you did like you were told devilment like this wouldn't happen.

Then my father stood. His wife stepped aside.

—Clear out of this kitchen! Or I'll get the stick to yez! And pull that door after yez!

Tess and I were down in the girls' room. Tess was sitting on the edge of her and Hannah's bed. Tess's legs were crossed. Left over right. The left one was shaking. The girls' door was open and so was the toilet door. Hannah was sitting on the toilet bowl and crying. Her cries echoed up and down the blue corridor. She cried that Tess brought this on herself. Did she not say many times that something like this was bound to happen! And next Hannah cried that we'd never see brickeens like those again! Why, oh why did Tess always have to ruin everything for everyone! Stephen was in the boys' room. Stephen was most likely whispering to dying brickeens on the windowsill. He was bored with this drama. Tess was staring at the floor. I reached out and held her shoulders and begged her to look up. She had stopped crying but her hand still gripped the ripped blouse. And that left leg still shaking. Her wet scraggly hair fully hiding her face. Like the river before we ripped the lilies from it. Rushes wilting in Tess's hair and rushes scattered at my feet and muddy water dripping from her hair and dress onto that bedroom floor.

—I saw you, Tess, I said. —I saw what you and him did.

Tess looked up.

—Don't tell them, Jimmy. Don't ever tell. If they find that out they'll kill us—

—I won't tell them, Tess, I promise I won't ever tell anyone—

And I never did tell that Kevin Lyons's hands shoved my sister's blouse out along her raised arms and the same hands reached around my sister's back and unclipped her bra and tossed it like a cigarette butt into the meadow. Nor did I tell that I saw my sister unbutton Kevin Lyons's shirt and shove it over his shoulders and down his arms like she was skinning an animal. Nor did I say my sister reached in and pulled Kevin's cock out through the zipper she had just unzipped and she laughed and kissed him fiercely on the mouth before she leaned over and gave him his first blow job.

The adults made no inquiries with regard to the why, the how, the what. The adults just went to work. We were banned from going to the river for the rest of the summer. Mascara, blush, and eye shadow were burned on the range. Pinups of pop stars on the girls' bedroom wall were ripped down and burned. Teenage magazines the girls read were burned. Tess had borrowed those magazines from school friends. And

Tess's scrapbooks were burned. I forget what she pasted into them, but she had quite a few. The adults didn't touch her paintings. Those stayed, one here, one there, on that otherwise bare wall. And the pink skirt vanished from the wardrobe. I've no clue what the adults did with that. And one morning my father took the platform shoes into the far corner of his garden and pounded those daring heels to bits with a crowbar. Then he picked up each shoe and tore off the cheap flashy straps and buckles, and he cursed under his breath when he flung them at his raspberry bushes.

The Lyons family had their troubles. Kevin vanished for three days. One story was that he stayed with his uncle Roger, and because Michael and Roger didn't speak, Michael never visited Roger. But I think the real story was that the eldest son hid out in hay barns and stole eggs from henhouses and ate unripened blackberries and crab apples. Every morning of the three days he was missing, his father and my father had the same solemn conversation in our yard while they smoked and half-glanced at each other across the bed of Michael's Nissan truck.

—Any sign of him, Mike? asked my father.

—Not a sign or a word, Tom.

—You didn't ring the Guards, Mike.

—I'd like to not bring them on me, Tom.

—It's good you didn't do that. He'll pipe down, my father said.

—Didn't we all have to, Michael said.

—He'll be back in no time. Don't I know it, my father said.

—I was trying to train him, Michael said. —Now God only knows what's going to become of him.

—He'll pipe down, he will, my father said.

—Odd fucking life, ha! Michael said.

When Kevin did come home his parents bought him new clothes that we considered cool—a snug Dingo denim jacket, flared Dingo jeans, a wide leather belt, platform shoes.

Then it was autumn. The red tractor brought the hay pikes in from the meadows and we forked the hay high in the barn. Potatoes were dug and pitted. The autumn rains and the wind returned. The cows stopped giving milk. The evenings grew darker and colder. The two sheepdogs didn't sleep on the cement yard anymore; they curled up in the warm barn when the stars appeared above the elms and frost sparkled on the cement yard—and at last I was on the red bus. What I had dreamed about for so long. I wore my Confirmation jumper, pants and shoes, and I sat on the top deck, where the tough and the cool sat. I wanted very badly to be one of them, though I discovered soon enough this was never going to happen, but I didn't want them picking on me, and so you learned how to pretend, you learned how to flatter, and you learned how to act like you didn't care. Anthony sat upstairs, on the long backseat. That's where the girls who smoked sat. Anthony ignored me. That's the kind of brothers we were then and the kind we'd be.

Kevin was king of the bus and king of the schoolyard. Boys wanted to be his friend. Girls turned capricious when he appeared. Every lunchtime he fought who challenged him and he fought who he challenged. The fights happened between the two prefab schoolrooms, which were far from where the teachers ate lunch in the main school building. His fighting method was to kick his opponent in the head, then get that dazed opponent in a headlock, force him to the ground, and kick him in the head some more. Tess was on the bus. She sat on the bottom deck, beside the bus conductor. Not even Kevin messed with him. Our parents demanded that Tess sit there. She was repeatedly warned to bring no more trouble upon any family.

In the schoolyard I was one of Kevin's targets.

—Will you look at small Jimmy Dwyer, he'd shout.

—Take a good long look at Fatso Dwyer, he'd shout.

I skedaddled. Skedaddling being the only skill you fully mastered at that technical school. But how many times did he knock you down on their schoolyard? He sneaked up behind and tripped you and the instant your fat belly hit the gravel and dust filled your nose and your eyes clamped shut and the world as you saw it and felt it detonated like a bomb inside your stupid head he planted his right foot on your stunned heap of a body. Then boisterous laughter from him and his followers shot up around you.

One morning in the metalwork room he shoved a compass needle fully into your left arse cheek. Laughter and pointed fingers followed you for the rest of that day. In the boys' bedroom that evening your mother walked in and saw the dark stain on the Confirmation pants that you'd thrown onto the floor and you turned from your mother, who then saw the even bigger dark stain on the white underpants that were stuck to you, and you turned back to your mother, who tightly folded her arms and asked what mischief were you up to at that school.

—Boys messing in the metalwork room, you mumbled.

—Of all the people I know, you need to stay far away from those kinds of boys, she said, and left the room.

One October evening he laughed and danced along the bus aisle. I was sitting halfway down. He stood over me, reached into the left breast pocket of the jacket, and pulled out a shiny packet. He shook the packet before my eyes.

—You know what I have here, young Jimmy, he said.

—I do, of course, I said.

I brushed the packet from my face and watched the red leaves spinning against that dirty bus window. Boys and girls clapped their hands, banged the backs of seats, and howled. Beyond the spinning leaves, the mobs of cattle. The shining patches of water in fields and bogs. The red rusting roofs of hay barns. For what the fuck do you do? You could tell yourself that humiliation on a rickety bus crammed with howling, smelly teenagers in a cowed place was nothing compared with the lives of starving African children, but the adults were happy those starving children existed; starving children gave them the perfect tool for control.

—You don't fucking know, Fatso, he said, and he pushed the package under my nose. I again pushed it away, and I was smiling when I stared at the spinning leaves.

—A French letter, he said. —I'm keeping it for your fine sister. I'll use it on the two of them, when I get them in the same corner, and I'll get them in the corner. Mark my words. I've noticed that the younger one of the Dwyers is budding at last—

—Fuck you, I said, and sprang out of the seat.

I'd like to think I swung at him, but what a joke that is. Kevin Lyons could trounce me, do it in seconds, but it was the week after this that he was expelled from school. During lunch, the wheels of the English teacher's French car were punctured with a penknife. Kevin was blamed, though who knows if he was the one who did it or if the teachers just needed someone to blame. The news went around the schoolyard that when the English teacher, who was also the mechanical drawing teacher, accused Kevin, he laughed out loud and held up his middle finger to the teacher.

You liked that teacher. The only one you did like. He told you once you were good at mechanical drawing. And he told you that you weren't a bad writer, but you needed to practice very hard. You stored up those things, along with all the others.

The evening he was expelled, that English teacher took him into the science room and locked the door. I was in the group of boys standing outside. The English teacher allowed us to stand there. He was teaching us a lesson. Beyond that door, the sounds of fists, grunts, the clatter of falling things. Then silence, and seconds later the key turning, the door opening. Kevin stood in the doorway. I did not see the English teacher. He was sitting down in there. He was catching his breath. Kevin's hair was wet with blood and sweat and plastered down on his forehead. The left eye was blackened. Blood from his upper lip dripped onto the collar of the denim jacket. We stared in silence, awe, and dread. Like a rabble, we stared, the upturned plastic chairs behind him, glass from broken beakers at his feet, his bloody, bruised face, and the right sleeve of the jacket nearly torn off. The jacket that helped to make him. He had tried to beat them, but they weren't to be beaten, and seeing him in the doorway that evening, I felt for him. And I looked up to him. I did, because I despised the adults even more than I did him.

The crowd parted. He walked on through. He gripped the torn sleeve. The bloody mouth smiled.

Anyway, behind the striking new pump house the top branches of the poplars swept back and forth like water on a strand. My mother whitewashed the pump house. She made plans to plant shrubs around it. Plans that never came to pass. But cool springwater rushed rapidly and silently through buried pipes, up the fields, into water troughs, and we didn't have to schlep buckets of water to cattle from the old well, all the way up those fields. We also had water piped into the kitchen. The last job Michael did was install the stainless-steel sink and the immersion heater. My mother talked endlessly about the fine hot water in the kitchen tap. How lucky she was in her life. How good God was to her. My dead mother was in heaven.

6

In January 1988, Brendan and I finally made up our minds to apply for Donnelly visas to the States. It was a Saturday night and a Sunday morning, and we were eating chips under a crowded awning and watching people like ourselves walk across O'Connell Bridge.

—Where will we go if we get one?

—People are heading to Boston, Brendan said.

—We'll be a statistic, I said, and we laughed.

Brendan lived with his parents in Cabra. He had a steady girlfriend, with a job that she liked fine. She didn't want to go anyplace. Brendan and I had jobs, many didn't, but our jobs bored us. I still worked in the bar. He worked in the same printing shop as his father. Back then, Brendan and I were best friends, but we haven't talked since the day I drove him in the Camaro to Detroit Metro Airport, though at the airport gate we put our arms around each other and promised to keep in touch. Back then, in Dublin, we went to the bars. Brendan read Freud and Nietzsche, and he told me about them and I read them, and in the bars we talked about them, and how boring life was, the way young people do, and that night under the awning, Brendan said if he got a visa he'd go and have a bit of fun, try to save some money, then come back and marry. I said I'd suss it out as I went along. No. I forget what I said, although I don't forget that Una Lyons was huge on my mind, but I kept it to myself, I never even told Brendan—even though more than a year had passed since she and I had last seen each other.

Brendan and I got visas and we planned to leave for Boston inside three months. Stephen was still in Manchester, Anthony was in Killarney, and Tess was nursing in Cork. I rang and told them I was going. The Friday before I left, I took the train down to say good-bye to Hannah and my father. On the train sat young people like myself, visiting places they still called home—places that had stopped being that the day they took the train out of there. I bought a novel at the station but put it aside, because spring sunlight flashed through the train car, and beyond the window calves suckled cows in green fields, and farmers sat atop tractors and plowed their fields and gardens, and the crows and the jackdaws preened in the fresh clay and feasted on the fat worms the plows threw up.

Hannah picked me up at the Junction. Coleman Daly was on the platform. He lowered his orange flag and asked Hannah how our father was keeping.

—In great form, Coleman, Hannah said, and thanked him for asking.

The train was sneaking toward Cork. Coleman gently poked my chest with the butt of the flag and said he hadn't seen me in a long while, how was things with me? I turned from the train and cheerfully said I was heading off to the States. Coleman shook my hand, wished me luck, then stepped back, pulled off his cap, stared at the platform floor in a morbid way, and said it was a tragedy that young people had to go to that country again, since that's a cruel country, if you think about it, people go stone mad over there, go to all extremes, he himself had the chance to go out there once, fare paid, the works, but he knew that country wasn't for him, but saying all that, he had so many relations out there with so many years, and though he didn't know what states they lived in, or what they did to make a living, he was dead sure they were doing frightfully well.

On the drive home, Hannah said our father was not in the best of moods. He grumbled about his children not visiting, but he still took his walks, he read the paper, he had his appetite.

I asked what he'd said when she told him I was going to the States.

—That you're the sort who's happy no place, Hannah firmly said.

I turned from my sister and watched the road. A few minutes passed.

—He took this fit last week, Jimmy, and burned these things on the range. I wasn't going to tell you, and I'm not going to tell the others—

I turned to my sister.

—Like what things, Hannah?

—Things he kept in their room, Jimmy. I walked into the kitchen. He was standing over the range. The lid off and the flames flying up and the smoke filling up the kitchen—remember them tins of biscuits Mam's friend in London used to post to us every Christmas when we were young?

—I do, of course.

—So there he was, Jimmy, pulling things out of four or five of them tins, and shoving them into the blazing range. The tins were filled to the brim and lined up along the top of the range—

—But what things are you talking about, Hannah!

—Things! I don't know! I don't want to know. I knew I shouldn't have said a word to you—them small copybooks, Jimmy, that he once bought at O'Shea's, but he turns from the range and says to me this should have been done before his wife and Michael left him—

—And what did he mean by that—

—Your guess is as good as mine—

—But, Hannah, you said something to him—

—I told him to go ahead and burn whatever he likes, Jimmy, but try not to burn the house down, and I opened the kitchen windows and the back door and the kitchen door, and I went down the hall and opened the front door to let the heat and the smoke out.

Hannah sighed. I lit a cigarette and handed it to her.

—He's a lunatic, I said.

—He's our father, Jimmy.

I said I was sorry, then said we should put it out of our heads. Hannah said she already had. And so I asked about the other things, and she said the cattle were fine, her part-time job in the Tampax factory in Tipperary town was fine, and things between her and the boyfriend couldn't be better. The boyfriend was a neighbor. He worked as a fitter in the same factory. And when Hannah pulled up in front of the house she said they were going to marry inside the year. They'd already picked the children's names.

—That's great news, Hannah, I said.

The next night Hannah took him his supper in his room. She came back to the kitchen and said I should give him a while to eat. You know how he likes to take his time. Yes, I do. Was I in the mood to face him? No, never. Was I in the mood to say good-bye? A thing that had to be done. We were sitting at the table. I poured the tea. Hannah put biscuits on a plate. The telly was turned down. Hannah went through the people who were sick, dying, had got married, expecting before they got married, expecting but not married, who was new to the dole, who had left and where they'd gone to.

—You heard, I suppose, that Una Lyons is going to London, Hannah said. —She's marrying some English fella she met in Dublin.

—I didn't hear that, but good for Una, I said.

—You won't bother contacting Kevin in the States. He's out there a while now, doing well, so I hear.

—We were never friends, I said.

—I think he's where you're going, Hannah said.

—We'll see what happens.

—I hope you talked to Tess.

—I did, don't worry, Hannah.

—I should go down, Jimmy, and see how things are with him.

Hannah stood and opened the kitchen door. I was right behind her. She went down the blue corridor. I walked through the hall and out the front door. In the middle of the yard I knelt on one knee and petted the sheepdog. Her companion had died a few weeks before. Then I stood and walked to the edge of the yard and stared down the paddock. Weeds thrived around the pump house. Its roof and walls were covered with ivy. The poplars were very still. I turned from all of that and went back and knelt again and scratched the sheepdog's head. I whispered in her ear that I was sorry that her companion had died. The sheepdog wagged her tail and I headed around the back of the house. Where the wood was chopped and cut looked the way it did in my head. I passed the kitchen-sink window and stood at the barbed wire and stared up the field. The cattle were lying underneath the bushes. I took a few steps along the wire and found a rusty thorn and I shoved my thumb down very hard on it then shoved the thumb into my mouth and sucked the blood. Next I was staring through the back window at the kitchen table. Tea going cold in mugs. Biscuits not touched on a plate. The slumped sleeper couch against the wall opposite was once Auntie Hannah's bed. The dull and ignorant aunt you never warmed to. Above the couch, their smiling wedding photograph and next to that a black-and-white National school photograph of us in black turtlenecks. We looked like the Beatles on the cover of their second album. My mother's friend in London posted those turtlenecks. Hannah walked into the kitchen with Auntie Tess's white tray—that's what we called it. I don't know if Aunt Tess brought it on the train from Dublin one summer or if she posted it—Hannah's head was down like an altar boy's. I sucked my thumb again and went in the back door and crossed the kitchen and stood at the kitchen sink and washed my thumb and then washed his plate and cup and I washed the tea mugs and put the biscuits back in their packet and wiped my hands on the tea towel and stared for a while through the window at the Galtee Mountains. Then I looked down at my thumb. The blood had stopped. The skin was swollen and purple. Hannah said she was taking him down his mug of Complan. And she'd give him the tablets for his frail heart.

—When I come back up you go down and put it behind you, she added.

—Thank you, Hannah, I said.

Hannah came up.

—I'll go down, I said.

—It won't kill you, she said.

—It might kill me, I said.

I kissed her cheek and she mine, and I went through the kitchen doorway and shut the door behind me. I switched the light on and stared down that blue corridor my mother had painted. I think I helped her paint it, or that's something I'd like to think—the short blue corridor that saw no daylight unless the bedroom doors were open—and that night I went down it I swear I smelled his sweat from all his years of hard work. Sweat that insulated him like a coat of armor. Like the shell of the turtle. This thing you forever wanted to run away from. A way you didn't ever want to be. Back then when I slept in the bedroom with Stephen and Anthony he was the last to go to bed. Every night he knelt at his chair for an hour and prayed. When he got up he checked the back and front doors then slowly walked down the blue corridor in socks his dead wife had darned too many times. His rosary beads curled like a rattlesnake in the drawer behind his chair. Back then I waited for the almost soundless click of the kitchen door handle and his stockinged feet on the corridor floor. I stayed awake to hear. And those sounds still trap me in the oddest places—like waiting in the check-in line at an airport, or walking down a crowded American city sidewalk, or sitting alone with a book in the quietest corner of a used bookstore.

That Sunday night I dreaded my few cowardly steps. Past the room on the right where I once slept with my two brothers. Three big boot holes in that door from when Anthony once wanted in and Stephen and I wouldn't let him. Hannah and Tess's room on the other side, where Hannah now slept on her own.

I knocked on his door. He said to come in. I put one foot in the room, kept the other in the corridor, pulled the door against me like a shield, stuck my head in, and squeezed down on the door handle.

—Take your weight off that handle, it's in a tender way, he said.

I let the handle go, but I didn't move.

He was sitting in his chair beside the bed. His back was to the window. The chair usually faced the window. He liked to stare out at his dead wife's untended flower garden—his thin pale legs with the long and winding blue veins, the walking stick on the floor by the chair, and the red dressing robe that fell a few inches below his knees. The robe had black burn holes from the Sweet Aftons he'd stopped smoking the week after his wife died.

—You didn't come in to see me last evening or all day, he said.

—You were sleeping. Hannah thought it best not to disturb you, I said.

—So many are concerned about my well-being, he said. —What a lucky man I am. But you haven't been down to see us in a very long while.

—Busy in work, I said.

—You were always a great one for the work. When are you going back?

—Early train tomorrow, I said.

—A very short visit. Like the Holy Father himself, he said. —So when are you going away?

—The end of the week, I said.

—You're afraid to come into the room. You could at least dignify the man who raised you with that much.

I opened the door and planted my feet in the room. He told me to close the door but to be extra careful of the tender handle. I did as he asked.

My mother's Mass shoes were on the small rug next to the bed. She bought that rug in Dublin years ago. Mothers and their children had traveled there by bus on a zoo day trip the Irish Countrywomen's Association organized. It was springtime. My first time visiting Dublin. And it might have been my mother's. I forget so much. And get so much wrong. On the dressing table their battered prayer books and his rosary beads. On the walls, the pictures of the Blessed Family, Padre Pio, and Saint Francis, who once sat atop the television. The heavy red curtains Auntie Tess sent from Dublin were open. The curtains reached the floor. The same sort of curtains hung in the boys' and the girls' bedrooms. It was dusk. A blackbird was singing. He raised his face. That smile appeared. He said the blackbird sang morning and evening. He scattered bread crumbs along the windowsill for her. The blackbird was his wife saying hello.

—But all so soon, what day did you exactly say, or did you tell me that? he said.

—This Friday, I said.

—And why, he said.

—Why what, I said.

—Did Daly take the hearing from you at the Junction?

—The hearing's sound, I said.

—You have a job, he said.

—I don't like it anymore, I said.

—Aren't you the plucky fellow, he said.

—I wouldn't know, I said.

—You know it only too well, he said. —When I was your age, so many went off. The Christmas cards arrived for a few years with a few scribbles you could barely read and then them cards stopped arriving. People go away and don't come back. Only too well I know that myself—

—It's not that way anymore—

—Do you think it's a fool I am!

—That's one thing I never think, I said.

—Well, that's good to hear, so what exactly do you plan on doing when you arrive there? And how long do you intend on staying there?

—I'm not sure yet, I said.

—Not sure. It's not like you're going down the road a bit.

—I'll get a job. I'll go to school.

—Will you now. Go to school. So you will.

—That's what I'm thinking.

—And what does my plucky fellow intend to learn in school? From what I remember, you learned nothing there in all the years you went.

—I might study English, I said.

—Don't you know that already?

—Something else, then, I said.

—But why are you going out there in the first place? he asked. —Your mother, God rest her, would want you to stay where you are, in that fine job I got for you. She'd like you to be here for your brothers and sisters. I'm not going to be around for too long more. Did you go and visit Tess? You took the train down to Cork to see her—

—I rang her. She didn't want me going down there—

—You were very happy to not have to put yourself out—

—She didn't want me going down there. She said it'd make her lonesome—

—That's the best excuse I've heard in a long time. Since when did she know what she is thinking! That might be the one thing you know as good as I do!

—Tess's fine. She likes the nursing, I said.

—You didn't even bother to go down and see her, and you getting onto a plane for yourself—

—I told you she didn't want me to!

—Keep the voice down. Do you hear me. The ears are sound as a bell. More sounder than your own. But what difference anyway that you are going. We never see much of you. You might as well be gone. When I think of it, you were always gone. My plucky fella cares greatly for us—

—I'm not so sure about that, I said.

—Now the truth of what I know since day one comes out—

—Whatever you think yourself, I said.

—Don't disrespect your father, he said, grinding the back teeth, wagging the bent finger, and shuffling the feet.

—Sorry, I said.

—There's little sorrow in you, he said.

The blackbird started to sing. He cocked his head. That smile appeared and he turned to look at a holy picture on the wall above their bed.

A few minutes later, he said, —You remember them John Garfield films, you do?

—I do, I said.

—You were young, but you were so fond of them. There's risk for you, he said.

—Eddie told me you were into the acting, the first day I arrived in Dublin, I said.

—What are you bringing up now—

—Your second cousin. Eddie in the union.

—Like I have been saying to you my entire life, you talk and think about things that are of no use, and Eddie never had a clue what he was going on about. The only one Eddie is faithful to is John Powers. He keeps that family in high spirits. Eddie's trouble is that he never got used to not being at home. He'd come down from Dublin for a few weeks in summer before he found the unfortunate old wife who could never give him a child, and we'd go for a few—

—He told me that day he was sad he had no children—

—There you are again, bringing up things that are of no concern to you—

—I'm only saying what he told—

—I don't want to hear another word about that, he said.

—Fine with me, I said.

—Well, if you want to know, after the few pints you couldn't stop Eddie from wailing that he would be a happier man if he'd stayed, and God forgive me now for saying this, but Eddie never told one word of the truth for one day in his life, not a word, lies for no rhyme or reason, that's the kind Eddie is, and sure what could you expect, because that's the way Eddie's father was, who was likewise faithful to John Powers. When Eddie's father died they found the empty bottles in every nook and cranny. They opened the wardrobe and the empty whiskey bottles poured out like the sands of time, and paper bags filled with whiskey bottles, hidden in the weeds, at the bottom of the haggard, empty bottles shoved into the rafters of the cow house and the henhouse. Of course, the father was on his own and Eddie was away in Dublin, starting his union for himself, and Eddie's mother dead since Eddie was a youngster.

He coughed loudly then took his hand from his mouth. He looked right at me.

—Born and raised in Brooklyn, John Garfield was, but you being the plucky young fella that you are, you'd know that.

—Of course, I know that, I said.

But I didn't.

—Brooklyn's not so close to Boston. Boston is a ways north of there, he said.

At the kitchen sink I gulped down two cups of water and stared out. No mountains and no fields. Only my dark reflection on that window-pane. Hannah's dark reflection appeared to the right of mine. She was a few steps behind me.

—It went all right, Jimmy, she said.

—Like you'd expect, Hannah.

—He still misses Mam so much. He talks about her all the time. He worries about us. He worries about you going. He doesn't want you to go. He is so sad over your going.

—He doesn't have an ounce of sadness.

—That's a very mean thing to say, Jimmy.

—If I call him the small, bitter, perishing patriarch, would that be mean, too, Hannah?

—You're trying to be smart now, Jimmy.

—What if I am, Hannah?

—I'd give anything to see Mam again, Jimmy.

I turned from our reflections. Hannah stared at the floor.

—It will be easier when you marry and have your children, I said.

And I said it in such a cold way. Said it the way he'd say it.

Less than a week later, Brendan and I were staying in a motel room not far from Logan Airport. During the day we rode the T and got off at stations along the way and wandered the streets. At night we lay on the motel beds and studied maps of the city, read the Boston-Irish newspapers, watched television, and drank duty-free rum from plastic cups. When the rum bottles were empty we rented space in a flat off Highland Avenue in Somerville through an ad in one of those newspapers.

The Davis Square T stop was a fifteen-minute walk from the flat, which was on the middle floor of a narrow three-story. The house next door looked the same. The houses had decks. And a deck was magic to us. The apartment was a one-bedroom. A carpenter from Cork lived there. He was illegal, and had been living out here a few years. Brendan and I rolled out our sleeping bags on the paint-splattered wooden floor in the sitting room. We bought a clock alarm and pillows. With regard to finding jobs, the Corkman told us to visit this bar on Central Square. Sure to find a lead there. And he kept telling us how lucky we were to have papers.

We visited that bar on Central Square. That was a place we'd come to love. We met people there from home. We met Americans, Europeans, Mexicans, and South Americans, and one Saturday night, I ran into a man from Dublin. Eamon was his name. He wore a sleeveless leather jacket with a skull and crossbones on its back. He and I chatted while pissing, and while I was drying my hands, he offered me a job painting houses in Concord. Six or seven big houses, inside and out. And he had a few more jobs lined up after that. The hourly wage was sound and under the table. I told Eamon I had no experience painting. Not to worry. A monkey can paint. I'd paint the outside. Pick you up at the Dunkin Donuts on Porter Square at half-six on Monday morning. Brendan met someone in the bar who offered him a job as a printer. We were set.

The accident happened on a Friday morning. This was around the end of July, about four months after I'd started. Eamon, myself, and the other painter, whose name I don't remember, ate doughnuts and drank coffee on the front porch of the house we were painting. We sat on wicker chairs and made jokes about the thick cushions. The Mexican gardener was mowing the lawn on the left side of the driveway. The mail carrier was walking up that long and wide driveway. We had never seen a female postman before, not to mention she was black. Her name was Tina, I remember that, and we chatted with her every morning for a few minutes. She liked our accents. We liked hers. The jokes went over and back. After Tina had left, Eamon said his team was playing hurling in Dorchester the next day. The other painter and I said we'd go. I had no interest in hurling, but seeing a match in Boston might be cool. Eamon said that afterward we'd head to this new Irish place in Brighton. A girl he knew from home bartended there. She'd set us up with free beers. The gardener was watering the flower beds along the driveway. He taught me vulgar words in Spanish. I taught him some in English. The house was a white three-story colonial. It had elegant bay windows and those lovely old shutters. Or that's the way I recall it. Like it was Howard's End. In the shaded backyard was a red brick patio and a small fountain fed by a constant stream from a fat stone boy's penis. I don't remember ever seeing the couple that lived in the house.

Eamon and I got on ladders at the shaded gable end. Three or four tall maples grew there. Our ladders were ten feet apart. He was painting the shingles. I was scraping old paint from them. The other painter was painting one of the two downstairs bathrooms. Eamon and I talked about the heat, like we did every day. He went on for a while about how he'd lost his hole in a poker game two nights ago, before he told me that every summer, when he was a child, he visited his aunt, uncle, and cousins in County Dublin. The aunt used to take Eamon and her children for picnics in the foothills of the Dublin Mountains. The day Eamon's youngest cousin turned eighteen, his aunt left letters for her husband and children. She put a few things in a bag and took the boat to Liverpool. She never again came home. For years the aunt had visited her sister in Liverpool. The aunt had met a woman there very early on. This woman and Eamon's aunt fell in love and began to correspond in secret. They were in love for twenty years before the aunt left the family. She waited to raise the children first. Eamon said he never once blamed his aunt for leaving on account of his uncle being a complete bollocks.

I told Eamon about Aunt Tess. That she never married. That she was a matron in a Dublin hospital, and every summer she visited my family for a week, and my father brought me with him to pick her up at Limerick Junction. Me because I was her godson. And I told him that my aunt's hair was the color of copper, she had fine manners, wore bright red lipstick, dresses with exotic patterns, and that my father and she spoke little on the drive home from the Junction. Only my aunt inquiring how their sister was faring out in the City Home. Fine. Grand. And I told him that my aunt Tess smiled when she turned around in the front seat to ask me how I was doing in school. What subjects did I like? What was I going to be when I grew up?

And I told him Aunt Tess flung herself under a city bus across the street from the Garden of Remembrance, that my aunt Hannah told me this before I left for Dublin, and Aunt Hannah passed away a few months later. And I told him that when I first arrived in Dublin I'd sit in the Garden of Remembrance on my days off work and gaze into the dirty pool and then look up at the Children of Lir changing into swans, and when I sat there I tried very hard not to think about Aunt Tess flinging herself under one of those red city buses lined up across the way. No. I saw her standing in the July sunlight at Limerick Junction. She was waiting for my father to pick her up. He was forever late for everything. She wore her beautiful clothes. At her feet were two suitcases and the bag I later brought to Dublin. That a so-called friend later stole. The medal still pinned inside the bag. I wish that fucking thief luck.

And I told him Coleman Daly stood beside my aunt and she and Coleman chatted and smoked and their smoke made its lazy way across the tracks and vanished into the bushes and the meadows. Coleman's navy blue uniform coat was open. His hat lay upside down on the bench behind him, his right hand deep in his pocket, shoulders back, the noble belly stuck out. Coleman addressed my aunt as Miss.

But I never got the chance to tell Eamon I'd visited Aunt Tess's grave in Glasnevin, that Aunt Hannah had only told half of it, which didn't surprise me, but I don't know if Aunt Hannah even knew, and now I'll never know if any of them at home ever knew, but about a month before I left for Boston, I visited the hospital where my aunt once worked, and was put in touch with a woman who was best friends with my aunt.

Mary was retired. We met on a park bench in Drumcondra. The bench was against the tall stone wall of Saint Patrick's College. Mary brought her dog—bronze hair, the height, head, and folded ears of a terrier, and the thick, long body of some other breed. The dog's name was Daisy. I shook hands with Mary and looked down and rubbed Daisy's back. Maybe I turned to Daisy because I felt guilty. Or maybe I was afraid of what Mary was going to tell me.

Mary said my aunt Tess was the solitary sort. She gave her life to her patients. She loved the hospital. Never once missed a day's work. And next Mary said my aunt became involved with a married Dublin man she tended to in the hospital. And it was then I stopped rubbing Daisy's back and looked up at Mary.

—Tess fell in the big way, Jim, Mary said. —And not long after, he stopped talking to her. Would have nothing to do with her anymore. It broke Tess's heart.

This man was mending after a motorcycle accident. And my aunt gave their child up for adoption. The boy was born a month after the man and Tess stopped talking. This boy was now a man, and Mary opened her purse and shoved into my hand a slip of paper with his phone number on it. I shook hands with Mary and said I was heading off to the States. Mary squeezed my hands, wished me luck, said that no one was as brave as Tess, and the only good thing about the young people leaving again was that you had the chance to tell things. Tell because what did any of it matter to those who were going away.

And I never got the chance to tell Eamon that two days before I left for Boston I took a bus to Clontarf to see my aunt's son. His house was at the end of a tree-lined street. He was somewhere in his thirties, a mathematics professor at UCD. Mary had told me that. And he had red wavy hair. I saw it for myself. The same color hair as my father's. Or I imagined that's what my father's hair looked like when he was this man's age. A lighter shade than my sister Tess's hair.

And my cousin had the blue eyes and the thin, long bottom lip of my father. My cousin did say he knew from a young age that he was adopted, but he had no desire to meet my aunt until his adoptive mother finally convinced him that it was the proper thing. My aunt and he met twice, in the space of three weeks. This was ten or twelve years before. I never mentioned my aunt's death to him. And I didn't say that the time they met would have been around the time she died. I don't even know if he knew how my aunt had died. My cousin's name was Sean.

And I never got the chance to tell Eamon that Sean had agreed to see me only out of politeness. Like the best way to be rid of me was to see me. The family who raised him was more than kind. He was blessed with them, Sean said. His mother and father were his real mother and father. I was sitting on a couch in his sitting room. His wife and two children were playing in the kitchen. Crashing plastic blocks followed by the children's yelps. When I'd rang the doorbell the wife answered. Stout, college-educated, country-raised, which you knew by the way she spoke, she didn't look at me when she led me to that sitting room couch and left. Five minutes later, Sean arrived with the tea tray. Collar and tie, the shirt creased and buttoned at the wrists. He put the tray on the coffee table between us. I stood when the door opened. We awkwardly shook hands. He sat into his armchair and rested his arms along its plump arms. His fingertips clawed at the fabric and I made this jokey remark about how nice it was to see a cousin I never knew existed. He didn't find my remark one bit funny. He looked out the window at the sea. His face turned pale, the fingertips clawed away. I'd made the remark because I was nervous. Sitting on that couch. Rubbing my palms together. Like I might wipe away my dead aunt's blood. But my hands would stay stained with her blood every day from that one on. Like it was me and not some stranger who knelt beside her on North Frederick Street after the bus did its dirty work. My beautiful aunt, who said no to the plot. No to this one long, dull wank of a life.

And not once during that short visit did Sean smile.

But who can blame him?

—A very sad woman. Suffering for her mistakes, Sean said in the end.

—But she would have been delighted to see you, I said. —She would have looked forward to it for such a long time—

—A woman who couldn't control herself. I didn't have much to say to her—

—She took me and my brothers and sisters for walks in the fields when she visited in summer, I said. —She knew the names of the wildflowers. Every one of them. Very hardworking. Kept to herself. So I'm told.

—My children need to be in bed, he said.

He stood and opened his sitting room door.

—Passionate was what she was, I said.

I was standing, talking to his back. Then I looked down at my opened hands. They were shaking. My sore thumb was throbbing.

—That's a very fancy way of putting her appetites, he said.

Beyond him his lavender wallpapered hallway. I made fists of my hands and shoved them down my pants pockets. I faced the sea and grunted like an animal.

—The smell of the sea is lovely, I said.

But the smell was foul.

—I don't mean to be mean, but I'd like if we never talked and never saw each other ever again, he said.

—You don't ever have to worry about that, I said to the sea.

A shout came from Eamon. I looked over to see a shower of yellow jackets swarming around his face and many more shooting out from underneath the shingles. Yellow jackets crawled up and down his bare arms and climbed through his long hair. They made a ferocious sound. A sound as loud as me shouting that his ladder was tottering. And the paintbrush fell from his hand and the bucket of paint clattered onto the stone path. And when he fell backward I was still shouting.

On his way down his head hit a crotch in one of the maples, and the instant it hit, his legs jerked out, like in a tap dance, and when he landed on the stone path, I was watching the bloodstain on the maple, and if his body made a sound when it hit the path, I did not hear it, and I don't remember climbing down the ladder, but when I was on the ground, the other painter was kneeling by him. He was crying and begging.

I ran in the back door and dialed 911 on the hall phone, and then ran down a corridor along a narrow rug and stood on a sunlit wooden floor in a room lined with stuffed wooden bookcases and carefully walked around a glass coffee table covered with magazines, and picked up a caramel-colored cushion from a long and finely wrinkled leather couch that sat before a stone fireplace, and when I turned from the couch I stopped to look at a framed poster on the left side of the fireplace. For three or four minutes I stared. Squeezing the cushion under my arm. Though I often think I never saw that poster in that house. That the poster had caught my eye in some store window I passed on a Boston street, and in the mess called time it ended up here. The poster was a painting by Rothko. I found this out three years later when I was turning the heavy pages of an art book late one night in the library of a community college I attended for two years when I first arrived in Michigan. There was blue and green in the painting. I leaned over and kissed it.

Outside, the other painter had folded up a drop cloth and covered Eamon up to the neck. Paint from the can was splashed all over the place. I gently lifted Eamon's head and fixed the cushion underneath it. His pupils moved rapidly, and when I laid his head back, blood spread along the cushion. I wiped my bloody fingers on the edge of the drop cloth. I remember thinking that was one fucking cushion no one would ever again sit on, lay their head on, or lay their back against. The other painter was saying a Hail Mary. The gardener was kneeling and saying it in Spanish. I didn't know then that his prayer was the Hail Mary. The ambulance sped up the driveway. Sunlight glimmered in the still maple leaves. The fresh coat of paint on the house looked ravishing. And the fat stone boy pissed away at his leisurely pace, like he was keeping time.

7

Zoë walked over to him and said her name. They shook hands. When he said his name he tugged at the bill of the cap. Zoë reached into the tote bag for her sunglasses. She slipped them on and stepped out of the shadow of the house, into the bright sunlight. He picked up the backpack and the flowers. I had opened wide the two car doors. There was a whiff of flour when I did, but there was no flour dust on any of the seats. That morning I'd taken the car to the gas station and filled the tank, checked the fluids, and done a mighty hoovering job. Zoë politely asked him if he'd rather sit in back or up front. He said back, and then Zoë and he had a few words about directions. She turned from him and stared at me across the car roof, and she smiled when she said she would navigate.

—Fine by me, I don't have a clue, my dear, I said.

She placed the tote bag at her feet. He moved into the middle of the backseat. I watched him in the rearview mirror. The white t-shirt beneath Una's red shirt. The hair around the ears newly clipped. And I remember thinking when I backed down the driveway that afternoon that I had dreamed up the conversation he and I had about Kevin Lyons—*needs and wants you to go see him*—but when the car was in the street I knew our conversation had been real, like the two sloppy lines of cars and SUVs parked beneath the dusty maples. Zoë rolled her window down. I rolled mine. There was a tape in the deck. It had been jammed in there for a while. I put the volume on low. In the mirror, he rolled up his sleeves and curled his right arm around the backpack and drew it to him. The flowers were sprawled across his lap.

I drove under the long roof of maples, turned right at the end of the street, made a left at the United Methodist church, where the tiger lilies were fading, then another right and another left, and at the bottom of that steep street the freight train lights flashed and the barrier came down.

The freight train came through town at the same time every afternoon. I used to hear it from that flat. And when it came through at 12:40 in the morning, I often heard it. Zoë half-turned and asked him if he traveled much by train. He said he could not remember the last time he was on one, he took the bus. His face in the mirror, when he was speaking, made me think that for some to live was to be constantly fucked over. And I hated it in me: that in one breath I pitied him, but in the other I despised him, because of that message he'd brought to my doorstep. Zoë was talking about her aunt, her mother's sister, who had moved from a Chicago suburb to Florida. Zoë hadn't seen the aunt in a long time. Then Zoë turned and asked him his aunt's age. He said he couldn't remember. The train cars clattered past. Many were badly rusted, but many had this beautiful graffiti. In what cities or towns did they do it? What time of the day or night did they chance it?

I'd made a plan to ring Stephen, Hannah, and Tess. I hadn't spoken to any of them in a very long time—but Hannah might know something about Kevin Lyons, because news about us who'd left often found its way back, though whether the news was true or not was another story. And Stephen was best friends with Seamus Lyons in National and vocational school, but I wasn't sure if they kept in touch after Seamus and Tommy moved to London to work in hotels, and Stephen ended up going from Manchester to Berlin, then to Sydney, with a blond Australian woman he'd met late one night on a train during an ecstasy trip in Prague. And I needed to ring Tess. Tess always rang more than the others did. She'd rung around Easter—but you were busy with school and the bakery.

A few of the train cars had the names of states in big letters. Ohio. Montana. Oregon. He was telling Zoë about a bus trip he took one winter's day from Maysville, Kentucky, to Detroit. When the bus arrived in Detroit his connecting bus to the Upper Peninsula had already left. Two in the morning, freezing cold, the bus station mobbed with stranded travelers, he sat on a bench outside all night and waited for the morning bus.

—And what were you doing around here then, I said.

In the mirror he was staring out the window to his right.

—Picked apples up north, he said.

I didn't mention that apples weren't picked in the U.P. in the dead of winter.

A car windshield on the other side of the tracks shimmered between the crawling train cars. It blinded me, but I kept staring into it, turned the music up slightly, and tapped my fingers on the steering wheel. He and Zoë were talking about some ocean town in Florida I'd never heard of.

You hurt her but you don't know why
You love her but you don't know why

Five days after Brendan and I arrived in Michigan, I rang Hannah. Brendan was at his new job, we had just got the phone connected, and after Hannah and I talked, I went outside. I'd walked a few streets before the freight train stalled me, and when it passed I climbed the embankment teeming with pine needles, chicory, crabgrass, discarded beer and wine bottles with faded labels, beer cans, and empty cigarettes packs. How did it all end up here? Maybe from people like the man I was driving to see his aunt. Him and the forlorn that wandered down after dark to stare at the rails in the moonlight. Rails shining like the scalded blade of a butcher's knife. I walked for a while along the tracks but stopped every now and then to stare out at the town. Insects buzzed. The sky was blue and foggy. Crows circled the four or five church spires. And all around were clusters of trees. And I remember thinking how changed this scene would be when the leaves fall, for who knows, good or bad, what the fuck's ever going to transpire.

—He dressed up in that old suit and found his way back to the Junction. Completely off his rocker, Jimmy, Hannah said on the phone.

Then she broke down. She was talking about our father. He was buried seven days before.

—He never changed, Jimmy, she said. —Not one bit. But he loved his grandson. He did. In the end he wanted to spend all his time with him.

—Christ, Hannah, was what I said.

—You have to ring Tess. Do you hear me, Jimmy—

—I hear you, Hannah. I'll ring her—

—The boys are always fine, but ring Tess—

—I told you I'll ring her—

—She is dying to hear from you, Jimmy—

—Is she all right?

—She's fine, but you have to ring her, are you listening to me, Jimmy—

—I'm listening, Hannah, I promise I will, but tell me what happened—

—He put on that old suit, Jimmy. The last time he put that thing on was for Mam's funeral, and before he arrived at the Junction, he ended up at his home place, and before that he was in at Breen's. He says to me that morning he wanted to go home, and I said to him he was at home, but he says home where he was born and raised, his real home, up on the hill with Auntie Tess and Hannah, and I said to him, Jimmy, how can you say things like that, and he says Michael will give me a lift there if you don't have the decency to oblige me, says it in that mean way of his, and I says to him, Jimmy, who is this Michael fella you are going on about, and he says, who do you think, Miss, are you that much of a fool, is it five ungrateful fools I have brought into this world, Michael Lyons, who do you think, and I says straight out to him, Jimmy, that Michael Lyons is dead and gone with years, dead and gone since I was a girl, so Michael Lyons will be giving you or no one else a lift anyplace.

Hannah told him to go back to bed, to try to sleep, she had the child to take care of, she would bring him his tea in a while, and bring him his dinner when her husband came home from work, she was going to roast a chicken. Peas in the garden bursting out of their pods like a fat man in a shirt way too tight.

She shut his bedroom door and went about her work. He got out of the bed and opened the wardrobe and put on the good suit, his tie, his good shoes, picked up his walking stick, sneaked down the blue corridor, out the front door, and across his dead wife's flower garden. My sister was chatting with the child in the kitchen. She had the radio up loud. She enjoyed the gossip on the morning talk shows.

She and her husband didn't work in the Tampax factory anymore. The Tampax factory had relocated to someplace in Mexico, but her husband worked for a French airline out at Shannon Airport, and Hannah worked weekend night shifts in a bar, in Tipperary town, and she raised the dry cattle.

He headed out the path to the road and was only moments on it when a neighbor, Big Johnny Ryan, stopped to pick him up.

I took the red school bus with Johnny's son, who was called Little Johnny, called that since he was a child, and will be by them until the day he dies, though Little Johnny was the tallest boy on the bus. He became a Guard in Waterford city.

Big Johnny was at least one generation below my father, and I'm thinking that my father and Big Johnny's father, also known as Big Johnny, were friends, or at least they would have chatted to each other while they waited in line at the creamery, back when they both took the milk there in a horse and cart.

My father asked Big Johnny would he mind giving him a lift back the road to Breen's.

—Not a bother, Tom.

My father went into Breen's. Big Johnny went about his business. He had his farm to take care of. A farm with all the modern equipment. Big Johnny made a very good living from farming, for he had many acres. And that's forever key.

Big Johnny's daughter married a German she met in Dublin. They were attending medical school and after they were graduated they moved out to LA, where the German died five months later in a boating accident on the Pacific. And after Big Johnny's daughter buried him she rang her mother and father and told them she was coming home inside the year, and never again was she going to leave. Big Johnny and his wife had a bungalow built for her. Far back from the road, up high on a hillside. The most panoramic site on all of their land. But the week before the daughter was due to arrive home and move into the bungalow, which had a new Honda Civic parked underneath the sycamores out front, she rang her father and mother to say she had joined an order of nuns. She was going to spend the rest of her days helping the troubled people of Rwanda.

Oh, her treachery, they all said, to treat her mother and father so cruelly, them who had wasted all that money building and furnishing that bungalow, not to mention the medical school bills, the brand-new Honda, and the heap of money they would have got for that fine site, but in the end, they all agreed, the real blame was with Big Johnny and his wife. From the start they'd spoiled her, so she knew no better, because, they all said, when you make too much of children they grow up to be heedless, ungrateful brats.

Abandoned the beautiful bungalow remained. The thistles, nettles, and dock leaves grew tall around it. Weeds taller than the windowsills. Dust settled on carpeted floors, new armchairs, couches, beds, dressers, mirrors, and so on. And the lovely Honda cloaked in a thick layer of sycamore dust. The tires deflated. And the same tall weeds around the house grew around the Honda. Then late one Friday night a gang of drunk and high teenagers from the new housing estate outside the village made their way up there. Their purpose was to steal the Honda, but they failed to get it to start, which bothered them to no end, and so they found rocks and smashed every window in the car, and they also located a hatchet, or one of them happened to have one handy, and they hatcheted the outside and the inside of the car to ribbons. But still they weren't satisfied. They went in search of more rocks and they lobbed those through every bungalow window.

Strangers and a few neighbors knocked on Big Johnny and his wife's door and offered to either rent or buy the bungalow, fix it back up themselves, but Big Johnny and the wife said no one would ever live up there. That was that. And every day Big Johnny and his wife drove by the bungalow, more than once, they did, and they never turned their heads. They let on that all that trouble and pain looming down didn't exist.

My father sat in one of the back seats at Breen's and ordered a small Powers and a half pint from the barmaid. He knew the barmaid's father and grandfather. He knew the men sitting back there. Men the same go as him, who he'd gone with to National school. Old-age pensioners who complained bitterly about the new housing estate the council had built outside the village that housed the thugs from Limerick city. Children running around this so-called estate. Children loud and filthy like animals. Those people brought the crime and the drugs. There was never any trouble here before that lot invaded like a shower of rats. Never an hour of trouble did we have. Tinkers held higher morals than that lot. And they would have all agreed that this was usually the case with people raised in the city.

A commercial lorry driver on his lunch break was reading a newspaper and eating a sandwich at the bar. My father approached him. The lorry driver did not know my father, but he knew Hannah and her husband. My father asked the lorry driver if he'd mind driving him to the place where he was born; it was only back the road a bit. The lorry driver said no problem. He finished his lunch. Off they drove.

When they arrived less than ten minutes later, my father rolled down the lorry window and stared up the long and steep path that led to the cottage where he and his two sisters were born. The land Aunt Hannah sold before she went into the City Home. My father could not really see the path against the summer bushes and the weeds, but he went on staring up there for a while before he turned to the lorry driver and said he'd had his fill of it. He'd had his fill of it for a long, long time. Then he asked the lorry driver if he'd mind driving him back to the Junction, which was fifteen or so miles away. The lorry driver's destination was Tipperary town. So no trouble at all. Sure the Junction's on the way.

The lorry driver left my father off in the Junction car park. My father took his wallet from his back pants pocket and handed ten euros to the lorry driver, who took it after some pestering, though he later offered it to Hannah, when he was telling her this. Hannah took it. If she learned anything from her parents, it was that every fucking penny matters.

My father went into the Junction. He walked down the long platform and sat on the wooden bench. Behind his head was the tourist poster of Beautiful Ireland. The one with the farmer tending his sheep on a hillside. That one because I remember it. This was one of those days when the summer feels jaded, days you can still wear short sleeves, but the nights are cool enough that you can get under the blanket and sleep like the dead, and all afternoon the lazy dust floats in the sunlight and the evening shadows are longer and darker.

The rest of it Hannah heard from Coleman Daly.

My father took off his coat. He folded it and placed it on the bench, and he rolled up his shirtsleeves, loosened his tie, and stared at the cows grazing in the meadows across the tracks. Coleman strolled out of his office and sat himself beside my father. Coleman lit a cigarette then unbuttoned his coat. They said they'd seen neither hide nor hair of each other in a dog's age. Then they talked about the fine weather. And they didn't mention the horses. My father lost interest in them the same time he did the Sweet Aftons. But Coleman was trying to find out what business my father had at the Junction. The Dublin train was an hour away, the Cork train even longer, and Coleman hadn't seen my father at the Junction in years, not since he picked me up at Christmas, or when I had summer holidays from the bar—nevertheless, Coleman wrangled it out of my father that he was waiting for Michael Lyons.

Coleman knew well who Michael Lyons was. Michael, Coleman, and Coleman's first cousin all worked in the copper mines, and of course Coleman knew Michael was long gone, but Coleman later told Hannah he thought our father was talking about Michael's son. Coleman did not know the names of the Lyons children, or what they were up to in their lives, but he would have known Una to see her. At one time he saw her in the same way he saw me, heading back and forth to Dublin on the train.

Coleman never married and some teenagers called him a queer behind his back. I don't know if Coleman was gay. When I think of him he is standing beside Auntie Tess, looking authoritative in his blue uniform with the shiny buttons. He enjoyed waving his flag at the incoming and outgoing trains, wishing the people who got on and off a good day, and doling out information with regard to times and connections. This job was heaven compared with the copper mines. And there's little fear of mercury poisoning at Limerick Junction. But Coleman finally figured out that the Michael Lyons my father was waiting for was the dead one, and so Coleman excused himself and went into his office and looked up my sister's number in the phone book and rang her and said her father was at the Junction dressed like a lord and waiting for someone who has not been alive in a very long time.

—Tom Dwyer will have a mighty long wait, Coleman said.

He laughed then. Laughed to be kind. Doing his best to temper things.

Hannah drove like a lunatic to the Junction. Her son buckled up in the backseat.

—Ye all brought me no luck. Ye cost me and your mother way too much. All the good and the not so good I did for yer sake.

Our father made those remarks on the way home. The last he said twice. Hannah ignored them. She'd never allow remarks like those to sink in and harden and darken over time like coal. And it took me a while to drag them out of her.

—But what did he say to you in the car, Hannah. He must have said something.

—I forget, Jimmy. He did say things. He was raving, I told you I forget.

—You don't forget, Hannah. Tell me the things he said—

And so Hannah gets him home. She rings the doctor. The doctor arrives. Fluid in the chest. And something along the lines of dementia. What's to be expected at his age. A storm in the head that will in due time exhaust itself. Dreams turn into distress when the hands and the mind are idle all the day long. A few days' rest and there should be improvement. If not give a ring. The doctor told Hannah things like that.

He died two mornings later. Hannah was bringing him his tea, boiled egg, toast, and the newspaper. Her husband had left for work. She could still hear his car going out the path. The child was asleep. And the moment she opened their room door she said she knew he was gone up to heaven to be with our mother. The room felt freezing cold and this caused her to drop Auntie Tess's tray. Which made this massive clatter and broke right down the middle. Split like a brittle bone. The egg, the mug, the tea, the toast, the unopened newspaper tossing and splashing across their floor. Hannah ran down the blue corridor to the hall and rang the ambulance. Next she rang her husband's job in Shannon and left a message. (This was before everyone owned a mobile phone, but not too long before.) Then she rang Tess and Anthony. They were only a few hours away. Next she rang Stephen. He was still living in Berlin, and could easily catch a Ryanair flight to Shannon. But Hannah had no way of ringing me.

Brendan and I took eight or nine days to drive from Boston to Michigan. We took the New York State Thruway. I forget why that route, but we stopped in Utica, Syracuse, and Buffalo, where we visited parks and battlegrounds, read inscriptions on the statues of generals and soldiers, and read about our refugees who built the canals and started the unions, and about the Indians who once owned the whole shebang, but were slaughtered, starved, and tricked out of it. A downpour hit us in Erie, Pennsylvania, and we stopped in the breakdown lane for almost an hour. It was like oil pouring down, the thickest, darkest, most blinding rain I've ever witnessed, and I sometimes think this was when he died, though I also think that thinking is nonsense. The morning after was filled with brilliant sunlight. We walked along the shore and looked across the calm lake to Canada. The sky was a shrill blue. We stopped in Ashtabula because of the Dylan song, we ate corn dogs, and I might have spent another day in Cleveland staring at the rubbish of rock stars. We took turns driving the Chevrolet Camaro. Four days before leaving Boston, we'd bought it from a guitarist I met in that bar on Central Square. On a few Sunday evenings he and I hung out in the foul alleyway behind the bar. He told me about the blues while we smoked opium. And that was the furthest you ever escaped from them. By the time we got to Buffalo the car floor was littered with the wrappers of burgers, French fry cartons, Coke cans, empty cigarette boxes, beer cans and bottles. I drove the Ohio Turnpike. Did it all the way in the left lane.

Two days before I left Boston, I rang Hannah to say Brendan and I were heading inland. It was going to take a few days. Hannah said I was mad for the road. My mother used to say that—mad for the road—but not once in a good way. And Hannah told me she'd run into Nora Lyons in Limerick city, she'd given Nora my phone number and address, and Nora was going to give them to Kevin. I told Hannah I'd recently run into Kevin on the street.

—How was he, Hannah said.

—Oh, fine, you know, I said.

—Small world, Jimmy.

—Maybe too small, Hannah.

Hannah said the news was Kevin was getting married to someone rich, and the Lyons family was flying over for the wedding. I said Kevin told me. Hannah asked if I was invited to the wedding.

—How's the father? I asked.

—A bit odder than usual, Jimmy.

—Well, I have to fly, Hannah, but tell them all I asked for them.

—You can move forward now, my dear.

Zoë nudged me.

—Thank you, my dear.

I turned the music all the way down.

—Hang a right. Follow the tracks out of town, Zoë said.

She turned to him and said her mother's father was a freight train driver.

—He was born in Martins Ferry, Ohio, Zoë said. —My father's father emigrated from southern Italy. He lived on the Lower East Side of Manhattan before settling in the Bronx, which is where my father was born.

—Don't know much about my people, he said.

—My mother's father was a devout Baptist, but when my mother became a teenager she could not abide the religious stuff, Zoë said. —She told me she put it all behind her the day she went to college in Boston. She went there on a scholarship and met my father her sophomore year. He was also on scholarship. They traveled to Italy together their junior year. My mother used to say that in Italy you really fall in love and you stay that way—

—Drove a truck once, he said.

—How cool, Zoë said.

—You drove it where? I asked.

—Drove all over. Drove it five years, he said.

—And what did you do after that? I asked.

—Worked with horses out in California. Ended up in Lexington, Kentucky, for a time.

—I didn't know you had anything to do with horses, I said.

—You and Walter aren't friends that long, my dear, Zoë said.

I looked over at her. She smiled and put her sunglasses on. In the mirror he was staring out the same window. He and Zoë began to talk about horses. Zoë knew about them. We passed the laundry where I washed the flour from my work clothes, the coffee shop where Zoë and I often met, and where I sometimes met other people from the university. And we passed the brightly lit liquor store where the large bottles of Chilean wine were the cheapest in town.

Zoë took off the sunglasses and told me to hang a hard right at the next light. I did and we were in a neighborhood I had never been in before. The houses were painted in bright colors. Trimmed shrubs and flowers grew in the smallish yards. Children's bicycles lay flat on the sidewalks, but there were no children in sight. The bicycles were pink and yellow. Ribbons hung from their handlebars like feathers from a headband. Maples blocked the sunshine. Their shadows moved coolly over my face. Next we were driving down a narrow street of small decrepit houses that all looked the same. Yards were barren patches. No trees grew on the sidewalk, and the tiny porches were chockablock with all manner of shit. Adults sat talking and smoking on porch steps. Their feet were almost on the sidewalk. I drove slowly. I was afraid I might hit one of the laughing children who ran along the cracked sidewalks and into the street.

—I think my mother misses where she grew up, Zoë turned to him and said. —As she's gotten older she does. I wish she married again. But she won't. She lives in a gorgeous house. The house I grew up in. My mother still finds it hard without my father. When he left, her life shrank. She says she's too old to begin again, but she will live for thirty more years. She takes care of herself. But you must miss home, Walter?

—Don't think about it much, he said.

—And you, James, of course, you do—

—I ran away, my dear, I said.

—New information, my dear, Zoë said.

—Your driver is a white dude from Western Europe. His life is a long, sweet wank compared to many Americans—

—Get over yourself, my dear—

—I'm sorry, my dear—

—Me, too, my dear.

We had left the town and were driving down a wide two-lane, freshly tarred road. You could see glimpses of the large houses behind ivy-covered stone walls. Lazy American flags hung on poles at the end of driveways with shut iron gates. The yellow line down the middle of the road was dazzling.

Zoë asked him about a turn. He told her and Zoë said she'd let me know. They both guessed it was five or six miles ahead.

—Dad was a preacher, he then said. —When I was born. So Mom used to say. Didn't stay a preacher for long, don't think.

—Where was this, Walter? Zoë asked.

—Florida, he said.

—I should visit my aunt there, Zoë said.

—You and Walter have so much in common, I said.

—I won't, Zoë said, and sighed.

—You could, couldn't she, Walter, I said.

I glanced in the mirror.

—Could do, he said.

—How foolish of me, Zoë said.

—We could drive down there, my dear. Follow the coastline. I have always wanted to make that trip, I said.

—It might be a challenge for this vehicle, my dear, she said.

—Look into the alien corn, my dear, I said.

—Economics, my dear, but Walter gets to see his aunt, Zoë said.

—Grateful, he said.

—An uncle on my mother's side was going for the priesthood once, I said.

—More new information, Zoë said.

—I've told you this, my dear, I said.

—Go right ahead and tell it again, my dear, Zoë said.

—It happened before I was born. He was in the seminary, but he left it. I don't know why he did, but he immigrated to this country—

—Why here, my dear, Zoë said.

—Here or England, I said. —But England was not welcoming then, but they would have shamed him out of home. And so he arrives here, marries late in life. He ended up in Vermont. Before there, he lived in Butte, Montana. He worked for a mining company. I think he did the books. Maybe the woman he married was from Vermont, and he met her in Butte. They had no kids. They lived in Burlington, I believe.

—My dad loves that town. He visits it every year, Zoë said.

—I've never been there, I said.

—Never been up there, he said.

—He taught in a Burlington high school for the rest of his life, I said. —But at home, because he was going to become a priest, he was going to lift the family up, give my Free State peasants some status. Then a few years before I arrived here, he died. His wife wrote some cousin in my family to tell them, but I forget how it was all found out, but his wife lived for only a year after him, she might have died of a broken heart, but when the failed priest first arrived in this country he used to send money home to the family, then one time he did not send home enough money, and my granduncle, his older brother, wrote and reprimanded him for not sending home enough cash. And they never spoke again. No money. No letters. Nothing. That was the end. But the failed priest wrote poems and ballads. He did when he was young. My mother put one in my bag when I first left for Dublin. I didn't know it was in there. I'd never seen it before, but I found it folded in my ironed underwear when I unpacked. I still have it. This ballad about boys climbing over stone walls in the moonlight to rob apples from the oppressor's orchard. Ha!

—Very intriguing, my dear, and, yes, I would have remembered it, Zoë said.

—You will remember the cornfields, my dear, I said.

—Directions are under my control, my dear.

I hung the right. The sun was behind us. High walls of corn grew on both sides of the road. A quiet and empty road not unlike the ones I grew up around, that country stillness, the wildflowers growing free on the headlands.

—Left up ahead. Rusty stop sign. Grateful, he said.

He fiddled with the bill of his cap. His throat made a nervous sound when he stared down at the flowers and shook them. Like when people must suddenly worry that the baby is dead, not asleep. The lovely scent from the flowers filled the car.

The STOP was fully erased. Outside my window were two rows of trailers. The ground around them was bare. Two skinny dogs slept in a wire cage very close to the road. Flies circled their heads. Cars and pickups were parked haphazardly. Most of the trailers had antennas that looked like trash can lids turned upside down. I hung the left.

—Left two miles up. Second turn, he said.

—No trouble, I said.

This road was narrow and potholed. Walls of corn growing on both sides.

—Got one kid, he said.

—You do, how sweet, Zoë said.

—Up in Boston? I said.

—Never once been up that way, he said.

—Not even once, I said.

—Not once, man, he said.

—But surely once, man, I said.

—Never, man, he said.

—Never took the bus up there, man, I said. —Drove a semi. Rode up there on a fucking horse, man.

—Like I said, man, never, he said.

—Stop it, James! You're acting crazy and rude!

She pinched my arm.

—Bad manners, sorry, man, I said.

—You should apologize, Zoë said.

She sighed and stared out her window.

—You're kind, he said.

Zoë turned to him.

—Thank you, Walter, she said.

I turned the music up a little. The walls of corn sailed past.

—Here, I said ten minutes later.

—Grateful. House on the right, third one down, he said.

I took the left onto a graveled road.

—You're sure you'll remember all of this, my dear? I asked.

—I won't forget any of it, my dear.

Dust swirled at the windshield. It stuck to my lips and eyes. We rolled our windows up. We passed two small houses before we topped a small hill. Cornfields lined the horizon. The road vanished into them. At the bottom of the hill, on the right, was a white Cape house, with vinyl siding and a dark brown roof. It was about thirty feet back from the roadside.

—That one, he said.

—None of it was that hard, I said.

—A pleasure, Zoë said.

I stopped before the house. There were three windows. A narrow stained-glass door between two wide windows and a smaller one. The curtains were drawn. Three wooden steps led up to a small covered porch. Hosta in pots on each step. The grass was cut. The unpaved driveway was empty. Cornfields bordered the yard.

—Sorry for being an arsehole back there, I said.

I didn't look in the mirror or turn. I rolled my window down. Zoë rolled hers.

—All right, man, he said.

Zoë got out. She lifted the seat. He got out. Zoë sat back in. She shut the door.

—What a cute little house your aunt lives in, Zoë said.

—Grateful, Zoë, he said.

—When should we come back and pick you up, man? I said.

—Hour and a half. Two. Grateful, he said.

He had carefully laid the flowers and the backpack on the yard.

—We'll just drive around and chat. That's what we'll do, I said.

He backed a few steps into the yard, looked right, and pointed at a line of trees that grew out of the cornfields.

—River where the trees are. Nice river. Right side of the road, he said.

—I have sandwiches and water, my dear, Zoë looked at me and said.

—I never thought of that, my dear.

—I guessed you wouldn't, my dear.

Zoë took the sunglasses off and dragged her fingers through her hair. Her fringe fell over her face. She dug into the tote bag and pulled out the corner of a sweater and wiped the dust from her sunglasses. I turned from them and stared into the still corn and wiped the dust from my eyes and lips with the back of my hand then turned back to him slapping the cap twice against his thigh. He stuck it back on, fixed the peak, picked up the flowers and the backpack, and headed across the yard. I drove away slowly. The shirt crammed Zoë's mirror for a second. I asked her for water. She passed the bottle. I took a long swig.

—You okay, my dear?

—I'm fine, my dear.

—You're not, my dear. You looked baffled and you acted very strange back there—

—Rows and rows of corn, heat and dust, the homeless, sorry again for being rude—

—So what exactly is the deal with this Walter character, James—

—You have a lovely way with the homeless, my dear, who would have thought it—

—A skill one learns growing up in Connecticut, my dear, but what's going on—

—He knows this place so well, Zoë. The signs, the river, and I understood that he has never been out this way before. I guessed he was a downright liar, and I'm fully convinced the old lady on the street is a lie—

—You should be more cautious about inviting strangers into your apartment—

—I was a little stoned. They say it makes us kinder, my dear.

—But he does not really seem like a bad guy, my dear—

—I agree, my dear—

—Now tell me what's going on. And then we find this river. I brought a blanket.

—But what if I don't want to tell you, my dear?

—You said before we left you would, my dear.

—I said might, my dear.

—Might. Whatever. Just tell me, James.

I stopped the car, pulled up the handbrake, and looked at Zoë.

—Walter knows someone I once knew, or sort-of knew. Walter works for this someone—

—What exactly does he do for him, my dear—

—I didn't really ask. All I know is he has to deal with a trouble-some bird—

—I'm confused, my dear—

—A whippoorwill, Zoë, but this someone wants me to visit him. I don't even know what part of the country he lives in, but he sent Walter with the message. Someone would think he was being funny. A hilarious caper. But I told Walter I was not going. Someone is the last person in the world I want to see.

—You're kidding me, James, right, Zoë said.

—I'm not kidding, my dear—

—And this someone is?

Zoë took off her sunglasses. I fingered a cigarette from my shirt pocket. She pressed in the cigarette lighter. She held it up to the tip of my cigarette. I took a drag.

—I grew up very close to this someone. He is the oldest son of my father's best friend, but his father is even more dust than mine is. He arrived in Boston a while before I did, and I'm not sure where to start—

—Just tell me three things about this someone, my dear—

—I smell a nice river, my dear.

—Only three, James.

—If I tell you, my dear, can we please stop talking about him—

—Yes, I promise I'll stop.

I turned from her and stared into the cornfield.

—When he was a teenager, he pushed my older sister into a river. He was the first person to show me a condom. I didn't know what it was, because they were banned. He was a complete prick to me in high school. And the second time I saw him in Boston years back he was with a woman who was not the one he married a few weeks later.

I turned back to Zoë.

—I've told you more than three things, my dear.

—And I get why you might not be excited to see him, my dear, but let's find this nice river.

8

The first time I saw Kevin Lyons in Boston was at the benefit for Eamon, which was held on a Sunday afternoon in the bar on Central Square. This was the second or third week of September. Eamon was in a Dublin hospital. Shortly after the accident, a medical team flew in from Dublin and took him home. Money was raised there and here. The couple who owned the house in Concord gave money. I forget how much, but no one complained. Eamon was illegal. So was his friend. In Boston most of the Irish and those I met from other countries were.

Nights after his fall, I'd wake up sweating like a pig and I'd fling the sleeping bag aside, stumble into the toilet, piss for a long time, wipe my face and neck with a damp cloth, then head out to the deck and sit in the armchair that Brendan and I had picked up from the street. Four or five Salvadoran men of different ages lived on the second floor of the house next door. The parties on that deck started after two in the morning, which was when those men clocked out of restaurant kitchens. In a glow of flashing lighters they'd shout and wave.

—*Venido, amigo! Venido, Diego!*

I went over every time. Big, boxy American cars pulled up onto the footpath. Ecstatic voices and quick footsteps rising on the narrow stairs. The deck rocked, like we were on a boat at sea. Candles shivered along the rails. And the loud music, the sweet weed, the laughter when empty bottles crashed onto the pavement below, and then candles quenched, music switched off, and back down those stairs, whose steps were crammed with soggy boots and soiled clothes that reeked of dirty dishwater and rotting food in Harvard Square alleyway trash cans.

But on nights when the deck next door was dark and silent, I'd sit in the armchair and see my father lagging along the blue corridor, his walking stick tapping the walls like the keys of a typewriter, and I'd see Hannah leaning over the sink, my mother's worn tea towel draped over her right shoulder, and I'd see Una the way she was in that doorway on Drumcondra Road, and I'd fall into the strangest sleep, where the traffic on Highland, my small flat on Botanic Avenue, with the records playing, the rank smell from the Royal Canal when I walked its south bank to Binns Bridge after dark, the dammed Children of Lir glimpsed from the top deck of a 16 bus, Tess's voice on the answering machine, saying if she wasn't so afraid to get on a plane she'd be over to see me, and my mother's neglected flower garden all became tangled up, and I'd jolt awake to glaring sunlight, flies buzzing around my ears, honking traffic, and unfamiliar voices rising from the street. I would have to be at Porter Square in less than an hour. The other painter and I had jobs to finish.

The bar was packed for Eamon's benefit. When I opened the door, someone was reading out a phone message from Eamon's mother and father: *Thank you all very much for your generosity toward our son. He misses you very much. On a day like today Eamon would want you all to enjoy yourselves.*

We bowed our heads and were quiet while an American priest said a short prayer.

Someone gave me his seat at the bar. I waved to Brendan and the Corkman at the other end. They were chatting with two women I often saw in there. Beautiful American women who thought Irishmen were cute. People kept coming over to say how sorry they were that I had to witness that. I said I wished there was something I could have done, but it happened in a flash. They all said the same thing—nothing to be done, that was life.

The other painter was sitting at a table behind me. He wore a gray suit. His eyes were red. His friends sat around him, rows of pints lined up on the table and the ashtrays brimming. His girlfriend sat next to him. She wore a short denim jacket with wide lapels. She minded the two children of a wealthy couple and did their housework. She drank and smoked too much. But that's what most of us did.

The other painter and Eamon grew up on the same street in Malahide. They went to the same schools. It was Eamon's idea to come to Boston and start a painting company. They had saved money at home. Their families helped. But the other painter said he and his girlfriend were going back. Never should have left Malahide in the first place. Should have stuck it out. Waited till the day when things improved. That afternoon, I told him he should stay. But he said it wouldn't be the same. Eamon got the jobs. He could talk to Americans.

On my way to the toilet I ran into Allison. She was a Catholic from Derry, and was studying American literature at University College Dublin. She wore t-shirts with images of Lou Reed, Dylan, Sinéad O'Connor, Che Guevara—people like that. We used to talk about books, the Troubles, apartheid, and The Smiths. I often slept on the single mattress on the floor of her tiny apartment at the top of a tall house on Inman Square, where I pressed the tiny dark freckles that dotted her belly and thighs. Pressed each one like a doorbell. She was in the States for the summer only, and she'd just come back from Texas, where she'd gone to rodeos and met real cowboys. She was telling me about the cowboys when she grabbed my hand and led me into the women's toilet. In a stall we kissed and did something else. Then she fingered a joint from her jeans pocket. Thirty or forty minutes later we were back in the bar. She waved at someone. We kissed and agreed to meet up later. I watched until her black hair disappeared in the crowd. Musicians were tuning up in the corner: an acoustic guitar player with a hungry beard, a beautiful-looking American woman with a fiddle, and a heavyset gray-haired American woman with a mandolin, whose t-shirt said Ronald Reagan was a war criminal and an asshole. The Corkman stood next to them. He was ready to sing. People egged him on. His voice was lovely and lonesome.

Our story's so old, again has been told
On the past let's close the door

When the song ended I got the urge to escape, and so I nudged my way through the crowd. Laughing people swayed into me and asked where the fuck did I think I was off to. I laughed and swayed and said I was heading outside for a breath of fresh air. I'd be back in in a few minutes. No worries.

The bar door shut behind me. Sounds faded like when you sink underwater. I raised my face and squinted in the hot bright sunlight. Loud laughter exploded from inside an Indian restaurant a few doors down. People and lovers went by. Shorts and t-shirts and sandals and backpacks and Red Sox caps and sunglasses went by. Cameras dangling from necks. People holding the hands of their tanned children.

Behind me the bar door opened. Laughter, smoke, and music leaked out.

Of all the stars that ever shone
Not one does twinkle like your pale blue eyes

I turned to find Tina. She looked younger out of that postal uniform. The tight knots in her hair made me see the thorns on the barbed wire behind the house I grew up in. Tina smiled when she said it was getting to be too much for her in there. I said I knew what she meant, and I bent and kissed her damp forehead and thanked her for coming. She reached her arms around my neck and kissed my sunburned cheek and said she needed to get on home. Kids needing dinner. Husband working the graveyard shift. I said Eamon used to look forward to seeing her walk up that driveway every morning.

—A neat guy. We gotta go on, she said.

—Nothing else to do, I said.

—You gonna be all right? she asked.

—Fine, Tina. Thanks, I said.

We were holding hands. She lowered her head and dropped my hand then turned and headed up toward Harvard Square. I knew I'd never again see Tina, and I watched until she vanished among all the other people. Next I was sitting on an empty bus stop seat a few doors up from the Indian restaurant. I was mesmerized by the ads and the huge smiling faces plastered on the sides of passing buses. I was beautifully stoned and the hot sun felt so comforting and I thought those faces were it. Students were sitting outside a café two doors up from the Indian restaurant. Newspapers, books, notebooks, cups, and sunglasses atop round iron tables. From the restaurant the consoling smell of cooking rice and Indian bread. I folded my arms, stretched my legs, and shut my eyes. Moments later I opened them because someone was sitting too close. I moved and looked in the other direction. The sky behind the vain and delicate downtown skyscrapers was a painful blue.

—Jimmy.

Someone touched my arm. I turned.

—Kevin, I said.

We shook hands.

—I've been in there a good while, he said. —I played hurling with Eamon in Dorchester a few times. I saw you in there earlier and wanted to say hello, but people were talking to you. Then I was asking around and someone said you'd gone outside—

—I don't remember you ever playing hurling at home, I said.

—I stopped after the father passed. Eamon is a nice fella, he said.

—He is. He gave me a job, I said.

—People were very fond of him, Kevin said.

—They say he'll spend the rest of his days in a wheelchair, I said.

—Never walk or talk again, Kevin said. —I heard you saw it. How are you?

—I'm okay, fine, and you?

—Fine, he said. —My mother ran into Hannah in Tipp town not so long ago. Hannah said they hadn't heard from you in a while. She gave your phone number and your address to the mother, so I have them now.

—How are they? I asked.

—You know how they are, he said.

—You're out here a while now, I said.

—Nearly two years, he said.

—You're liking it, I said.

—I'm a new man. It's like everything that happened before this never happened. You know what I mean, Jimmy? he said.

—I think I do, I said.

There was that glint in the eyes, the same as in Una's—their father's eyes.

He wore a blue button-down shirt, polished loafers, and a creased pair of khakis. The hair was thick like the father's. If he kept his mouth shut you'd think Boston was always his home.

He said he had good news for me.

—Good news is good on a day like this, I said.

—I'm getting married, he said. —She's a lawyer. Born and raised not far from here. Blonde. And not from a bottle. The green card. The works.

He laughed then slapped his right thigh.

—Good luck to you. Happy to hear it, I said.

We shook hands again.

I remembered him in the creamery yard. I was standing with my father and another farmer in the doorway of the store. The men were waiting to pick up bags of fertilizer and talking about how awful it was that those men in Mitchelstown were closing down the creamery but how could you stop men like that from doing whatever it was they took a whim to do.

Kevin whipped his shirt around his head and made loud yelps. The bike had been taken apart and rebuilt. It had no mudguards, no brakes, and the back wheel was smaller than the front. The frame was painted a bright red. It would have been the bike his mother once cycled. Tall, sturdy, the frame thick like a shovel handle. Bikes long ago abandoned to dairy houses. Covered in the dusty heavy topcoats that dead grandfathers once wore.

He cycled very fast, in perfect circles, each circle wider, each yelp louder, and the farmer said to my father that young Lyons had been caught robbing more than one shop in Tipperary town that past week, and but for the priest and Nora going in to beg the shop owners not to prosecute, the young fellow would have been in massive trouble.

—No one can control him. Come to no good, that lad will, the farmer said.

The farmer lit a cigarette then held the pack out to my father. He took one and said nothing. We kept staring. My father must have been thinking about his best friend, who was buried not so long ago.

—You have to come to the wedding, he said. —We'll have it on the harbor. Great food, great band. Una and the husband, the mother, the twins will all be there. You'll be there, you will.

—How could I miss it, I said.

—So no job for you now, he said.

—I'll find something, I said.

—I heard in there Eamon's friend is going back—

—After we finish the last of these jobs—

—I have work for you, he said. —I have a few properties. The fiancée invested in them. I fix them up into nice flats with a crew of lads, all from home, all illegal and mad for work. They're great gas, and we could do with another painter—

—After these jobs are done I'm never again getting on a fucking ladder, I said.

—Work in the office then, he said. —You look like you might be good with figures.

—Never, I said. —But Brendan is heading to some town in Michigan. He got a printing job near Detroit. The money's too good for him to turn down. He asked if I'd go with him. I'm thinking I might—

—Why the fuck travel out there? Stay here. I have a job for you.

—I want to see what it's like. I want to visit Chicago. You get tired of this, I said.

—You don't know a soul out there. You know me. I'll pay you well—

—I have to think about it—

—What exactly is there to think about, young Jimmy—

—I need to go back in there, Kevin. There's someone expecting me—

—Listen to me, Jimmy. I'll look after you. Will you give me a ring this week—

He opened his wallet and handed me a card. I slipped it into my shirt pocket and said I would give him a ring. Then we stood.

—I'm only trying to help you out, young Jimmy, he said, and he smiled.

—I know you are, Kevin, I said.

He rubbed his hands along the seat of his pants then glanced at his glinting heavy watch.

—I have to go, young Jimmy. An early start. And a few phone calls to make this evening. I'll be looking out for your ring. And I'll put the wedding invitation in the post. You look after yourself, won't you—

—I'll do my best, I said.

He hurried along the sidewalk. That strut he'd learned in the vocational schoolyard. He looked back when he was opening the door of a new car. Then I was staring through the bar window. They were all singing, arms around each other, window vibrating. Some people moved. Allison stood with her back to the bar. Her right foot tapped the rail. She was touching the forehead of a tall man who was laughing and fingering the hem of her Dylan t-shirt. I'd never laid eyes on the man before. But Allison and I owed each other nothing. Whatever it was we had was only there and then.

I went into the Indian restaurant and asked the host in the starched white shirt and silky black bow tie to please seat me away from the street and the window. When I walked across the wild battle scenes on the carpet I knew I was heading out to Michigan with Brendan. I didn't want to go to that wedding. Didn't want to see Una and her engineer. Didn't want to ring Kevin. But you would have to ring him. Your neighbor from home. Have to. All that. Your fathers the best of friends. All that.

The waiter put the plates of food before me. I thanked him. The buzz from the booze and the pot was fading in its dismal way. I tore into the warm bread. I'd forgotten how hungry I was.

I rang him a few days later. We arranged to meet on Friday of that week at his new offices. He told me the address, and mentioned that the offices were under construction.

—One of them is yours for the taking, Jimmy, he added.

I thanked him.

That Friday I got on the T at Davis and sat across from a group of chipper college students. At Harvard Square they slipped out the opening doors and skipped laughing along the platform. The train picked up speed. I watched them, feeling that dreadful envy, but down in the dark tunnel between Harvard and Central everyone I ever loved and everyone I didn't give a damn about vanished.

His office building was on a side street not far from the T. On the pavement was a large Dumpster. Two chutes led from it to two fourth-floor windows, where men with Irish accents were shoveling mortar into the chutes. The front door of the building was open. On the phone he'd said for me to come up to the second floor. He'd be there.

I headed up a stairs. On the second floor landing was a new stained glass door. A plaque: O'NEILL AND LYONS. I opened the door. The floor of the large room was covered with drop cloths. Stepladders and tins of paint. The high ceiling and the walls smelled like they had been painted that morning. On the right side of the room was a desk, with a lamp and a phone. Behind the desk, a leather office chair. On the wall behind the chair was a photograph of the Limerick hurling team. I went around the desk and stared at the photograph. I felt sure it was one of the ones I saw on the wall of his father's shed. I checked my watch. Half-eleven. I was dead on time.

The door to the next room was open. One wall was lined with filing cabinets. A card table and four metal chairs in the middle of the room. On the table the *Boston Globe*, a tin teapot you'd see in every house at home, mugs, a milk carton, a box of Barry's teabags, a bag of Irish sugar, and an opened packet of Jacob's Cream Crackers. I went over and ate one in two bites. A large rattling fan was jammed into the open window. To be heard in that room you'd have to shout.

I wandered down a short, newly painted corridor and stopped before a large framed map of Ireland. Around the map were portraits of famous Irish people. In their time they were mostly hated, or so few had ever really learned about them, but now money was to be made from them. Beside the picture was a small photo of the Lyons family. I only glanced at it. Michael was wearing the trilby.

At the end of that corridor a door was ajar. I pushed it in gently. This room was smaller than the others. The sunlight was dull, because the big window faced a red-brick alley wall. I liked this room the best. Before the window was another new desk, and on it a bottle of ouzo and two empty plastic tumblers. To my right a man's jacket and a black cloth bag with strings hung from a coat stand. Mortar rolled along the chutes and plunked into the Dumpster. The boisterous talk and laughter from the workmen above. The noisy fan. And now the happy voices of workers set free for lunch.

I noticed another door to the right of the desk. I hadn't when I walked in. Maybe because the door was the same shade of white as the walls. I walked around the desk and carefully pushed the door in. This room was like the first. It had the same type of desk as in the others, but this one was bigger. It sat before a huge bay window. A lovely view of treetops and tall Boston buildings.

Kevin was half-sitting on the end of the desk. His hands were flat on top of his head. His shoes were on, his shirt opened, and his pants and boxer shorts were around his ankles. Small American flags were printed on the shorts. Kneeling on the carpeted floor before him was a woman around our age. She wore denim shorts. Her hair was dark and in a ponytail. Her feet were bare. On top of the desk was a pair of jeweled flip-flops, the sort you'd get at Target. The fan and the noise from the chutes and the voices from the street and the workmen stifled whatever noises they were making. And it was when I was pulling the door carefully after me that I remembered him saying his fiancée was blond.

And that was the second time he saw me. And what he saw was a retreating shadow.

I was down those stairs quickly. At the T's hot mouth I stepped into a phone booth. Allison had rung three or four times that week. She was heading back earlier than planned, and wanted to meet one last time. I hadn't rung her back. I was busy working. I stayed up for four nights in a row and painted sets at Bloomingdale's for their fall furniture collection. And when I wasn't working I was drinking beer and wandering sidewalks after dark with anyone who would take me. I took every drug that came my way. I did because I wanted to. And I enjoyed all of that in a way I will never again enjoy anything. An electronic voice said Allison's number was no longer in service. I put the receiver back and pressed my forehead against the burning metal box. Drops of my sweat marked the filthy phone booth floor. My shoes were cheap.

Half an hour later I was standing in the hallway of the flat. Brendan was packing in the kitchen and he asked how the meeting with my old neighbor had gone. Did I like the office he gave me? I said the old neighbor left a note, he had an unexpected meeting, and I added that the sooner we hit the road, the better. Brendan asked what we should do with the heap of unopened mail on the hall table.

—This I can handle, I said.

I took the pile and a trash can out onto the deck. I sat in the arm-chair with the mail in my lap and riffled through it until I found the thick wedding invitation, which was the first envelope I ripped to bits without opening. And I dropped every piece into the trash can.

9

A mowed path ran between the cornfield and a wooden fence. On the other side of the fence was the river, which was really a stream. Zoë and I sauntered along the sunlit path then stopped in the shadow of an oak whose roots were knotted up on the bank. Zoë said this was the perfect place. I pulled the striped blanket from the bag and spread it, and after we ate the sandwiches we sat with our back against the oak and talked about books we should be reading, music we should listen to, movies we should watch, the upcoming election, and then we talked about my job at the bakery, the grant-writing gigs Zoë's dad sent her way, the classes we had to take and teach in the fall, the dissertations we were to start writing in the next year or so, and we laughed, kissed once, and said how boring that talk was. And so we got up and walked farther along the path. I carried the bag, and we were holding hands when we stood at the fence and looked into the water and across the bank at the Friesian cows and the two silos, and after we began walking again Zoë told me she'd mentioned the photograph to her father that morning. She'd never brought it up before, though she thought it was fine to now; the incident had happened years ago. Anyway, her father denied the photograph and the woman existed. He told Zoë he was true to her mother right till the end. When Zoë insisted she did see the woman, the swimsuits, the motorbike and the helmets, her father said she was confused. The man in the photograph was one of his buddies, or her divorced uncle who sometimes took girlfriends up to the cabin.

—It was not my uncle, and not one of Dad's friends, Zoë said.

—He doesn't want to hurt you, or maybe he feels guilty, I said.

—But it's a lie, James. When he's drinking, he tells me how much he still loves my mom. He says their marriage should never have ended, he regrets it did, but I'm just not going to call him or answer his calls for a long time.

—That will send the proper message, my dear.

On the walk back, the shadows of the corn stalks darkened the path. I sliced my hand up and down through the swarming midges and made jokes about *The Three Musketeers*. At the oak Zoë took the blanket from the bag and spread it. I leaned over her shoulder and unzipped the green dress down her curved and bony back while she fumbled with my shirt buttons and unzipped my pants. And things worked. And it was over within the usual time and you felt sore in the usual places. You were both lying back and that feeling was washing over you—maybe like when a well slowly fills back up. Zoë had put her sunglasses on. We passed a cigarette back and forth. And we didn't talk for a long time.

I sat up and buttoned my shirt. Zoë sat up. I zipped her dress up.

—Only connect, my dear, she said.

—If only, my dear, I said.

We were laughing when I knelt beside her and crushed a mosquito that was digging into her upper shoulder. A drop of blood appeared. I dabbed the blood with my sock. Then I put my socks and shoes on, stood, zipped my pants, buckled my belt, and said we should hit the road before some trigger-happy farmer found two townies having their sweet way with each other on the bank of his so-called river.

—You have watched too many bad American movies, my dear, Zoë said.

—I'm ready to be back home, my dear, I said.

I was looking across the stream, into the field. The cows were gone. A milking machine was buzzing.

When the brown roof appeared, Zoë took off the sunglasses and said she was not breaking up with her boyfriend in Austin. They had been together for too long. In three years he'd finish medical school and they'd move back east.

—I can't start over again, my dear, she added.

—You don't have to say anything for my benefit, my dear, I said.

—I know I don't, my dear.

Zoë slipped the sunglasses back on.

I pulled into the driveway. We talked about knocking on the door but decided to wait. He and his aunt would see us out here. A few radiant stars shone on the edge of the dusky cornfield. Frogs were croaking.

—Whatever happened between you and that woman, Sarah, my dear? You have never mentioned her.

—Yes, I have, my dear.

—Not once, my dear.

—You'd remember it, my dear.

—I would, my dear.

—You mention the starving millions to Sarah and she starts talking about the awful food in her private high school cafeteria—

—It's not an uncommon response in our little world, my dear—

—Her family didn't trust me, my dear. They saw me as immigrant trash. I'd struggled at the community college, and had just started at the university. Sarah had written her dissertation, and the family complained that I should be more accomplished, that I lacked ambition. Of course, they were dead right there. But why didn't you go to university in Ireland? Don't they have them over there? Those sorts of questions they asked me every time we met. And I couldn't explain it. And why the fuck should you have to. Once her lawyer brother-in-law railed at me as to why the bloodthirsty Catholics didn't all leave Northern Ireland. Leave it if they were so discontented. I tried to explain to him it was about home. And there was a long and complicated history to it. He didn't get it. Nightmares, Zoë.

—Your average, ignorant American clan, James—

—It was me who was ignorant, Zoë. They were being who they were, and if we don't knock on his aunt's door, my dear, we might be sitting out here all night watching stars and fireflies and listening to frogs that don't turn into shit.

We stepped out of the car and headed across the yard. I walked ahead.

—But you must miss her, my dear—

—No, I don't, my dear. She hooked up with an old professor. He had recently divorced. It was his third, and Sarah got some sweet position where he worked.

—How convenient, my dear—

—But I needed her, my dear. And she needed me. Or I'd like to think she did—but we were in different places. And when it was good it was fine. When it was bad it was unbearable. And she mostly acted like she was doing me a favor, to tell you the truth. But I was new then. I was lonely, I could put up with things. Put up with people. I suppose I was afraid, and wanted to fit in. And Sarah helped me fit right in—

—You were not in love with her—

—Who and what I thought I was supposed to be—

The steps were wet. Or it was the shadows of the flowerpots. I pulled open the screen and knocked once on the stained-glass door. The small empty porch and the glass lit up. The door opened and a tall, skinny woman with a long, furrowed sunburned face and blond streaks in her hair stood there. She was probably in her late fifties. I held on to the screen. I smiled. The woman did not. Behind me I felt Zoë was smiling.

—We're here to pick up Walter, I said.

—And who are you? she asked.

—We got held up. A nice river, like your nephew said, I said.

—There's no nephew of mine here, she said.

—The gentleman with the backpack, Zoë said. —We dropped him off here and told him we would return. We're late. The river was beautiful. It was hard to leave it. But you are not Walter's aunt?

—He's not Walter. I'm no aunt. And he ain't no gentleman, she said.

—Well, fancy that, I said.

—He left a while ago. Made him leave.

—We should have been here earlier, Zoë said.

—So if Walter is not his name, what then is it, I said.

—Jeremy, she said. —And I ain't seen him in almost twenty years. Not since the day he left. But he came to give money to our son. Said he wanted to do it years ago. Got close to doing it before, he said, but got cold feet. Cold feet. But I said to him it was too late. Years too late, because we don't have no son anymore. My husband is here soon. And your vehicle is where he likes to park.

—I'm sorry to hear about your son, Zoë said.

—Me, too. I'm very sorry, I said.

—Second time he got into a car, she said. —Drove too fast and drove into a telephone pole. If the pole wasn't there, his car would have went on into the cornfield. But I have another son, and a girl—

—So Walter is Jeremy, I said.

—My son's name was Walter, she said. —The man you dropped off here is Jeremy. His dad's name was Walter—

—He said his dad was a preacher, Zoë said.

—Don't remember anymore, the woman said. —And I didn't ask him where he'd been all these years. Don't need to know. Don't care. He got up one day and left. Didn't say anything about where he was going. Why he was doin' it. But I don't want to know why he done it. All's I know is he did.

—Do you know where Jeremy went? I asked.

—I don't know, and I didn't want to take his money, she said. —He left it here. Don't want his money. Right on the table. I'll give it to my church. And my husband parks where your car is at.

—We should be getting back, Zoë said.

—I don't mean to be unkind to folks, the woman said. —But I haven't had the best day.

—We apologize, Zoë said.

The woman waved her hands at the bugs, stepped away from the door, and shut it. The key turned. The porch and the hall light were quenched. I released the screen door. Zoë and I headed down the steps and across the yard to the car.

—Christ, Zoë.

—Bizarre, James.

I backed up that driveway in a flash.

—That gave me the creeps, my dear, but how sad, Zoë said.

—Very sad, my dear, I said.

—Way sad for her and for Walter, Zoë said.

—Loosened from our dream of life, my dear.

—We must be mindful of those we don't know who show up after dark, my dear.

—I hear you again, my dear, but let's not talk about them.

—Okay with me, my dear. Today was mostly perfect.

—One of the best in a long time, my dear.

I made the turn at the trailer homes. Lights shone in small windows. Barking dogs tore at the wire fence. I rolled the window up.

—I must ring the family tomorrow, I said. —I should find out about Kevin Lyons.

—How long has it been since you've spoken with them?

—A long while.

—Why a long while, my dear?

—I don't know, my dear, I don't live there anymore.

10

My father and Michael had identical alarm clocks. They bought them the same day, at the Market Yard in Tipperary town. Cheap clocks, enamel white, big-faced, with the round handle, two bells, and the little hammer sticking up between them. My father kept his clock on the bedside table. It woke him every morning. It didn't wake my mother, who rose earlier and needed no clock. Every night, my father carefully wound his clock, and a few months after he died, Tess posted the clock to me. When I knifed the box open and saw what it was, I taped the box back up and shoved it into the farthest corner of the wardrobe floor.

Tess once flung that clock down the blue corridor. I was standing outside the kitchen door when the door of my parents' room banged open to their angry voices and then Tess running out and flinging the clock, which bounced against both corridor walls, the left one first, before it spun and skidded along the floor and stopped dead at my feet. The alarm was going off and I picked up the clock, flicked the alarm off, and pressed the clock to my ear. It ticked away fine. Tess was back at their door, screaming into their room, words like they were not going to tell her how she was to live her life. This was September, in the year they built the pump house, the week before I boarded the red school bus. The row Tess and my parents were having was about Kevin.

Michael gave Una his clock when she moved to Dublin. I remember it sitting atop *Bury My Heart at Wounded Knee*, on the windowsill beside Una's bed. I bought that book at the Sinn Féin bookstore near

Mountjoy Square. I read it and told Una about it. She wanted to read it. I don't know if she ever did, but I do know I never got my book back.

I wound that clock once. It was a Sunday evening, about eight or nine months after I first visited her. Earlier that afternoon we were walking the canal bank on the Whitworth Road side. A swan bobbed out of the reeds and spun into the middle of the water. Una and I remarked on what a thrill it was to encounter the swan, but in the spinning, we noticed the arrow below its left wing. Not a full arrow, but a shaft butting out about two inches. The feathers around the arrow were soiled black. We didn't at first see the arrow, because the soiled feathers were below the water, whose surface was covered with plastic shopping bags, half-sunken and rusty shopping carts, bald tires, but also frog spawn, petals, leaves, and dust from the wildflowers and the trees that grew on the canal bank. We held hands on our slow and silent walk back to her flat, and the instant we got inside, she threw herself onto her bed, curled up, and turned her face to the window. She moaned low and steady. I shut the two windows, made tea, and sat on the edge of her bed, mug in hand. I would have said the tea would help, and that I'd ask one of the Dublin Corporation men in the bar if they might do something about rescuing the swan. She didn't move, speak, or take the tea. I stroked her hair, and when she was asleep, I went to her wardrobe for a blanket that I laid along her and fixed around her shoulders. I slipped off her shoes and stockings and tucked her feet under the bottom edge of the blanket. I did it like I had seen my mother do with my father when he arrived home drunk and bitter from Tipperary town, on those autumn days he sold cattle at the market. And before I headed back to my own flat I poured the cold tea down the sink, rinsed the mug, pulled the curtains on her windows, wound the clock, set the alarm, and placed the clock back on top of my book.

She and I used to meet two or three times during the week. She made dinner. Grilled pork chops, tinned peas, and instant mashed potatoes. Spaghetti Bolognese every now and then. I washed the dishes and cleaned up things.

We visited the city center cinemas. I paid for the bus fare and the tickets. She bought the sweets. And we walked the neighborhood to the west of Upper Drumcondra Road: left on Milbourne Avenue, right on Ferguson Road, left on Home Farm Road, right on Valentia Road. We stood on the footpaths and admired the yards and the houses. We held hands and kissed when the streets and footpaths were empty, and we talked about living in one of the houses. Marble fireplaces and sun-lit kitchens and glowing wooden floors. We took the 16 bus into the city center and stared at shop windows, and we sat silently for hours at this one café window on O'Connell Street. Rain and sun came and went, and all those strangers walked on by.

Not once in Dublin did I meet Kevin. When he first arrived in the city, he lived south of the river, but after their uncle Roger died, he moved north, to Phibsborough, where he bought the three tenement buildings with money inherited from Big Roger. Una told me that Kevin lived alone in a room on the top floor of one of the tenements. He and a few men he had hired were doing them up. The men drew the dole, and Kevin paid them under the table. And Una told me that some of the men were on the run from the law, and that Kevin lived without hot water or electricity. He taped sheets of cardboard over windows where the glass was broken. He'd a big problem with pigeons, but worse than pigeons were the rats that all his poisons and traps couldn't kill.

The day after my mother's burial, Tess and I, hungover as fuck, and still wearing our funeral clothes, took a walk in the fields behind our house. We talked about the names we gave the cows when we were young. When a new cow came along, our father asked us to name it. Tess and I went through the fourteen names. We laughed and argued over which of us invented what name, and we walked over to each cow and said something kind. Then we crossed the ditch onto the road. Big Johnny drove past in his tractor. He pulled into the headland, got down, shook hands with us, and said he was sorry to hear about our mother. We thanked him and inquired how his son was doing, and how his daughter was faring out at medical school in Dublin. Never better now, lads. Big Johnny got back on his tractor. Tess and I went on walking, and I was about to tell her about Una. It was at that place on the road where the tall elms on the ditches give way to sky and light and open fields, and a few miles ahead, the hill where Auntie Tess, Auntie Hannah, and my father were born. Tess had stopped walking. She was staring at the hill.

—You and me will always have each other, Jimmy, won't we?

—Yes, Tess, always—

—Always be like we are, won't we, Jimmy?

—Yes, Tess, everything like before—

—We'll look after each other and talk to each other like always—

—We will, Tess. We'll always be that way.

I couldn't tell Tess then. Couldn't tell—but the mind constantly stumbled toward Una. Such luck to be in love on that day. Love like that will smother all your other pain. And I did not stare at that hill the way Tess did. Her head raised. Eyes wide open. Like she was about to kneel on the road and adore it. Its top fields were ablaze with evening sunlight. Their miserable hill—but why did Tess have to talk like that? Ask you those sorts of questions? Cheat you into words you could not then and would not ever honor. I wanted to be lying beside Una in her single bed, making up stories about the voices passing on the footpath, reading Kafka and Blake to each other, blowing cigarette smoke at the open window, the smoke wandering across the ticking face of her father's enamel clock, then me slipping out of bed to boil a kettle of water for tea, boiling eggs, and placing the scalding eggs in the two yellow eggcups, with the hairline crack in each. Una had brought the eggcups with her the day she left home. She said the eggcups got cracked on the train on the way up, but you knew to look at those cracks that they had been there for a long time. Those were settled cracks. And boiling kettles of water for late-night baths in her tiny bathtub, washing the sticky hairspray out of her black hair. She cried every time I washed her hair. And I never asked her why.

This is how it more or less ended. It was five or six months after the swan, so seven or eight months after her uncle Roger's death, nine or ten months after my mother's death, and I forget how many months after she gave me those ugly shirts. Una had written a poem. It was lying facedown on the table: eight short lines, written in pencil, titled "My Wounded Swan." The petals, the frog spawn, the shopping carts and bags and bald tires with big holes were in the poem. Bombs made the holes in the tires. She was in the toilet when I picked the poem up. No. She was gone downstairs to see if the postman had arrived. Her soft footfalls in the doorway. She entered the room, dropped the post onto the floor, snatched the page from my hands, ripped it, and cast the pieces up in the air the way a magician might, like the pieces might change into pigeons, swans, cows, rats—whatever it is you want. Then she picked up her purse and walked briskly out the door. She did not close it. I ran after her and leaned over the banister. She was already in the hall.

—Sorry. Would it suit you better if I was not interested? I shouted.

Her windows shuddered when she banged the hall door. I went to her kitchen window to see if I might see her on Drumcondra Road. See her fine arse shifting in those high heels she wore on her days off work. But she had gone up Dorset Street.

I lay on her bed. The second hand moved on the enamel clock. Life going by. Shit floating down a river. Then the room was dark expect for the lit-up hands and numbers. And I don't know if I was dozing or watching the face of the clock when the sound of her key in the lock brought me back to them. She switched the light on. I got off of the bed, stood beside her, and asked why she had ripped up the poem and vanished in a huff.

—You wouldn't understand, she said.

Her spiked hair was stiff from the cold. Her face glowed.

—Look who you are talking to, I said.

—You don't understand, she said.

—I understand, I said.

—You don't, and you should go, she said.

—I'm not going unless you tell me what the fuck it is that I don't understand.

—You just don't. If you did, you wouldn't have to ask, she said.

—You owe me to tell me what it is I don't understand—

—I don't owe you a thing, and none of what we're doing is going anyplace. You should go, we are wasting each other's time—

—I'm not going anywhere. We should save for that house we like on Valentia Road. Get a loan for that, we should let people know about us, I'd murder a dragon for you!

—You don't have that in you. Don't be fooling yourself. And we are not saving for anything. And we are not going to tell anyone anything. I don't want to stay here, I don't want to be a stupid accountant for the rest of my life, I want to get away from here, I hate living here. You don't see it, you have no idea, you are insecure—

—I see it. You're the one who's insecure, and you're mad! Utterly and fucking mad!

—Well, if I'm so insecure and so utterly and fucking mad, why are you here, why don't you go, why aren't you gone already!

A creak on the stairs beyond the door made us stop talking. Footsteps moving to the next floor. She looked toward the door. The spikes in her hair were trembling.

—I'm sorry, Jim, she said.

Then the creak on the ceiling, where she now stared, and clenched her fists.

—But I am sorry, Jim. I am.

—Sorry for what, Una?

The sound of a television upstairs and someone telling the evening news. A toilet flushing upstairs. I looked from the ceiling to her. She looked away, her fists still clinched.

—Fuck you, I said.

I banged her door and the hall door when I left. Of course I did.

We did not talk after that, but every night on my way back from work I stood at the hedge for I now forget how many nights and stared up at her two windows and his two above hers. The curtains on the four windows were drawn, and each time her shadow appeared on a curtain a shock galloped through me—like when I was young and I gripped the electric fence wire that kept the cows in. Dare you to grab it, Jimmy, Tess, Hannah, and Stephen shouted and laughed. Dare you! Dare you, Jimmy! Jimmy's a coward! Jimmy's a coward! And the waves of electricity flowed through me and the warm piss flowed down the inside of my leg—but I knew which shadow was hers, and which one was his, but not once did I let myself imagine them together. No. I imagined her standing alone at her sink, washing a cup, a plate, putting the eggcups on the rack, shaking the water from her hands, drying her hands and heading to the toilet to change into her nightdress, her underclothes in a pile on the green linoleum floor. And when the light was quenched at her sink window, and the light next to her bed was on, I knew she was in bed. She'd wind the clock the moment she was under the covers. She'd read for half an hour. I stood and stared for exactly fifteen minutes. Then I headed back to my flat and lay on my bed in my underwear and listened to the records I bought on Saturday afternoons at a record shop on Henry Street.

About twenty or thirty times I followed them into the city center, on Saturday afternoons, which was the day and the time that she and I used to go. I'd wait at the corner of Grattan Parade. They'd come out from the hedge. She first, then him. He'd latch the gate. I'd duck down Grattan Parade. They'd start walking. Not once did they take the bus, though she and I took it every single time. That, I insisted upon. It was the speeding bus rising like a chariot over the arched canal bridge, charging up Dorset Street, past the spruced-up, mad, brave, violent, funny, cowardly, thieving, big-minded, bitter, foul-mouthed, small-minded fuckers, past the shops, the steel curtains, the shitty bars and chippers, left at North Frederick Street, where at the far corner the paperman's fingertips were blackened with ink, where a big clock hung above the bar, past Walton's music shop and the line of red buses parked face-to-arse, then past the Garden of Remembrance and the Ambassador Cinema.

I walked behind them, on the opposite side, and only once did I run into them. It was on Henry Street. I got waylaid in the shopping crowd. They had stopped at a shop window. She thought it was a coincidence. I know by the way she acted. She was wearing a long and loose khaki coat with straps and buckles. A coat I'd never seen her in before. It didn't suit her one bit. He would have bought it for her. And she introduced me to him. I shook his hand. He was taller than I was. Four or five years older. I bowed a little. I could do that. Parents and teachers were toppers at teaching you how to bow. He had the blond fringe swept to the side, like the lead singer dude in Spandau Ballet. The pleated slacks, loafers, white socks showing, a sports coat, with three buttons of the shirt open. Yes. I was so polite. And she acted like we were these neighbors from home who happened to meet in the middle of this Saturday shopping crowd, buying their potatoes, their peas, and their pork. Like I had never washed that sticky, hideous hairspray she bought in one of those big shops out of her hair—and his sports coat was checkered, I remember it, the sort wankers might wear to the horse races. He did not strike me as mean. He was dull. Certainly that. And his teeth were crooked, though I suppose he was tall enough that you wouldn't notice. When she said Hello, Jim, he put his arm across her shoulders and pulled her to him. She fell gamely into him. She had told him nothing about us. I saw that in their faces. And all this love and hate for her made me feel so miserable but so brilliantly alive. The country was in bits: unemployment lines, the North, strikes, riots, bombs, immigration, divorce, women's rights, gay rights, inflation, and the price of everything—oh, the woeful price of everything.

The next Saturday evening I was in the flat. I never drank whiskey, but I had bought a half bottle, and I sat cross-legged on the floor, with that bottle within reach, and put on albums and played the songs we liked, though mostly the songs I liked.

In my solitude you haunt me
With reveries of days gone by

Then this urge to write a letter to Tess. I got up from the floor, turned the music up a notch, took out the letter paper, and sat at that table. Beyond the window a streetlight lit up the evergreens and the moss. The well-dressed civil servant bachelor countryman, sixty or more, who had lived in a flat downstairs since he was around my age, knocked loudly on my door and told me to turn down that terrible racket. Who did I think I was! Have some respect! You have no respect! I stood and turned the music down, then opened the door, shouted at him to go and fuck himself. I don't recall his face, but I do recall the sound of his feet going rapidly down the stairs before I shut the door. He didn't expect that behavior from me, who, up until then, had been such a polite country boy, like when I ran into him in the hall on Saturday evenings, him drunk, flat out on the floor, his overcoat all over the place, his tie loosened and hanging sideways, and I helped him up, dug my hand into his right pants pocket to fetch his keys, then unlocking his door, my arm around his waist like he were my lover, and he pleading with me to shove my hand back into his pocket and give his balls a thorough fondling this time, for his poor balls got fondled only by himself—so I turned the music up louder and got remarkably into writing the letter. Tess had posted me her letter two weeks before. She wrote that she could not stop thinking about the card games we played as a family when we were children, that the card games were such a happy time.

My father initiated them. He was dealer and scorekeeper. He placed pennies on Auntie Tess's tray then put the tray on a stool and we pulled chairs around and played poker. My father stayed in his chair. That chair by the range that was moved only by my mother to sweep up the dust and the gray hairs that fell from her husband's head. Tess had a long winning streak at the cards. The rest of us detested her. Jealously, of course: Tess going about the house like she was Saint Anthony on top of that television that broke down every second week. Tess sat in the passenger seat of the car on the way to and from Mass. She sat beside my father at Mass and on the nights we did not play cards. But when Tess's winning streak ended and Anthony got onto one, the card games halted. My mother was thrilled. Those games brought tensions upon her home, and when those arrived, my mother cried, begged, pleaded, but mostly she said prayers for us. My mother never understood why her children didn't behave exactly like her.

My father took walks with Michael. But this was also the time that Auntie Tess died in Dublin. And I was the one who handed them that news.

The postman's green van turned in from the road. Out along the path I skipped. The van stopped. The postman rolled the window down and rested his hand on the door. A withered, twisted, gray hand that I'd never noticed before, though I'd taken letters and bills from him many times. And then the postman's head popped out and said he had a thing of great issue for my father and mother. The head and the hand slipped back in. And when the hand came out again a small brown envelope was pressed between the bent thumb and the joined and twisted fingers.

—Run in and hand this to them, young fella. Great issue. It's from Dublin.

I took the envelope. The hand rubbed my hair and the cold rushed into my fingertips and flowed into my balls before landing in my toes. The window rolled back up and the van reversed at an impressive speed.

I saw that hand again, not long after Sarah and I split up. I was with someone. We had left a party a few hours before and were wandering the bank of the Huron River. An early spring morning. Lilacs were blooming. We came upon a fuchsia bush and plucked fistfuls of blossoms and flung them on either side of the path like we were sowing seeds. Then the snapping turtle, right in the middle of our path. Its shell was coated with dried orange mud, and we said nice things to the turtle, encouraged it to move, but it didn't. So I reached down and picked it up. Held it on either side. The head slipped out; and there it was, the postman's hand, the head swiveling left and right, trying to snap at my fingers. River grass and slime dripped from jaws that opened and clamped shut like that contraption on the back of a garbage lorry. And I tottered on the riverbank when I flung that turtle high, with all my might, and before it hit the water, its body spun and its short legs clawed at the air like the arms of a baby. I laughed out loud when I did it. The person I was with screamed at me not to do it. The water bubbled around the turtle before it sank.

I ran back along the path, waving that envelope high in the air. Waving it like I was carrying the Olympic torch! The dogs barking when I got closer to the house. I told them to shut up and I opened the hall door and ran to the kitchen door and opened it. Only the two of them in the kitchen. My father didn't look up from the newspaper. My mother was wiping the table with a rag. Dishes and cups piled high on the rack behind her. The window clouded with steam so that you could not see the mountains. A pot of tea brewing on the range. My father's mug sitting on the edge of the range. My mother didn't look up from wiping.

—You want to be heard outside on the road, she said.

—Jack the postman gave me something of great issue. From Dublin, I said.

I was winded. All excitement. Looking up at my mother.

—Too lazy to drive in as far as the door, that fella is, my father said.

He put the paper aside. I held the envelope out to my mother, and when she saw it, she dropped the rag onto the table and took a step back.

—Hand it to your father and go outside immediately.

—Fine, I said.

My mother folded her arms. My father held his hand out. I walked over and handed him the envelope.

—Close them two doors after you. And keep that trap of yours shut. Are you listening to me, my father said.

—Of course I'm listening, I said.

I finished my letter to Tess. I wrote that she was the best that the two of them threw up. She was the shining one. And I wrote that every experience is a gift. Can't mess with what transpires. Ride the fucking wave. Ride it to wherever it lands you. Where it lands you is where you are meant to be—I must have been reading people who wrote things like this—and I concluded my letter by saying that the Lord above knew I needed her to keep going, and the Lord above knew that Hannah needed her to keep going, and Stephen needed her to keep going, and even Anthony needed her to keep going. And of course the Lord above knew her dear father needed her to keep going. Tess also wrote that she couldn't sleep at night, from worrying over him. She wanted to go back home, sit beside him, comfort him with mugs of tea and bread and soup, until those fourteen cows came home.

I thought my letter was good. I was slightly proud of it. I was drunk. It was this beautiful, melancholic state. I was outside of me. I was someone else. The foolhardy hero wronged by Una and the tall New Romantic Englishman. Yes. The letter was good. No. It was pure rubbish. Too emotional. More about me than Tess. But Tess would not see it like that. Tess would recognize it as a fortress. At the end of the letter I wrote: Love. Endure. Love. Endure. A full stop at the end of each word. I licked the envelope shut, thumbed the stamp in the corner. I had a good supply of stamps, envelopes, and writing paper left over from all those letters I wrote to my mother. A task I didn't have to do anymore. All the miserable lies I wrote her regarding Una. *Never see Una. Have tried ringing her bell many times but no answer. Maybe the bell is banjaxed.* My mother's letters were folded up neatly in a shoebox, at the bottom of my wardrobe. And Una and I wrote each other a letter once a week, but I threw them out the day after she tore up her poem and I said Fuck you to her.

—The hours of folly are measur'd by the clock; but of wisdom, no clock can measure, she once wrote to me.

—Drive your cart and your plow over the bones of the dead, I once wrote to her.

I reckoned I should post my letter to Tess, for if I didn't I'd second-guess what I had written, and the letter would sit on the table for days, and I'd come home one night, brooding after standing at that hedge, and I'd fling the letter into the bin.

The post box was on Drumcondra Road, halfway between my place and Una's. I passed that green box every day, walking to and from work, for as long as I lived in that city. Every letter I wrote to my mother was dropped into that green box. And every letter I dropped in I'd wait to hear fall on top of the other letters. It was a tiny, consoling sound. All those people writing to someone. Lies or not, what the fuck did it matter. People paying their bills. Sending money to political parties, to Rome, the African missions, pleading for prayers, like my father, who posted five pounds every six months to the Society of the Little Flower.

You knew very well
What was coming next

I took a final belt of whiskey and put on my jacket and stuck the letter in my pocket. I walked down the stairs and out onto the street. It was very cold. I zipped the jacket up and shoved my hands deep into my pants pockets. The sycamore leaves brightened by streetlights and hardened by frost coated the footpath on Drumcondra Road. I pressed my ear to the freezing post box, shoved the letter through the slot, listened to its soft fall, then headed on up Drumcondra Road.

I stood at the hedge and watched up at the two darkened windows of her flat. Both windows of his flat were boldly lit. Her shadow appeared twice on the curtain of his right window. I bent over, my hands on my knees, straightened up, took one breath, then another. I opened the gate back and broke a sprig from the hedge and brought it to my nose. It smelled like burned car oil. I threw the sprig down, shut the gate behind me, and walked across the cement slab that looked like an icy pond because of frost and moonlight and rays from the streetlamp falling across the hedge. I had my key, and I quietly unlocked the door and entered the hall. The lights were on. I crossed the hall and sat on the bottom step and stared at the shut hall door and the big white letterbox on the back of it. There were the smells of suppers and the lonely hum of televisions. The black coin-box phone across from me rang four times. No one came through a door to answer it.

Then my ear was pressed to her door. I was sure I could hear Michael's ticking clock. Dust was settling on my book underneath it. Chief Spotted Elk's dead and twisted body was frozen in a snow-covered field in South Dakota. And I felt sure I could smell that hairspray.

Then I was standing outside his door. I pressed my ear to it and heard him say something about a weekend in Manchester, a friend of his mother's owned a B&B there. I didn't hear what she said back. I knocked hard on the door. I had to be forceful about this. Acting like Saint Francis, like Brother Ass, was not going to do the trick. The sound of running water, the smell of roasting lamb, and their merry voices poured out the opening door, and as I watched it open, I had this urge to run back down the stairs, across the slick cement slab, out the gate, and through the streets until that city and all of them were behind me. But what do you do when you are standing at the edge of the sea in the dark, panting like a fool in the wind, staring up at the bright stars? Where the fuck do you go then?

She stood between the door and the frame. She gripped the edge of the door with both hands. A look of pure dread darkened that lovely face.

—No, Jim, no, not now, she gasped.

—What is it, dear? Who's there? he said, and turned the water off.

—It's Jim, I said.

I pushed the door back all the way, walked in, and shoved my hands into my pockets. She had stepped away from the door. He turned from the cooker. He looked me up and down while casually drying his hands on a tea towel. She moved to my right, next to a counter. She looked at the floor, shook her head back and forth, her arms flat against her sides. She acted that way when she was nervous.

—For God's sake, Jim, is this you? she said to the floor.

—And is this you, Una? I asked in a reasonable-enough way, though my words were shaky.

—You have not been invited. You have to leave, Spandau Ballet said.

—I need to speak to her—

—The bloke on Henry Street, your country neighbor.

He dropped the tea towel into the sink.

—I need to talk to Una, I said.

—Should I call the Bobbies?

Spandau Ballet was looking at Una. She moved. Her arms remained. He moved. Him on my left. Her on my right.

—No, Paul, please, no Guards.

—I don't trust this bloke.

He picked up the tea towel and began to twist it into a rope.

—He's fine, Paul. I know him, she said.

—I need to talk to you in private, I said, looking at her.

—There is a more civilized way to do this, he said.

He had untwisted the tea towel and was twisting it back up again. I looked at him.

—Twenty minutes, I said.

My words came out quite firmly.

—Give us twenty minutes, Paul.

She had turned to him.

—Are you sure you are safe with him? Look at his eyes.

—I know him. Our fathers were best friends, she said.

—Okay, Una, I'll go for twenty minutes, but I don't want him here when I return.

He dropped the tea towel into the sink. It took him less than a minute to adjust the knob on the oven, and then he walked in front of me and whispered into her ear. Put his left arm low around her. She hooked her thumb into a back loop in his tan pants. He picked up his leather wallet and a bunch of keys from the counter and took his overcoat from behind the door and buttoned it all the way up. Then he picked up his umbrella and shook it and faced the door then turned.

—So this is how Irish neighbors behave. Melodrama is what this is, he said.

He banged the door. On the counter, tomatoes and a head of lettuce trembled. A finely chopped purple onion pile. The sizzling lamb. The sad scent of rosemary.

And the truth is that I forget so much of what she and I said.

—He'll be back in fifteen minutes, she said that. —He will call the Guards if you are still here, that, too.

—But I can't stand it, Una, I'm sorry, I can't, I said that.

—Neither can I, but we have to go in different directions, Jim. For now we have to, she said that.

—Don't say that. Why would you say that? I can't stand it, can't—

—Neither can I, but we're better off this way, she said that.

—Three years, Una. Three, I said that.

And she came and reached her arms out and laid her hands gently on my shoulders. Then she turned her back and stepped away. Like she had touched her fingers to the roasting tray in the oven.

—He did that to me. When I was young, after Daddy died, she said that.

—Who and what are you talking about? I said something like that.

—Uncle Roger. My mother sent me over there with his clothes washed and ironed. His underpants, socks—the whole lot nicely folded. Seamus saw it all. It went on for months and months, Jim.

Seamus followed me. He was so young then. I don't know if he knew what was going on, but he'd follow behind me every time but never once came into Roger's house. He'd stand at the corner of the window and watch in at us. And we never once talked about it. Never will. We rarely talk anyway. But I'd see the shadow of his head on the window-pane. Roger never knew Seamus was there. And Roger would press me against the kitchen wall and stretch my arms along the damp wall, and there was this frightful smell of diesel when he pressed his big hard belly into me. I'd turn my face away and he'd press his lips on my cheek, press them very hard, then he'd lick my cheek, Jim, my face in a vise between his lips and that damp wall, and he'd force his right hand down my skirt and shove his filthy fingers in. Christ—but that was when I could slap him, Jim. With my left hand, I did. But he'd step back, laugh and rub his cheek, smell his finger, and say, You have a fine left hand, Miss Una. But I have great use for it. And he'd laugh and say, All the time in the world, Miss Una. All the time in the world. That's what he'd say, Jim—

I laid my hand on her arm. She stepped away.

—Go, Jim, will you please go, go before he arrives back.

—No. Look at me, Una. Won't you look at me?

—I won't, Jim. I want you to go away.

—But I don't want to go—

—Please go away, Jim—

—I won't go away, Una. I'll never go away, I can't stand it—

—But I want you to go, Jim. Listen to me. Just go.

—You're a selfish bitch, Una, I said.

And I don't remember leaving that flat, going down the stairs, through the hall, out the hall door, standing on the icy path, opening that stiff iron gate, and I don't remember if I went left or right.

I never walked past or looked at that house again. Nor did I take the canal path, but walked to and from work by Clonliffe Road. And when I took the 16 bus into the city center I sat on the opposite side, though when I turned from watching the street I'd think she was sitting five or six seats up. A slender pale neck between a black hairline and a collar did it. And thick black unruly hair circling out from a crown did it. That person was sometimes a man, which was immaterial, but for about a year after my mother died, when I was walking Dublin footpaths, I'd see her walking toward me. Streets she never walked on, never knew existed. Vigorously making her way through a city crowd. Wearing her black Mass shoes and the plain black Sunday coat. Her black hair in a tight bun. The saintly head held high. And when we met I'd lift my arms and she'd lift hers in the same cautious way, and I'd say to her then what I'd never said in life. I'd say I was sorry for all of it. Sorry to be a part of it. And that I never meant one word of it.

11

The day after Zoë and I drove Walter to the country, I came back from the bakery and rang Hannah. I asked how she was. Fine. I asked about the children. Fine. Have everything they want but they want more. I asked about the husband. Fine. Not enough hours in the week for all the work the French airline wants out of him. Plenty of overtime for everyone these days if people are not too lazy to take it.

—I painted the house from top to bottom.

—What color did you paint the corridor?

—The same shade of blue that it was—

—Any news for me?

—So, Jimmy, you didn't hear about Seamus Lyons.

—Where would I hear it, Hannah?

—Seamus passed away in London over a month ago.

—Christ, Hannah.

Seamus going downhill with years. Family tried to intervene but Seamus would listen to none of them. Got mad into the drugs. On top of that he downed a bottle of vodka a day. On a good day more than one. But it was the drugs that did him in. Lost a new condo in a posh part of London. The condo worth a fortune. Lost a new car and the high-up job in the five-star hotel. Ended up on the streets. A few days went by before the body was identified. They cremated him in London. Then an obituary in the *Limerick Leader* a week ago. A few lines saying Seamus had passed.

Hannah heard all this when she ran into a neighbor of Nora's at the new shopping center in Limerick city.

—Ring Stephen and tell him, Jimmy, will you?

—I will, Hannah.

—I should have done it myself. I meant to do it, but I'm so busy. And I can't get the times right. You remember them cycling the road on the bicycles they made from the scraps of other bicycles?

—I don't know if I do, Hannah—

—Sure maybe you were gone by then.

—I'll ring him—

—The phone won't bite you, Jimmy. You can reverse the charges with me if you like, you know that.

—I know, Hannah. Sorry I haven't rung in a while. Busy like yourself.

—Your own business, Jimmy, I know what you're like, but you wouldn't believe the changes around here. Big mansions going up along the road. Mansions and no one having children anymore. And everyone driving a brand-new car. And bypasses around every town. People going abroad twice a year for holidays. People buying summer places abroad. Can you believe that, Jimmy?

—Money's good for the nerves, Hannah—

—And strangers everywhere, Jimmy. You never know who's driving or walking the roads anymore. The Polish behind every counter. You never know a word they're saying. And you have to check the change after—

—They have your religion, Hannah. Immigrants looking for work—

—You could never take a joke, Jimmy, that was always your problem, but I nearly forgot to tell you this one. Guess who's back around again.

—No idea, Hannah.

—Una Lyons. She's back, Jimmy. That's what they're saying, although no one has seen her, but about two months ago the cottage and the shed were bulldozed to the ground and Una's mansion is going up in that spot. That's what people are saying anyway. Una's mansion's what they're calling it. The biggest one around. She must have the money to heat all them rooms. Or she must have a huge wardrobe. Wouldn't surprise me one bit with her. From what I remember and hear about her. I drove by the place a few times. The walls already up—

—The silver birches, they're gone, Hannah—

—Everything's flattened, Jimmy, but making the dinner is what I need to be doing. He'll be in the door from work any minute. And have to look at the cattle. Was out in the garden all day. The children are out there now playing. A lovely day for it. Everything turned out grand this year.

—But Tess and Anthony, so how are they?

—Tess gives out that you never ring her. Still does after all these years. She still doesn't understand that's the way you are. And she's still afraid of her life to get on a plane, but did I tell you she broke up with her man?

—You didn't. Kieran's his name—

—That's him. She was great with him for a good few years now. A nice fella. And she left the nursing job. Good for her that she can give up a job. She's thinking of selling the house and she is going to her art classes for herself. And your older brother is fine. Auctioneers making rakes of money nowadays, so he's rolling in it. Bought a new house down near Dunmanway. Paid to get an old farmhouse done up in the modern way. Haven't gone down there to visit yet. Don't know when we'll have the time to do that—

—Christ, I should have rung Tess ages ago—

—Jimmy, you know what I think—

—What, Hannah?

—I think she'd be better off if she was married and had a few children. She doesn't know what to be doing with herself. Too into herself, she is, but I put flowers on the graves last week—

—You ever hear a word about Kevin Lyons, Hannah?

—I heard he got married again, but not for very long. In the front door and straight out the back door with him. Nora's neighbor must have told me that. Who else. But they say the family is taking Seamus very hard. Nora hasn't put her head outside the door since she came home from the cremation in London, but the neighbors are very good to her like—

—I should let you go, Hannah, I don't want to hold you up, but I'll ring soon again—

—But you'll ring Stephen for me—

—I'll ring him, Hannah. I'll do it now.

—You promise me, Jimmy.

—I said I will, didn't I—

—It's always lovely to hear your Yankee accent—

—Don't forget to tell himself and the children I asked for them.

—I'll do that, Jimmy. They'll be glad to hear that you're still in the land of the living.

I sat in the chair and lit one of the two joints the mother at the bakery gave me that morning. Nora grew flowers on the two front windowsills of the cottage. A rosebush grew on the right side of the path leading to the door. Red petals scattered on the glassy uneven flagstones. The leaves of the silver birches in the sunlight shone like tinfoil. And the blue corridor was a bright blue. Your mother chose that color because of the poor light. I got up and stood at the screen door. The sun shone brightly on the grass. Squirrels playacted in the evergreen trees. The traffic rolled along Huron. Around this time yesterday he was standing at the corner, clutching the robbed flowers. He had no clue then what he was about to discover. I turned from the screen door and took another hit. Then I lowered the music and rang Stephen.

The twins were going to the kindergarten down the street. Just walk them down around the corner. They talked like fucking Aussies. Talk exactly like their mother. Bought a piano last week. Secondhand but in fine condition. Put a new roof on the house last weekend. Friends from Glasgow and Derry helped out along with friends from Auckland, Berlin, and Tel Aviv. So the roof was on in no time. Then a barbecue that night that went on into the small hours. Played and sang the old songs and smoked. Neighbors came over. Backyard barely big enough to fit everyone. Sharon's family visited from Canberra. Sharon got a promotion in the job. Now one of the head salespersons.

—But no word from you in a very long time. So what's new, Jimmy?

—Watching squirrels, Stephen, but I was talking to Hannah. I do have news, and it's not good.

—I thought there must be a reason why you rang. Nothing to do with family.

—No, not them—

—That's good to hear. I'm feeding the twins. Say hello to the girls.

He put Katelyn and Aisling on the phone.

—Say hello to your uncle Jimmy in the USA.

—Hello there. Is your dad behaving himself? Do you like the new piano?

The kids mumbled for a few seconds. Then they pleaded to watch television. He told them they were to go outside to the backyard and play on the swings. The fresh air was good for them. He spent two weekends putting up them swings, so they should make good use of them. Swings don't grow on trees like the lemons do. He had to chat with their uncle. Their mother would be home soon. She was getting ice cream, and they could eat it if they did what they were told. Have to chat with his brother for a while. Didn't hear from him that often.

—They do sound like Aussies, I said.

—I know. I'm opening a beer. I've just finished feeding them. They're always fucking ravenous—

—But the not-good news, Stephen. Seamus Lyons died in London. He was into drugs. The hard ones. He was doing very well—

—I'm putting the phone in my pocket, Jimmy. I'll put it on the loudspeaker. I have to keep an eye on the girls.

A glass, a cup, or a plate crashed in a sink. A few notes from the piano and feet crossing a wooden floor. A door sliding open. The girls laughing. They were on the swings. He was pushing them. Higher, Daddy! Higher! Higher! He told them to make sure they were holding on to the ropes. This went on for a few minutes before he said that was enough of the swings for one day. Their mother would be home soon. Home with the ice cream. Did he already say that? Why don't they kick the soccer ball around. Kick it, but not too hard. Had to talk to their uncle. Chat with his older brother.

—Sharon is working all the time, Jimmy. When she comes home she's knackered. She eats her dinner, drinks a beer, takes a shower, says a few words to the girls, and hits the bed. I bathe the girls. I make their lunches. How's Hannah?

—She's fine. Her kids are fine. The husband is making good money. You know the economy there is flying—

—I need to ring her, Jimmy. Sharon sent her a card three weeks ago. Hannah posts things for the kids. Clothes and sweets. We give the clothes to the Goodwill. Sharon would like the kids not to be within five miles of sweets—

—Sorry to be the one to tell you about Seamus. I don't know if you were ever in touch with him—

—Not since Manchester. That's the last time. So years ago. He came up from London one weekend. He was acting wild, wild like we were when we were younger, but I knew Seamus could be wild, and he was mad wanting coke. And I kept telling him I knew nothing about coke, well, I did, but I didn't want to be near coke myself, and so we were out in a bar, and that was where things went wrong, Jimmy. There was this good band playing. They were playing the Irish songs. The old fucking songs. And Seamus was telling me he didn't talk to Tommy anymore. The two of them worked in different hotels and never saw each other. Tommy changed more into going to Mass than he was even into Mass at home. He found a church in Shepherd's Bush and became a minister of the Eucharist—

—But what went wrong in the bar, Stephen?

—Well, as the evening wore on, Jimmy, Seamus kept wanting coke, and I kept saying to him to leave it alone, and then something happened in the toilet. I don't know, I think Seamus fucking asked someone if they knew anything about getting coke, but the outcome was that this person got very angry at Seamus and his friends were mad, too, and there were a good few of them. I tried to sort out the hassle, but I was drunk, but Seamus was even more drunk, and he was in the wrong, Jimmy, but you still have to stand up for him, and so we were told to leave, and we did, but I had a hard time telling Seamus that we had to, that there were a million fucking bars we could go to, and so we left, but outside he pulled me into the street, waving his arms and screaming, and a car came at us menacingly, and I pulled him out of the street in the nick of time and told him he needed to cop himself on, and he shouted at me that I was a bollocks and he shoved me against a wall and I shoved him into a lamppost and he said he never wanted to see my fucking face again, and I told him I didn't want to see his. Then he took the train back to London later that night, Saturday night, but his plan was to stay till Monday morning. I didn't say good-bye to him. I stayed in the room. The door was open and I could hear him shoving things into his bag and mumbling under his breath what a cunt I was, and I was a lousy fucking friend, but I didn't go out there and say good-bye to him, I didn't know that would be the last time I'd see him. How the fuck was I to know?

—You weren't, how could you—

—Poor Seamus. That whole family, Jimmy. They were mad. They never got over the father dying. Was that it? Do you ever hear a word from Kevin over there?

—He got in touch a few days ago. He wants me to go and see him. He sent a stranger with the news. But I am not going to see him—

—Sending a stranger. That would be Kevin. Make a fucking drama out of it. Too easy to pick up a phone. But go and see him. Why don't you?

—I was never close to him. I have no money—

—I'll send you the fucking money. He's sad over Seamus. He wants to see someone from home—

—Thanks for the money offer. However, I'm not going.

—However. However what. What the fuck's wrong with you?

—I'm an upside-down fucking beetle trapped inside a shut match-box—

—You're between chapters.

—That's one way of putting it.

—So you won't go and see him—

—I said no, didn't I—

—But did I ever tell you what Seamus told me about Nora the night before he went to London and three weeks after I went to Manchester?

—You didn't.

—We were out of our fucking skulls, and Seamus was crying, going on about how much he was going to miss everyone and he didn't really want to go because he was afraid he couldn't handle London, but he kept saying that he had to go, but Seamus told me that Nora tried to burn down the shed two days after Michael was buried. Can you believe it, two days after the funeral and small Nora with a canister of paraffin and a box of matches! He said Nora was screaming and crying, I gave my life to this man! I gave my whole life to this cold man! Can you imagine gentle Nora saying and doing something like that—

—I can't. Can't, Stephen—

—And so Kevin found the key to the shed, I forget how, but Nora caught Kevin right when he stuck the key in the lock. Caught him and she got the key back from him somehow, and it was later that same day that she tried to burn down the fucking shed. Michael still warm in the grave. And Nora flinging paraffin at the shed like she was lighting a funeral pyre. Imagine that, Jimmy.

—But Stephen, he might have been making it up—

—Fucking nonsense, Jimmy, and you know that, but after that thing in Manchester I rang him in London. This was about a month after. I got tired of being mad at him, so I rang him because I was going through a hard time myself, the job had ended, and I didn't know where I was going to end up next, this was before I heard news about the job in Berlin, and I thought it was so stupid that we fell out, because we were such great friends, and you hold a hot coal in your hand long enough you only end up burning yourself, but for a full week I left messages, but he never rang me. He was gone. He'd made his decisions. Or lovely snow-white spoonfuls of coke made them for him.

—The girls, they'll hear you. They'll learn all about who we really are soon enough.

—That they will, Jimmy, but Seamus and me were so fond of each other. You'd never think people that fond of each other could ever fall out. Fall out and never again talk. Makes me think, Jimmy, that our nature is not love. Love being a gaudy fucking present you give to someone once a year, like at Christmas. Something you do that pleases yourself. Making yourself feel better about yourself. Keeping people on your side till you find out they're of no use to you anymore. When Seamus and me cycled the roads as children we promised each other we'd be the best of friends till the day we died, that we'd let nothing ever come between us, no matter what blunders we made, no matter how the fuck we turned out. But you were very close to the sister in Dublin.

—You've asked this too many times before, and I've told you this too many times before. We were friends. We were young. New to the city—

—We all thought there was something between you and her—

—Here we go again—

—You were so moody then when you visited from Dublin, which wasn't too often anyway, but even Tess thought there was something—

—The mothers said we should meet, and so we did, like I told you many times before. We took Sunday walks. We went to see films—

—You and her had a thing for each other. I can still hear it in your fucking voice, the way your breath goes. You don't think I know you, so why don't you just tell me the truth—

—If you don't stop I'll hang up the fucking phone—

—I'm only joking you. You're always so fucking serious. You turned out exactly like our father.

—Stick the fucking knife all the way in, Stephen.

—But you know what I think now, Jimmy?

—I know I'm going to fucking hear it—

—Blank. We're from men who picked their holes in public, but you didn't know the first thing about them. Blank, I'm fucking telling you—

—He spoke directly to God morning, noon, and night. That's not blank—

—Whoever the fuck he spoke to, he went at life like an animal. Nothing in there. Going at life like an animal. All those years when all he did was grumble and grind his teeth and tell me to do this and do that and to get out of his way. Do this. Do that. Do this and that at the same time. But I gladly got out of his way. I got as far out of his way as I could—

—You did, Stephen, but there was something in there—

—Nothing was in there.

—There must be. There had to be. I need to think there is—

—You're going to college, so you obviously know better than me—

—I'm hanging up on you—

—Only pulling your leg, Jimmy. So rarely do I hear from you. Waiting for Sharon to come, Jimmy, so that I can wash the kids and put them to bed. But I am going to be thinking about things I don't think about anymore, thank fuck for that. But they were so close. You'd have to admit that they were so fond of each other. They were like lovers.

—Who are you talking about now, Stephen?

—The old man and Michael. Who do you think? But what do you think they talked about?

—They talked about John Garfield films, and they talked about their neighbors, and they talked badly about politicians, and they talked an awful lot about the horse races, and Michael talked about the jobs he was doing and told his jokes. The old man, he never laughed at them, but Michael went on telling them. You remember Michael and his hat in the church porch?

—The hat, of course, the fucking hat—

—He took the hat off that one moment when the Communion bell rang, and by the time the sound of the bell had faded he had the hat back on and tilted. I stood in the porch a few times when I didn't go to Mass with him and her, but I also remember walking through that porch and Michael standing at the back and the father would just ignore him. Walk on by. That was the only time the father did not acknowledge Michael. The rich house on the hill of love thy neighbor as thyself.

—But what was that hymn the father liked to sing? He sang it so well. The only one he ever sang.

—It was "Hail, Queen of Heaven, the Ocean Star."

—"Pray for the wanderer, pray for me."

—That's the one, Stephen.

—But the truth is, Jimmy, I don't remember Michael too well. I was too young, but I remember the morning he died.

—He died at the table. He was eating an egg. He was about to go to work.

—He didn't die at the table. He fell off a ladder. He was putting a new roof on a hay barn. And he had a heart attack and fell off the ladder. Up at Mearas. Close to where Auntie Tess and Auntie Hannah lived, up where the father was born—

—You're thinking about someone else. Michael died at his table at home. A man came to the door and told us. The mother invited the man in—

—It was Mick Maher. That's who it was. Maher, who stuttered when he got excited.

—It wasn't Mick Maher—

—I'm more than positive it was Maher—

—The only time I remember Maher in the house was when he visited because his two sons and Anthony had vandalized the National school. They put small holes in the windows of the new toilets. Stained glass, and they put round, small holes in each window. They used a pellet gun, I think, and there was war over it. They had to write apology letters to the teachers and the canon after. Why would those boys do that to the fine school toilets? How could they be so brazen? That's what the adults said, the mother and father included. But those boys were getting back at the teacher for all the beatings and insults she inflicted, for all her pain that she punished us with—

—But how's Anthony? I never ever hear one word from him.

—Hannah says he bought a house in Dunmanway. Like you, he's busy raising children. And he's making lots of money. Cash was what he wanted. And he didn't even have to leave home to find it. So all his dreams have come to fruition. I never hear a word from him—

—But how was the old fella after?

—After what, Stephen?

—After Michael died, what do you think?

—It must have been terrible for him, then the mother a few years after.

—But how's Tess, our fine thing of a sister?

—I'm going to ring her when I'm finished with you. She quit the nursing job. She's taking painting classes, and she broke up with her boyfriend. So Hannah tells me.

—I often think of her paintings on the wall of the girls' room.

—The only things that survived after the pop star photos were torn down.

—The paintings were lovely. The one of the farmyard, the hay barn at different times of the year. The one with the dogs lying under the trees down the paddock.

—But remember the one she did of the pump house? Remember that one, Stephen?

—That one was the best, Jimmy. The sheepdogs in that one, too. On either side of it, like they were guarding it, but why did they marry at all?

—Who?

—The father and mother, who do you think.

—Why are you asking me that?

—You dwell on these things. You have the luxury. You're going to college.

—To increase knowledge is to increase suffering, and fuck you—

—Fair enough, Jimmy, but I should go to Mass for Seamus. I never go. I'm raising a shower of nonbelievers. But I'll go for Seamus. Light a few candles. That won't cost me too much. Say a prayer. Sharon is nothing in that way, and she should be here soon with her sour mood and dark circles under the eyes.

—I'll let you go then, Stephen, I have to ring Tess.

—I need to give the kids their baths. Read them something or play them a song. That'll make Sharon happy, though it all depends on how her day at work went. You put women to work like men and they act exactly like them. Like pure bollockses. But when the girls and Sharon go to bed I can have a few beers and smoke a bit. Play the piano for a bit—

—You have lots of work in the buildings.

—Too much work, and you're at that bakery? Is that where you are?

—I take the hours they give me. I should get another job, but I study, or sometimes I do. And I take and teach a few classes.

—You were never one for hard work, Jimmy—

—Don't criticize what you don't understand—

—But, Jimmy, think of the mad conversations you'd have with Kevin. When you have children you have other things to think and to worry about. That might be the best reason to have them, so are you ever going to get married—

—Mother of Christ, Stephen—

—Hold on, I hear Sharon's car at the corner. I need to stand with the girls. They're all dusty and sweating from kicking the ball. When they're knackered like that they start crying. And I'm not in the mood for their tears. I too have my own tears. But you shouldn't be so afraid of the phone.

—I can't afford this call—

—It's me you're talking to, so fucking afford it. I'm just trying not to think about Seamus or any of you.

—I have spent my entire life doing that—

—We all know that, but I'll think about it when it's dark, and the girls and Sharon are safely in bed. But come over and see us. The girls would like to meet their moody uncle. I tell them about you and I tell Sharon about you.

—I miss you frightfully, Stephen.

—So come over and see us, can't you, Jimmy. We'll have a barbecue. We'll invite our friends and neighbors. I'm growing my own plant. I'll play the piano. Play you Gershwin and Chopin. Play you the old songs. You'll have your own room on the third floor. The house is huge. We'll pick lemons from the tree in the front yard and make fruity drinks like they do over there. The country where Bill is still the king. Bill who helped bring peace to our homeland. I'll send you the price of the ticket. Pay me back when you're a professor. And I surely think you should go and see our neighbor. He won't fucking bite you—

I pushed open the screen door and walked across the warm grass to the shadows of the evergreens. I tried to hear the traffic but Stephen was crying in the doorway of the girls' room. Crying and smacking the door handle up and down. In his other hand was his tie. The color was gone, but the wide end of the tie was touching the floor. Tess was sitting before the mirror. Her eyes were done, her shining hair tightened with hairpins. Hannah was down in the kitchen with Anthony and our father. She was frying rashers and eggs for us. And Stephen was crying that his shoes weren't polished. His mother polished them every Saturday night. Tess left the room and came back with the polish and the brush, and she knelt before Stephen and asked him to pull his pants' legs up and carefully she polished each shoe. When she was done, she stood and snatched tissues from a box on the dressing table and handed Stephen a few and told him to wipe his eyes, and she wiped her hands with a few and asked Stephen to hold his head up and expertly knotted his tie and buttoned his jacket. And Tess sat Stephen before the mirror and brushed his hair with her own hairbrush. His blond hair curled up at the shoulders. She rubbed mousse into it and pulled the stiff strands out between her fingers so that it looked like a clown's hair. Our eyes met in the mirror and we sniggered. Our hands covering our mouths. Auntie Tess's red curtains were drawn all the way back. Tess liked to look out at the cows grazing beyond the barbed wire. The click of the kitchen door handle made me turn from watching the cows. My father's slow steps were on the corridor. Tess parted Stephen's hair at the side and layered it around his ears. She squeezed his shoulders and whispered into his ear that he looked like a pop star. The used tissues were at their feet. The head of my father's shadow touched Tess and Stephen. Tess laid the hairbrush on the dressing table and folded her arms. Stephen stood and shoved his hands down his pants' pockets. They both stared into the corridor. My father could not see me sitting there on the edge of the girls' unmade bed.

—Don't make me late for your mother's funeral Mass, he said.

I was standing underneath the maple and smoking. Birds and insects made their slow summer noises overhead. Two or three cars passed. The maples cast their shadows on the parked cars and SUVs. The couple across the way were sitting at their porch table. Each was reading. One looked up, then the other did. They waved, I waved. Both studied at the university. I gave them free loaves from the bakery. They invited me to dinner on their porch. We ate, drank wine, discussed movies, books, classes, students, professors, politics. We enjoyed each other's company. And they all the time asked that I tell about where I grew up. And so I told them about the small farm, the vegetable and flower gardens, evenings after school spent picking stones from meadows, planting, spraying, digging, pitting potatoes, hay being cut and saved, calves being born, the routine shit about the Catholic church, the IRA, breaking the necks of chickens, knifing the throats of pigs, the one state-owned TV channel and the one state-owned radio station when I was a kid, the time indoor plumbing was installed, where you did your business before that, the belligerent teachers, milking cows by hand every morning before boarding the high school bus, and milking them again in the evening. Of course, I told only what I wanted to tell, told it with humorous pomp, but then afterward that stinging, chronic feeling that you'd hurt someone who loved you in an especially cruel way. But you told it in the first place to hurt that someone.

The couple said it was amazing. They even said it was exotic.

They were five years younger than I was. A smiling copper sun with fat cheeks was pinned above their door. Green creeper plants dangled from baskets on their porch roof. I looked down the sidewalk and wondered if the elderly woman was sitting on her porch, but it was too early for her. On the sidewalk across from her house a tall man with a backpack walked toward downtown. Only for seconds did you think he was Walter. And then you were thinking you'd seen the last of Walter. But you hadn't.

I put the cigarette butt in my pocket and waved again at the couple. They waved back. They were beautiful to look at, in that sunny, faultless American way: good-natured, freethinkers, secretly and viciously ambitious, though taking their time with graduate studies before the careers and the house down payment their parents would furnish. For a while you wanted to be them, except that you could never be them, but the imagining, then the finding out, was always what fascinated. From the beginning you were on this road. I was whistling when I opened the screen door. The cool air rustling the vents made me see leaves being blown across an empty deck floor in autumn. I sat in the chair with a beer. Then I stood, turned the music down, and rang Tess.

—Should I ring you back, Jimmy?

—Do you mind, Tess?

—Not a bit, Jimmy.

Tess rang back.

—So the news is you got rid of another man, I said.

—It's high time you rang me. It's ages since you rang me—

—Are you miserable, Tess?

—I could be better, Jimmy, but I've been a lot worse. Kieran was a fair-enough man, but he wanted children, and I said to him when we first met that I didn't want them, and I haven't changed my mind, and he had no problem with not having children when we first met, but as the time went on he started to say he wanted one, just one, but I said no way, and he used to get mad at me and say he never met a woman before who didn't want children, and there must be something wrong with me, and I said to him he's at liberty to think whatever it is he likes—

—You'd be a kind mother, most of the time.

—I never wanted one.

—You heard this terrible news about Seamus Lyons?

—Hannah was on the phone the moment she heard it.

—And you quit the nursing.

—I did, Jimmy. And I'm selling the house.

—Hannah told me that, too.

—She left no news for me, but I bought the house for nothing over ten years ago, and I'll get a good price for it now. I'll buy a condo. Something that fits me. Then I'll see what I'll do. I was knackered from the job, and I'm not going to go back to it unless I have to. I've saved a good bit, too, and I will have to get a part-time job somewhere, but I'm fine for now.

—Any other news for me?

—So Hannah didn't tell you about Kevin Lyons selling the houses in Dublin about six months ago?

—She never said a word about that.

—She'd too much to tell you, Jimmy. You know the way she is, she just keeps yapping away about whatever comes into her head—

—And she's constantly run off her feet—

—She's not happy unless she is, but she complains to me that you don't ring her.

—She says the exact same thing about you.

—She says it more than I do. I know to expect it. I know what you're like more than she does.

—You do, Tess, but Kevin bought those tenement houses for nothing.

—He did, and he did them up and rented them out to yuppies. And he let some rental company look after them after he left. He got into trouble before he left for not paying taxes on them, and he wasn't paying his workers their stamps.

—In Boston he and his wife bought houses, the first wife.

—Kevin's been on the mind the past few days, Jimmy, to be honest. Maybe it's because of Seamus. Or it happens when you break up with someone. You start thinking about the other ones. I had it for Kevin in a very bad way at one time.

—I know that, but you behaved yourself.

—I did and I didn't. You don't even know the half of it.

—We're lucky to know the quarter of anything, but you never told me the didn't part.

—When I could tell you, you wanted nothing to do with us, but Kevin and I were sneaky, Jimmy. We had to be. If they found out I was seeing him there would have been holy war, as you know. They would have locked me up and buried the key.

—They thought you and him were not suited—

—Who knows what they thought. Them showing their will at every twist and turn. Wanting to be the boss of your life. Wanting us to live the way they'd lived. Never wanting one thing to change even when the changes were happening right in front of their eyes.

—But you were good at keeping it to yourself—

—Like I said to you, we had to, Jimmy, although I did get over him. It took me a long time, but many's the night I stayed awake over him, but you're right, he was not for me, but no one could tell me that then. And Kevin had to have more than one woman, more than one of everything, houses, cars, suits, and so on, and he would have wanted children, and more than one of them. I wasn't fully a fool, I knew he was the wrong man for me, but at one time and for a long time I thought the two of us were meant to be.

—So when was the last time you saw him?

—A bit before he went out there.

—And so now you tell me all this.

—But you'd put me and us behind you, Jimmy. From the day you left home, you did, don't let on differently, so Kevin rang and said he was going to the States and he wanted to see me one last time. We hadn't seen each other for a year. He'd visited Cork a few times, but I finally had put a stop to it, and when he rang to say he was going, I was seeing someone new, we were serious enough like, but I told Kevin to come, so he drove to Cork, and we met at a bar a good ways from where I lived and worked in the hospital. That was the last year I lived in Cork, before I moved up to here, and so I got someone to cover my shift in work. I lied to that person and told her there was trouble at home, and I needed to go immediately to see my father and sister. And I dolled myself up, Jimmy. I put on the red dress. I knew he'd like that one on me. Or maybe it was another one. No, Jimmy, it was the light red one. Not the other red one. I paid good money for that dress. But I knew what perfume to wear, perfume he'd bought me once, and he'd say to me to spray a few tiny drops on my right wrist, only a few so that no one else could smell it but him, and when we'd meet, the first thing he'd do was bring my wrist to his lips, and Jimmy, I was in heaven then. I don't think I've even felt anything like that since, and I did the hair up and everything, but didn't I run into the girl who took over my shift. I had to put petrol in the car, and she walked straight out of the petrol station and there I was pumping the petrol, and she on her way to cover my shift, doing me that big favor, and I knew by the way she looked at me that she knew I'd told her a pack of lies. She knew because of the way I was dressed, like I was not dressed like there was trouble at home. I was dressed for a different sort of trouble, if you know what I mean. And the two of us smiled and chatted away, and I told her I was on the way home to see my father and sister, but she knew, Jimmy. She saw that I was dressed like a hussy, and thank God she didn't know the fella I was going out with then. If she did, I was in even bigger trouble, and I probably told her other lies now that I forget.

—But Tess, maybe she didn't know a thing.

—That would be nice for me to think, Jimmy, but I could see it in her face that she knew, but when I finished pumping the petrol I drove to this bar about five miles away, the place we arranged to meet, and we sat at a table at the back and drank one drink. Mine was a vodka and tonic. We sat there for hours, till way after dark. And all I tasted through that straw was the bitter lemon. You see, I thought I was well over him, Jimmy, that he couldn't do that to me anymore, but to tell you the truth I was in tears. The face in a pure mess and all the makeup running. I looked like the crying clown. That's what I was. A crying fool of a clown. I brought it all on myself, but after we left the bar, Jimmy, we were sitting on the plush leather seats of his car in the dark car park. He had a bit of hash and we smoked it, and he kept putting his hand down and I kept pushing that hand away, I knew well what was going on inside his pants, but he eventually stopped and we said nothing for a long time. I was looking out the window, looking at the couples hand-in-hand walk in and out of the bar, and I was the one who broke the silence. I turned back to him and said that he was the torment of my life, and that I hoped I'd never lay my eyes on him again.

—He took that very hard, Tess—

—Very hard, Jimmy. I was a pure bitch to him. But it was very hard for me, too, of course, but after I said those things to him he started to cry. I'd never seen him shed a tear before, not even at his father's funeral, I didn't know he had tears inside him, but he wasn't putting it on, and he cried and said it was so hard to leave me, and I would never understand how hard that was, but I did wish him luck, Jimmy, and I got out of the car the moment after I said it. And I never looked back at his car, but it didn't pull away till I got into mine and turned on the lights and started the engine and drove away, like he still thought I might come back to him.

—You were in bits, Tess.

—Complete bits, Jimmy. I had to squeeze the steering wheel very hard because my hands were shaking that bad, and the tears like a downpour, and I got lost in the city, took every wrong turn, drove down every wrong street, and ended up out in the country. I didn't know where I was going, and I just kept on driving, Jimmy, because I was thinking then too that you were going to leave. I knew it. I knew since the day you left for Dublin that you would never stay. And in my selfish way I wanted you to stay. I never wanted you going away, but I knew you would and I knew you had to. And that night I didn't know which way to turn, and it was so dark, Jimmy, and I could see the sea out there in the moonlight, and I was frightened that something very bad was going to happen to me, that I was going to make it happen to myself, like I was going to land myself dead in the sea, because of the way the water moved in the moonlight.

—Christ, Tess. You're all right—

—Fine now, Jimmy. I can let things go. I can. So that's well in the past, but that night, Jimmy, I told my mother that I was sorry for all the going against them, the anguish, but their mad regulations would make anyone mad, the You're not going out wearing that, the constant How could you do this to me after all I did for you! All the vows she wanted me to make that I wouldn't let a man even near me, locking me in the toilet with her and making me swear that I won't ever let them touch me, cross your heart and hope to die, and you know how many times she told me that nothing would make her happier than me becoming a nun, that she prayed night and day that I would become one. But can you imagine that, Jimmy, me a nun!

—Not for a second, Tess.

—But I was afraid, too, that night, Jimmy, that I'd run into the man I was seeing. I'd drive the car around some corner and there he'd be, standing in front of the car, waiting for me, waiting to say, Caught you in the act, you bitch.

—A panic attack, Tess.

—Call it what you like, Jimmy. But I didn't want to leave Kevin in that car park, but I couldn't go with him. I did not want to leave home. I could never get on a plane, and if I could not get on a plane for you or for Kevin Lyons, I could for no one. And of course Dada was alive then. And I was not leaving Dada.

—Kevin wants me to go and see him, Tess. He sent someone to my door with the news. A down-and-out man—

—Sending someone, that's Kevin.

—That's what Stephen said.

—But Jimmy, why do you think Kevin wants to see you?

—I have no idea, Tess.

—Are you a fool, Jimmy?

—Oh, sister—

—He's in an awful state over Seamus. He wants to see someone from home.

—Stephen said something like that.

—Stephen's right, but I wish you would just come home, Jimmy. You could get a job here now, no problem. You could get all the jobs you wanted—

—I had a job, Tess. I live here now. I have to finish the studies.

—You never say much about what you're studying, or I forget.

—Poetry and some other things that don't talk to me anymore.

—It goes away and comes back, Jimmy, you know that.

—I do, Tess, you're right, but I'm not going to see Kevin.

—You're so stubborn. You always were.

—You're a fine one to talk, Tess. And so you heard the news about Una's mansion being built where the cottage was. They tore up the silver birches—

—Oh, I heard it from Hannah. The moment she heard it she's on the phone to me, but it's Nora I often think about. How was she going to raise those children? Where was the money going to come from? You remember their uncle Roger?

—I do, at the creamery. His red Zetor and all his milk churns. He had all that land. He and Michael didn't talk. They fell out over the land. The father left the land to Roger, although Roger was a few years younger than Michael was, but the father didn't like Michael.

—How do you know all that? From Una?

—Mostly overheard in the kitchen from the mother and father.

—So Roger's land and money would solve Nora's problems, but in the end she never even had to marry Roger—

—Because he died suddenly, and Nora inherited Roger's money and land, so they auctioned off the land and house and everything else Roger owned, and they moved down the country, bought that new place with the money, and Kevin bought his tenements—

—But Jimmy, I forget how Roger died.

—He died in the meadow. I remember hearing it. Died slumped over the steering wheel of the tractor. A heart attack. That's what they said. Went the way Michael did. The tractor was in low gear and humping the ditch like a dog.

—But Jimmy, people were not a bit nice about Nora and Roger.

—They weren't, but Roger was the devil.

—Una told you that, of course, but you won't tell your sister—

—Oh, sister—

—I understand, Jimmy, we all have things we don't want to tell, but when Nora took up with Roger, Dada never spoke to Nora again and Mama talked away nicely to Nora when they met after Mass, but when Mama came home she clipped Nora like I never heard her clip anyone. One time after her coming in from Mass, I remember, her saying Nora Lyons was a pure tramp, how dare Nora Lyons go up to the altar and receive—

—Stephen just told me Nora tried to burn down the shed a few days after Michael died, but they stopped her the moment she struck the match. Seamus told Stephen that.

—Stephen might be making that up, Jimmy.

—I said something like that, but he's not, but I hear you're painting again—

—Taking a class for the first time. But what about you, Jimmy?

—You lose track, Tess. The country is huge. I live in a matchbox—

—You won't forever. Should I send you money?

—I'm fine, thank you.

—Ask if you need it. We're all rotten with it now. We're acting like the only problem we ever had was that we'd no money, like the way we lived at one time was a different country with different people, but Jimmy, you're the sort who drives forward looking into the rearview mirror—

—I don't look in the rearview mirror—

—You do so. And you should go and see Kevin and then ring me. He never once looked in the rearview mirror, I can tell you that much. But I know you and him were never close. I know you never liked him. You and him are so different in manner. Then he's the few years older.

—I spent many schooldays running like a lunatic from him.

—Kevin had to be the biggest man in every room, but I admit I liked that in him.

—You still think about the two of them—

—Nearly every day, Jimmy, but we were all so hard on each other at times.

—And I still think about not ringing you after he died, after Hannah asked me to.

—I've forgotten that, Jimmy. You know I never stay mad at you for too long.

—I haven't, Tess, but I should wash the flour out of my hair and eat something—

—Talk to me for another few minutes, Jimmy.

—What's the weather like there today?

—A few showers this morning, but the sun came out around two, and the grass dried up, and I cut the lawn and took the dog for a walk by the river, and then I went to the bakery in the village and drank a cup of tea and read the paper. I'll be seeing a few friends later on. One of them is bringing some fella who wants to meet me. I'm told he's a

nice fella and he's nice-looking. I hope he is, but Jimmy, you should go
and see Kevin—

—I'm not going, Tess. You know very well I'm not.

—You have to go, Jimmy.

—I don't have to go anywhere, Tess.

—Jimmy, like I said to you, you're so stubborn. He just wants to
talk to someone from home. "Yea, ere my hot youth pass, I shall speak
to my people and say: Ye shall be foolish as I; ye shall scatter, not
save"—do you remember that, Jimmy?

—Patrick Pearse, Tess. I forget which poem it is.

—The teacher beat those lines into us with her meter stick.

—It's not "The Rebel" or "The Mother." Oh, I remember, Tess. It's
"The Fool."

—That's it, Jimmy. So will you do that for your sister? Kevin's our
neighbor—

—Christ, Tess. Everyone's our neighbor. Remember that.

—Fine, Jimmy, but you owe me that much.

For a minute we were silent.

—Jimmy, I'm sorry for saying that. I didn't mean it. Are you still
there, Jimmy? It's Tess.

—I'm here, Tess. I heard you. Fine, Tess, I'll go. I will.

The phone was ringing in the next room. This was six or seven days
after Hannah told me he was dead. I was sitting at the kitchen table in
the apartment, with a pen in my hand, looking through the help-
wanted section in the local newspaper. Brendan was at his job in
Detroit. The answering machine clicked on.

—Jimmy, it's Tess. I got your number from Hannah. You should
have rung me by now. Hannah told me you said you were going to
ring. Pick up, Jimmy. I know you're there.

I stood in the doorway and stared at the phone on the floor. Tess
was still talking. And my hands were pressed to my ears when I crossed

the floor and turned the volume down all the way. Then I left the room and shut the door and sat again before the newspaper. I drew stars around the restaurant jobs that looked promising. I did it like an eager child in possession of a box of new crayons and reams of blank pages, and when I was done I wanted to suss out those restaurants, and so I wrote down their names and addresses, then I shaved and showered, ironed my clothes, and stuck a map of the town in my pocket.

On Main Street people were eating and shopping. On both sides of one restaurant doorway impatiens grew from fake wooden tubs. I forget now if that restaurant was on my list, but I went through the double doors and stood at a host stand in a foyer with high ceilings and windows. Behind the stand, carpeted stairs led to the next floor. Shining brass railings and blond wooden walls and at my feet black and blue tiles. On the specials board the soup of the day was minestrone. A smiling woman with menus appeared. She asked if she could help me. I said I wanted to fill out an application. She fingered her hair around her left ear, reached under the stand, and handed me one. She directed me to a seat at the bar and said I could fill it out there. When I handed back the completed application she asked about my accent. We chatted for ten or fifteen minutes. Her long black fringe was swept back. She resembled a softer version of Chrissie Hynde. And she was wearing this white old-fashioned man's shirt. One with the stiff point collar. The kind my mother once ironed for my father for Mass. And less than a week after I'd filled out the application, I was bussing tables on lunch and dinner shifts. I had also signed up to take the GED. The community college was mailing its catalogue of winter classes.

The hostess was Sarah. She worked weekends in the restaurant. Two years passed before we really got together. Seven more months before we moved in—though that's enough of that. On the restaurant application I wrote my name as James. And everyone I came to know from then on called me that and I never once said they should call me any other.

I erased Tess's message that afternoon before I left the apartment. I never listened to it. And when we did talk, months later, I told Tess the answering machine was broken, and I was sorry for letting time slip away. This I blamed on settling into the new town, the hassles of classes, and the restaurant job. But why didn't I call? Why didn't I pick up? And why didn't I listen? I didn't want them getting in the way. That's why. And I was trying very hard not to think about him and those alive and dead connected to him.

I showered away the flour and I hard-boiled three eggs and spread them on thick slices of sourdough bakery bread with salt and butter. And then I rang Zoë.

—Stop by. Bring decent gin, my dear. I'll go half. I have lemons and tonic.

—I'll be right over, my dear.

I took a few hits from the joint. Next I was walking in the shadows of the maples. I said hello to people I often passed on that sidewalk, and they did the same: a sullen-looking student around my age, a tall elderly man who swept the downtown post office, and a hip young couple wearing colorful secondhand clothes.

A U-Haul truck was parked in the elderly woman's driveway. Two men carried boxes up the ramp. In the middle of the sidewalk stood a thick-chested middle-aged man in a worn t-shirt. Sunglasses were propped on his forehead and his hands were fists in the back pockets of his cargo shorts. He stared up at the men hauling boxes and furniture out the front door. I stepped around him, and I was at the corner, about to cross the street, when I turned back. I stopped a few feet from him. He was still looking at the door. His hairy forearms were golden.

—I haven't seen the woman on the porch in a while. I live up the street, I said.

—Mom can't live alone anymore, he said.

He grimaced at the man bringing the scarred headboard of a child's bed through the door.

—Only monks, nuns, and the unhinged can, I said.

He smirked, turned to me, then back to the door. The withered vines hung limp from the porch rails. The chair and the box were gone. I asked if he was born in the house.

—You bet, but most of the old neighbors are gone, he said. —Dad passed seven years ago at his desk on the back porch, his office desk. He sat at it every day after he retired, but Dad didn't crunch numbers anymore, he wrote thrillers no one would ever read. Mom and I thought he was crazy. I'm their only kid, and I was saying for years they should sell the house and move south. But Dad, he loved the back porch and the traffic behind the trees. I still don't get it.

I said the traffic didn't bother me either, but I didn't say I'd seen the paperback books and the metal desk. Nor did I say I'd found fifty bucks right where the U-Haul was parked. I politely asked where he now lived.

—Chicago, Evanston, he said. —Mom lives close by. The retirement facility takes good care of her. She doesn't like it, but we all gotta deal. I'm selling the house. Mom talks about things I know nothing about.

He tapped his forehead with his finger.

—Sorry to hear it, I said.

—So much stuff. My dad's stuff. I just need to get back home. Look up there.

He pointed to a string of dusty lights strung from hooks along the edge of the porch roof.

—Dad and I put them up one Saturday afternoon after we'd come back from a football game. I screwed in the hooks. He held the ladder. I was just a kid then.

He turned to me.

—You from Germany?

—Ireland, I said.

—Cool, he said, and his eyes went back to the men and the door. —My wife's folks are from there. We plan on visiting when the kids are older, hike the moors—

—Walk the bogs, maybe—

—What's the difference?

—The peat, I think.

—Sure, he said.

—Your mom and I never talked, but we waved at each other, I said.

—Mom does not remember anything, like Dad and I never happened, but I just need to get this place cleaned up. I got work back home. Getting a Dumpster in here later tonight. Gotta get rid of all this trash.

—Walter was telling the truth about the woman on the street, Zoë said, after I told her about meeting the son.

—But one fine day we'll be like her, remember nothing.

—I'll try to forget you said that, my dear.

We were sitting on the deck of Zoë's second-floor apartment. On the small table between us, the gin and tonics with wedges of lemon, two candles burning, and a plate with soft cheese ringed by delicate crackers. I told Zoë I'd spent the afternoon talking to my sisters and brother. Then I told her Kevin Lyons's younger brother was found dead in London.

—Cocaine nailed him, I added, and I hummed, "Riding out on a rail, feels so fine."

—That's terrible, my dear, I'm sorry to hear it.

—My brother and he were very close when they were younger. My brother's upset.

—I bet he is, but how are you dealing with this?

—I didn't really know him, my dear. He was younger. And I am gone from there such a long time.

Daylight was fading. Two fireflies blinked at the edge of the porch. The shadows of the candle flames darted along Zoë's cheek and neck. She put her glass on the coaster, sighed, and said, —James, I must visit Austin next week.

—And I must visit Kevin Lyons, I said.

—A change of heart.

—I promised my sister, my dear. They love to drag you back into things.

I went to the deck railing and watched the quiet street. The cicadas were drilling inside my head. On the first floor of the house across the way, children sat on a couch before a huge television and ate out of bowls. A mother or a babysitter sat between them. I flicked my cigarette butt into the street and picked up the sweating glass from the railing. I turned to Zoë and leaned against the railing. She was talking about museum exhibitions in Dallas. Her father and her stepmom were flying in there.

—We come and go like fireflies above a field of alien corn, my dear, I said.

—Don't be dramatic, my dear. What did you expect?

—Oh, the usual, my dear.

—Sounds like what you say to your bartender, my dear.

—Or your hairdresser.

—Do you consider my feelings?

—Indeed, I do, my dear.

—And I consider yours, my dear, but I need to deal with Austin, and you need to deal with this Kevin guy.

—When I felt lonely in Dublin, my dear, I used to think life would be perfect if I were that guy in the film *Marty*. He lived alone with his mother, in a New York City neighborhood. I can't think of that actor's name—

—Ernest Borgnine, my dear. The neighborhood is actually in the Bronx. My dad loves that movie.

—So did mine, and my mother, I said.

—I watched it with my dad many times, Zoë said. —It was set in the neighborhood he lived in as a kid, and so this is your answer, my dear. What next, Jesus? Buddha?

—Gin and tonics, my dear. The others never worked, but I was a teenager then, my dear, who wrote letters home to his mother, even though he didn't always tell her the truth, which kind of bothered him, but you could sit on the elderly woman's front porch on Sunday mornings, read the paper, dally over your coffee and orange juice, watch the maples shed in the fall, bud in spring, and spread out the brilliant way they do in summertime.

—That's the life you loathe, the one you've been avoiding—

—Fooling myself, my dear.

—You've had all these wonderful experiences, my dear.

—Another name we give to all our mistakes.

—Okay, Mr. Wilde. Look at Walter.

—Maybe he feels he's free.

—Do you honestly believe that, my dear?

—Not for a second, my dear, and certainly not after meeting that woman. He must be miserable, wherever the fuck he is. Maybe he took to the road again.

—I imagine he feels he's made a grave mistake.

—I'd like to know why he left, my dear.

—I bet he doesn't know anymore, my dear.

—True, my dear, but when I first arrived here, I had that job bussing tables in that restaurant, and I also washed dishes a few nights a week for months because dishwashers kept quitting, but I needed the money, so you did what you did to get it.

—Some of this you have already told me, my dear.

—Well, I was eventually promoted to food runner. It was better money. A step up. What I did was take the trays of food from the kitchen to the tables. I got a small percentage of the waiter's tip. I saw myself as down and out in the American Midwest, but there was this man from Nicaragua who worked in the restaurant—

—I'm not sure where this is going, my dear—

—Neither am I, my dear. Okay, I had insomnia that winter. And when my shifts ended I never wanted to go back to my flat, and so after work I drank whiskey, smoked pot, and played cards with the people who worked in the kitchen. I had a great time with them, although more than a few were dicey characters, but I didn't really know anyone else then, and my friend Brendan had gone back, and anything is better than tossing and turning in the dark, but when I did eventually walk home buzzed to the gills past the unlit houses I would think how different my life was compared to the past life, and that difference made me feel like I was living this fantastic life. Delusion kept me going, because what I never wanted was to go back home, and so I knew that wherever I ended up, I had to imagine it might fucking work.

—It was fantastic, I think it was, my dear.

—Well, thank you, my dear, but when I was on my way over here this young black man I worked with in the kitchen back then came into my head. He was barely twenty-one. I'd tell him about the books I was reading in my lit class at the community college. I loved that class so much, maybe because it was so new to me then, or the professor was so passionate, but I gave this man *Black Boy* by Richard Wright, and I gave him books by James Baldwin and Toni Morrison. I'd never read any of those writers before then, never even heard of them, and neither had he. And we had these long conversations about those books on cigarette breaks in the basement of the restaurant. Then he got into some serious trouble. He shot someone who fucked with his girlfriend. He didn't kill him, but he nearly did. Some row on a porch. The gun was there. And the fucking gun goes off. And you could never imagine this young man shooting anyone, I still can't—but the people at the restaurant went to his trial every day. I didn't go because of classes, but at the trial he told them his mother cleaned houses for white people. Someone in the restaurant told me that. And the law planted him in the belly of the beast for a very long time.

—I'm not sure what you want me to say, my dear.

—And I don't know why I'm telling it to you, my dear.

—This young man's death in London is bothering you, my dear, and you're going to visit his brother. Also, you're stoned—

—It's wearing off, my dear, but the gin has kicked in nicely.

—I wish you had brought me some, my dear. I could use some.

—Next time, I will, my dear, but the young black man used to call me from prison on Sunday nights. He rang at exactly eight minutes after eight. We'd talk again about those writers, and I'd tell him about new books I was reading. I wrote him letters, but I forget what I wrote in them. I suppose small talk about goings-on in the restaurant, and that I hoped he was doing all right, that one day it would be behind him. He could start again. He was young. Shit like that. Then I stopped picking up the phone on Sunday night. I'd stare at it and let it ring. I didn't want to think about him or about how difficult his life was. I couldn't manage it. And I started to leave the flat at eight. I'd wander around town for hours and wander along the railway tracks and the river.

—But what became of the man from Nicaragua, my dear?

—We want to think we can imagine people's lives, but that's utter nonsense, my dear.

—It might be all we can do, my dear.

—Well, the man from Nicaragua was illegal. In his fifties. He worked at least sixty hours a week in the restaurant, and he worked in the French restaurant on Main Street. I don't know how many hours he could have possibly put in there. He might have gone back by now or they might have kicked him out. He had a wife and too many kids back home, and he sent his money back to them—

—Like your granduncle once did, my dear—

—Exactly, my dear. It was a Nicaraguan busboy who spoke English told me the man sent the money back—but the man did the work Americans would never do, like scrubbing the greasy kitchen floors on his hands and knees, dragging the greasy kitchen mats that weighed a ton into the alley and hosing them down with boiling water, schlepping out the trash bins, there's nothing uglier than restaurant trash bins crammed with food at the end of the day, and dumping out the hot grease from the fryers. He finished work long after everyone else did. But at Christmas we dropped names in a hat. And I picked his name, my dear, and I wanted to get him something good. He always smiled at me. I smiled at him, though we could never talk because of the language. And that was one dreadful winter. Hard heaps of snow on the ground for months. And I was broke. I drank cheap beer and went to classes hungover, and I spent most nights with a waitress who dressed funky and lit scented candles around her bed. She bought sex toys and we fucked each other blindfolded to the Piano Concerto Number Five. Then I hooked up with darling Sarah—

—Please, my dear, finish your story about the guy from Nicaragua.

—Well, I bought him a pair of gloves. I wrapped them up nicely in Christmas paper and gave them to him, but when he opened the package, he lifted his hands up to me. Palms out, fingers spread, and he had six fingers on each hand. I'd never noticed that about him, but on each hand, next to his small finger was another bigger finger sticking far out. And when I saw those extra fingers I thought about when a planet skips out of orbit. I was reading about retrograding planets in Astronomy 101, and I thought that was such a natural thing to happen, like here you are but you're someplace else, and then here you are back in place again.

—And how did the man react, my dear?

—Oh, he smiled and handed the gloves back to me, my dear. I told him I would exchange them for something else, but I never did. I forgot about it. I just didn't bother. School was back in session. Time went forward.

—Do good, my dear.

—Indeed, my dear. But remember I told you about the houseful of men from El Salvador I lived next door to in Boston?

—The Reagan years, my dear.

—Well, one of those men needed a job for a few weeks, and he asked if I could get him a job on this Irish painting crew I was working on. He needed the cash. He was trying to get to San Antonio. He'd family there.

—More gin, my dear?

—Fine with me, my dear.

I crossed the porch. Zoë poured for both of us. I went back to the railing.

—I said I would do my best to get him the job, my dear. But there was this Irish guy I knew, who like the Salvadoran was illegal, and who'd asked would I try and get him this job on the crew. There was only one going. And I got the job for the Irish guy. I told the guy from El Salvador I tried but they were not taking anyone on. I didn't even like the Irish guy. He was a racist and a dumbass. And the guy from El Salvador got picked up soon after. Someone else who lived in that house told me that. The guy had tried to get a job in the wrong place and some fucker grassed on him.

—None of us live without regret, my dear.

—That's true, my dear, but since I got the message from Kevin Lyons a few days ago, I'm opening these doors that I thought were all in the same house, a house I thought I knew every corner of, because I built it myself, but the doors open into all these weird fucking places, like in nightmares and children's stories.

—It might then be good for you to see this Lyons guy, my dear.

—So my sister and brother say. I went out with Lyons's sister, my dear. When I lived in Dublin years ago, I did, and he never knew anything about it, though he was living there then. None of my family knew about it, but they suspected, and I come from people who never forget, but I kept my mouth shut. I always did and I still do. I never even told my beloved sister, Tess, who was once madly in love with Kevin Lyons.

—The tangled web, my dear.

—Indeed, my dear, but Lyons's sister and I loved the idea of having a secret. A secret kept the others at bay. She taught me it was fine to have your own life. She gave me the ugly shirts that I gave away to mysterious Walter or Jeremy, or whatever the fuck his name is—

—The woman who gave you no horse, my dear.

—How selfish of her, my dear.

—You loved this one, my dear.

—Never marry a fucking Celt, my dear.

—I'll keep it in mind, my dear.

—All immigrants are conniving assholes, my dear.

—I'll also keep that in mind. Thank you, my dear.

—You're more than welcome, my dear.

—Can I tell you something, my dear?

—It's high time you did, my dear.

—When Dad and I made up later in the summer he left my mom, I would go to his apartment. Luke had his own room there, I had one, and my dad had parties every weekend that summer. He was enjoying his freedom.

—Maybe he was just lonely, my dear. He needed people around.

—Whatever, my dear, but he invited me to every party. He said he wanted me there more than anyone else, and he invited his work friends. I knew most of them. I had since I was a kid. They were very kind to me. They knew what was going on. But there was this one guy, who attended every party, a guy who was close to our age now, but if he didn't have the good fortune to be a nephew of one of my dad's colleagues, who knows, my dear, this guy was a dumbass.

—Accident of birth. Gifts from the gods.

—He flirted with me, my dear. And I liked his attention. I was miserable and so angry with my dad, and I was fighting with the guy I was dating. We were fine in North Carolina, but things changed for us at the end of the summer. Like unexpectedly he became someone else. Or I was the one who became someone else.

—These things happen, my dear.

—But this guy at my dad's parties was cute, my dear. A mover. All gung ho. At one of the parties we sneaked up to my room. We were drinking gin and tonics. The windows were open, and I could hear the voices of the men on my dad's patio below, their loud, self-satisfied voices. This guy took my t-shirt off. I yanked off his polo shirt. And the men on the deck were laughing and talking about the fine quality of the meat being grilled. The ice clinked in my dad's heavy glasses. And this guy wanted to be one of those men. He could not wait to be them, and he thought he was giving me something special, and I was charmed by his attention, like he was exactly what I needed. He didn't know that when we were making out I could only think of the thick hamburgers and steaks dripping bloody fat on my dad's new patio grill.

—Probably none of it was easy for your dad, my dear.

—Why are you so forgiving of him?

—Because it might make it easier for you. You love him. He loves you. Because I never liked my own father.

—You regret that, my dear?

—I got to live more than once, my dear. You won't like them all and they won't like you.

—Remembrance of things that are of no use, my dear.

—He was right there, my dear. That's all I do fucking remember.

—But you are worried about meeting your old neighbor, my dear. You're upset over his brother's death. And we should go inside. I'm chilly. I must finish the proposal. You have to be at the bakery in the morning.

—These things must be done, my dear.

I came away from the railing and blew out the candles then picked up the plates and the glasses. Zoë held the door open and I put the things down next to the sink, wrapped the cheese, stored it in the fridge, screwed the cork back on the gin, and flung the dregs in the glasses into the trash. Then I began to wash the glasses and the plates. Zoë stole up behind me and wrapped her arms around me, pressed her face between my shoulder blades, tightened her hold, pressed her face harder. I kept washing and saw her riding on the back of her father's motorbike along the strand at night. Water pounded the sand and stars shone in the heavens. And I recalled the carefree sound my feet made when Brendan and I rushed laughing up the quivering gangway at Dublin Airport the day we left. Then I turned off the tap. Zoë sniffled.

I held her hand to my mouth and kissed her fingers. They tasted of lemons.

—Are your allergies acting up, my dear?

—Stop it, my dear.

—Sorry, my dear.

—I'm sorry, too, my dear.

And we stayed that way for a long time before we released each other's fingers.

A thing like a dream woke me. My watch on Zoë's bedside table said 6:30. She was soundly sleeping. In the thing like a dream I walked down the blue corridor. It was pitch dark but my fingertips knew the damp and bumpy walls. I stood for a while outside my parents' door before I pressed down the wonky handle and slowly pushed the door in and stood at that threshold I hated to cross. Aunt Tess's red curtains were open and the room was lit with evening summer light. July or August light. Everything in the room was the same. The small holy pictures, the bigger picture of Saint Francis and his animals, their bedside rug and shoes. But the room was maybe three times its size. My father and mother were sitting on the edge of their bed. They were wearing their Mass clothes and talking to Auntie Tess, who sat on a chair beside them. She wore a fine tweed coat buttoned to the neck. I couldn't hear what they were saying, but their faces looked agreeable. To the right of Aunt Tess, the others sat next to each other on chairs that had been brought down from the kitchen. My sister Tess was talking to my sister Hannah. Tess was playing with one of the buttons on her purple coat. Stephen was chatting with Anthony and Seamus and Tommy Lyons. Seamus was the way I recalled him. Smiling. Stocky. Hair like Ray Davies in the mid-sixties. Una was talking to her father. She wore those long earrings fashionable young women wore in the eighties. That's all I saw of her. And Michael was laughing. The hat rested on his knee. The little feather flashed from purple to blue like

traffic lights slipping from yellow to red. Nora sat silently beside her
husband. She wore a black dress. Her face looked solemn and her raw
red hands were joined on her lap. Hands of mothers I grew up around.
Uncle Roger sat next to her. His belly was huge. He was naked from
the waist up and his suspenders hung down. And I was slowly backing
out of the room when my mother looked at me and smiled. I smiled
back at her and called her what I once called her. But this was a thing
like a dream. And you understood that.

—Look, Tom and Tess, we have a visitor, my mother turned to
them and said.

My father then looked at me. The corner of his mouth slipped down.

—Whoever you are, you're welcome, he said.

—Oh, a visitor, you're more than welcome, Aunt Tess said.

She was looking at me and smiling the way my parents were.

—I should offer the visitor a cup of tea, my mother said.

Then I was back again in the dark corridor. Standing right outside
their shut door. At the end of the corridor, where the kitchen door was,
was a shining set of eyes. The eyes I saw in the elderly woman's driveway a few nights before. And the eyes rose up to where they were
around my height. I blinked and I was that boy running and laughing
down the platform at Limerick Junction to Aunt Tess. My father was
behind me. I don't know how far but far enough. And I picked up my
dead aunt's bags and she said, Jimmy, you don't have to do that. I
gasped and looked up at her and said, But I want to. I want to. She
turned to Coleman Daly and smiled. Coleman's teeth were cigarette
yellow. And then I was standing in the empty schoolyard. Kevin Lyons
and I faced each other like in a Western. That tone and cast of light. A
train whistle blowing in the distance. At our feet the withered elm
leaves. At the side of that schoolyard, the stout branches of four or five
elms grew over a tall wall. He came to me and put his hands on my
waist. He pulled me to him and kissed my lips. I put my hands on his
waist and kissed his lips. He shoved his tongue into my mouth. I shoved

mine into his. And we ground ourselves into each other until we were exactly the same person.

When I sat on the edge of Zoë's bed and pulled my pants up, that's how those images had arranged themselves, even though I don't know if it happened in that exact pattern. Already I'd fixed them. Not so much unlike when you are awake and what you see you fix into what you can manage and make sense of. And so those dead and living people sat in that room. My mother said that. And my father and Aunt Tess said what they said. And I ran down the platform to Aunt Tess the way I once did. And Kevin Lyons and I met in the empty schoolyard and we kissed and became the same person. Definitely the schoolyard. The rustling elm leaves. The gravel shifting underneath my feet. And in their bedroom they drank their tea from cups and saucers my mother brought out only when the parish priest visited. Which at most was once a year. The failed priest who lived in Vermont posted those willow-pattern cups and saucers to her. My mother often said they were too beautiful to use, and she washed and cared for them like she once did her babies. Back when she understood and liked us more. When she changed our nappies then wiped and powdered us. When we suckled and bit her and grabbed her hair in our fists. But my mother would open the two doors of the kitchen cabinet to the right of the sink. She'd fold her arms, take a step back, and admire her cups and saucers. When she did that I imagined she was staring at a dead body in an open casket.

I tidied the bedclothes around Zoë. I was careful not to wake her. She had left ten bucks on the night table for the gin. I pocketed it. The air felt chilly. I turned the air conditioner down and sat back on the edge of the bed and stared down at her lovely face. I smoothed her black hair. *A stór*, I whispered, like my father used to once say to Tess.

The air in the street was warm. Birds darted from the trees on one side of the street to the cables on the other side. Then they flew straight back. The lawns were neat and clean. A few sprinklers were already going full blast. The ugly photographs of politicians, their names, their parties, had all faded in the sun. A boy was flinging newspapers onto lawns and porches. He skillfully maneuvered his bike up onto the foot-path then back onto the street. I passed five joggers and a few people in leisure wear walking their dogs. In the cool shadow of the Methodist church I stared at the wilted tiger lilies and regretted not having been more watchful, because every year I looked forward to the tiger lilies blooming, like in spring, when the snow and ice vanished, I longed to see and smell the lilacs. I could be happy then. Happy to use that one thing to forget the others. I walked by the old woman's house. A Dumpster was parked in the driveway. The yellow truck was gone. So were the lights on the porch roof. The son took them home to Chicago. Or they were in the Dumpster with his father's trash.

In the flat I made coffee. It was one of the days I didn't have to be at the bakery until 9:00, and not at 4:00 a.m. to measure the flour, butter, eggs, buttermilk, brown sugar, baking soda, salt, macadamia nuts, dark or white chocolate chips in the big bright metal containers that were shaped like tulips. And I didn't have to wheel the containers un-der the mixer that churned those ingredients with a whisk you might anchor a small ship with. And I didn't have to cut the cookie dough in the cutting machine, arrange the cut dough on the trays, then slide the trays into the oven. And while those trays circled the oven I'd stand at the bakery window, hands on hips, the way my father stood alone in the fields, and that glorious smell rose at the same time as the fiery red sun rose over the golf course across the road from the then empty park-ing lot of the strip mall.

The nine o'clock shift was different. I'd push the trembling heaps of dough into the cutting machine, shut the lid, press down hard on the handle, then open up the lid and fling armfuls of cut dough along the long wooden table, and the mothers who worked there full-time, and the high school and college kids doing summer jobs, laughed and joked and kneaded the dough into loaves. I'd arrange the loaves on the trays, and I and the mother who gave me the pot kept an eye on the loaves in the oven while we chatted and swept the floor and cleaned the table for the next round of bread. That bakery job might be the nicest one I've ever had.

I listened to the news on the radio. Then I washed myself at the toilet sink and changed into bakery clothes that when laundered still smelled powerfully of flour. I opened out the door, hooked the screen door, and sat in the chair. I went through the books and picked up the Good Book and opened it to the page I'd marked after I'd finished talking with Tess the evening before.

It is better to go to the house of mourning,
than to go to the house of feasting: for that is
the end of all men; and the living will lay it
to his heart.

I looked up to see Walter at the screen door. Sunlight glowed on the gravel at his feet. He was wearing the shoes he wore the first two times I saw him. And he was wearing the other shirt Una gave me, the one with the blue in it. The sleeves were rolled up. The baseball cap was on. The backpack was over the shoulder. I put the Good Book down.

—You're up early, man, I said.

—Guess I am, man, he said.

He took the cap off and pushed it into his back pocket. I crossed the floor and unhooked the door and told him to sit in the chair. When he was sitting I asked if I should call him Walter or Jeremy.

—Walter, he said.

—I'm sorry to hear about your kid, I said. —I am, and I don't know what else to say, only that I won't hold the lie about your aunt against you.

—Grateful, man, he said.

—If the telephone pole wasn't there, the woman said.

—Bullshit, he said.

—Bullshit is forever the right answer, but you'll have coffee, I said.

When I handed him the cup he thanked me. I said sorry when I told him I had to be at work soon.

—Talked to Mr. Lyons yesterday, he said.

—I'm going, man. The mind's made up, I said.

—Have the tickets and information here, man, he said.

He reached down and rubbed the soiled backpack like it were a blind person's dog.

—That's easy enough then, man, I said.

—Said to mention John Garfield.

—He did now, did he. Ever heard of John Garfield?

—Not so sure, he said.

—Actor. Forties. Fifties. Mr. Lyons's father and my old man watched his films on television on Friday nights when I was growing up. Joseph McCarthy's mother was born in the county where I was born. Garfield was blacklisted, so go figure. But where exactly does Mr. Lyons live?

—North of New York City. More than an hour. Down an unpaved road. Ain't far from the river—

—Ha! Between Boston and Brooklyn, I said.

—Tell him to expect you in four days, man, he said.

—Four days will work, man. I just need to throw a few things into a bag. And I have to talk to my boss at the bakery.

He unzipped the backpack and pulled out a large taped manila envelope. He handed it over to me, and I held it to my ear, shook it, and then glanced at it back and front. There was nothing written on it. I threw it onto the futon bed and looked away from it.

—He says everything you need is in there, man.

—Thanks, man. Do you want a cigarette?

—No, grateful, he said.

—I'm sorry again about it. You want more coffee?

He said yes. I filled his cup. I turned the radio off. When I sat again I offered him a cigarette. He said no.

—How's she doing? he asked.

—The elderly woman? I said.

—Your girl, he said.

—Oh, Zoë. It's Greek, you know. Means life, yes, life, but Zoë's good, and she's not my girl. Zoë's not anyone's girl. And the elderly woman is in an old folk's home in Chicago. All her life is all mixed up in her head, so her son told me, but as we speak she is eating breakfast and blissfully looking out over Lake Michigan—

—A real sweet lady, man, he said.

—Zoë is that, man. She liked you, she did. She enjoyed our day out very much, but I have to knead bread soon.

He finished the coffee and stood. I stood. He slipped the backpack on and pulled the cap from his back pocket and put it on. He adjusted the bill. I followed him to the door. When he was outside I hooked the screen door. He took a few steps and turned his back to me. He stared down at the gravel.

—It was about wanting to leave and never about where you were heading, I said. —That place only exists in the head. But you probably know that better than anyone.

—Don't know what you're talking about, man, he said.

—Sorry for saying it, then. But what do you do when you get sick?

—Don't get sick, he said.

—Some good news, man, I said. —Did Mr. Lyons mention a brother in London?

—Don't talk to him that way, he said.

—But what exactly does Mr. Lyons do now for a living?

—Makes money, I guess, he said.

—A noble profession, I said. —He offered me a job once. Years ago, in Boston. But it wasn't the job I wanted. What I wanted was to go away. I wanted a new start. Away from everyone who knew me. The starts are brilliant. What comes after, who the fuck knows.

—Wish I never found out about my kid, man, he said.

—It's awful news, man—

—He said I should come back here and see him and her, man. Make things right. Told him I tried to do it once before, what I told you and your girl in the car yesterday—

—Apple picking up north, I said.

—Yes, man. Then he called me a—hell, man.

—He called you a what, man?

—Said I was weak. A coward, man. And he laughed. Just wish I never found it out.

—He was being a jester. He can be that, but finding out is the right thing, man.

—Ain't, man. Wished he never told me to come back here. Wished he never called me those things. I ain't ever been such a good person. He ain't one either.

—I won't argue with you on your opinion of him. Nor will I go into it, but you're also very upset at the moment, man. You've had a hard blow. We gotta deal.

—Still gotta deal with the bird and do some other work for him.

—The whippoorwill, man, I'd forgotten.

—Thought I could make it right but only made it worse, man.

—It's better to know, man. In the end it is, or so they always say.

—It ain't better, man. Won't ever get better now. Know now that's the way it is. Can't ever again live it any other way.

—I don't want to be rude to you, man, but I'm going to be late for work, and I shouldn't be when I'm asking the boss for time off, but will I ever again see you?

He turned and stared at me.

—You talk exactly like him, man, he said.

—You told me that a few nights ago, I said. —But I used to despise him, and probably envy him, man, if you want to know. When I was young, I did.

After I said it I looked down. I did because my face turned red. Red like the fat stupid boy that Kevin Lyons shouted and laughed at and ran after in the schoolyard. When I looked up Walter was smiling. The only time I recall seeing him smile. And it gave me the chills. This big, brutal, shameless smile. The missing and the rotting teeth showing you something you had already seen and knew. I unhooked the screen door and stepped outside. I wasn't sure if I wanted to say something kind, or if I just wanted him to go away so that I could go to work. It felt chilly standing beside him in the shadow of that brick house, though the sunlight on the grass looked bright and warm. I stood for four or five minutes, flicking my cigarette ash onto the gravel, neither of us speaking. And when he walked steadily down the driveway I got that smell I got from him the first night he visited. He walked around the corner of the house, and the moment he was about to vanish, I called out goodbye. I did it loudly. He heard me. He must have. He did. But he said nothing. And he never looked back.

Part Two

1

Anton was building a stone wall at the end of the long, sloping yard. Behind him the stream flowed under a narrow cement bridge with crumbling low walls. The gravel path began at the bridge and wound around the yard and up the side of the house to a two-car garage with a wide deck atop it that joined a front porch. I was standing on the porch and watching Anton. Birds sang and butterflies flew here and there. On all sides of me grew mighty trees.

Two hours before, Anton had introduced himself at an airport gate in Newburgh. I followed him to the parking garage. He drove east on Interstate 84, and when the steep tree-covered hills appeared on the other side of the magnificent six-lane bridge I asked him the name of the bridge and the hills.

—Newburgh-Beacon, the Hudson Highlands, we're crossing the Hudson.

The steel rods flashed past and far below gleamed the wide river. There were small boats and a long barge heading toward New York City. Anton said he'd known these parts of the river his whole life.

He turned south on Route 9, and less than an hour later he led me to a room that was down a short hall from a kitchen with a new stove and fridge. The room walls were painted mocha. There was a single bed, a nightstand, a gooseneck lamp, a wardrobe with knots in the wood, and an old school desk and chair at one of the two windows. I dropped my bag on the bed and went to the desk window and re-marked upon the light falling through the trees. He said the trees

stretched for miles beyond that window, that the house sat on the edge
of a state park. I turned from the window and asked if Kevin Lyons
was around.

—He's somewhere. Beer in the fridge, and stuff for a sandwich. I
got work to do.

Anton slapped mortar between the stones.

—Reminds me of the father, Kevin said.

He stood where the porch met the deck, his right hand in the pocket
of his faded khaki shorts. The other hand rested on a gas grill whose
cover was coated with withered pine needles.

—Kevin, I'm very sorry to hear about Seamus.

—Thanks, Jimmy. We don't have to talk about it now, if you don't
mind.

—Whatever you like, I said.

I walked over. We watched each other. His t-shirt had the logo of a
lumber company. The hiking shoes looked expensive. The hair was
shorter, the face a little heavier, though the body looked the same. And
the father's eyes that I hadn't thought about in so long. We shook
hands. He said he was sorry he didn't hear the van drive up, he was
working in the basement, and he asked how long I could stay.

—Four days, I said.

—The first wedding was a fantastic day, he said, and smiled.

—I got the urge to go, I said.

—Water under the bridge, Jimmy, he said. —I know your father
passed away around that time. I wanted to get ahold of you, but now I
should take the workman a beer. Follow me.

He went first through the sliding glass door on the deck. I stood on
the mat inside the door. He went behind the kitchen counter and opened
the fridge. The walls of that big room were white and bare. Five railway
beams ran across the ceiling. A thick red-brick wall butted out halfway.
The kitchen was on the left side. On the right a raised fireplace built into
the wall, and a coffee table before the fireplace. Across from it a green

couch under the porch window. Next to the couch, a matching arm-chair, a bookcase with a few books, and a stereo. Floor lamps. Big and small rugs. At the window to my left, a wooden table and four chairs. On the table, a bowl piled with fruit. And that entire room was filled with sunlight. It poured in the wide, bare windows. It flooded the wooden floor and the walls. I felt like I had entered a sanctuary.

He was rummaging through a drawer, searching for a bottle opener.

—No curtains, I said.

—No need with the trees, he said. —The nearest house is on 301. We're about five miles from the village of Cold Spring.

He crossed the floor with three bottles of beers. He handed me one, and I thanked him.

—You know Walter's name is really Jeremy, I said.

We went through the sliding door. When we were outside, he pulled the screen to.

—Walter showed up at a house I was renovating over a year and a half ago, he said. —He needed work. I needed a job done that after-noon. He did it. He's good with his hands, when he's in the mood.

We walked down the wooden stairs on the right side of the deck, then down the gravel driveway. He left a beer on a pile of stones beside Anton, who didn't look up. We headed toward the stream. The loud water rushed over the rocks. There were two big rocks you could hop over on. Under the cement bridge the water foamed.

—Walter painted that room you're sleeping in, he said. —He painted the front room and fixed up the basement. I built the bookshelf and sanded the floors in the big room myself. I asked Walter to mow the yard, but then I thought, Who gives a fuck up here where there's no one to see it but me. And I asked him to paint the porch and the deck. He'll do it when he needs the money—

—He said something about the whippoorwill, I said.

—That bastard wakes me up every night. You'll hear it, he said, and he laughed.

—I can't wait to hear it, I said. —But Walter had a child who died about twenty years ago. He left around then. He never knew the child had died until I drove him out there last week.

—That's a tough one. I do my very best to keep him in work.

—He told me things about his life, I said.

—You're way more into hearing those things than I am, he said. —I have a reliable crew. Walter is the weakest one. He always looks a bit lost, like you never know what's going on with him. He comes and goes, but I feel sorry for him, so I keep him in jobs.

—And he's your messenger, I said.

—Only in your case, Jimmy, he said, and laughed again. —Someone on the crew told me he had family out where you are that he hadn't seen in years. It wasn't hard for me to find out where you lived. But I said to Walter that it might be good for him to pay his family a visit. I had to do a bit of prodding, but I offered to pay his way out there and back, and I offered to pay him a good bit more if he paid you a visit.

—I think your money went to a church, I said.

—I couldn't care less where it went. I wanted to see you, Jimmy, he said.

We walked the stream bank to a broken-down stone wall, which he said was a boundary line. No bank on the stream beyond the wall. Just water flowing over rocks and twisted tree roots. Next we headed up through the yard. Butterflies dallied like they had forever. A shower of well-fed robins flew out of the long grass.

—Let's head back to the porch, he said. —That's the best place at this hour of the day.

He sat into a wicker chair next to the grill. I sat into one beside him. It felt cooler under the roof. I asked how his mother was handling things.

—I spent three days with her not so long ago, he said. —She's having a hard time, but the mother is tough. Tommy is going to move home and live with her. Seamus was buried in London. It was the best way to handle it.

—Hannah mentioned that, I said.

—No one could save Seamus, he said. —I gave up on him years ago. The father used to say that Seamus was more fragile than the rest of us, and the mother never wanted Seamus to go to London. She went mad when he made his plan to go, but when Seamus got something into his head you couldn't stop him. He was wearing no shoes, no shirt, and no underpants—wearing only a pair of dirty designer jeans and lying on the top step of a church. Facing the big wooden door. And in spite of all his years of coke and vodka he was fat. They say he died from the cold during the night. I'd say he didn't feel much of anything, cold or what the fuck have you.

   —I talked to Stephen. They were great friends at one time, I said.

—I've no idea where Stephen is.

—Well settled outside of Sydney, I said.

—He went a long ways, but Una is building a new house where the cottage is.

—Hannah mentioned that, too.

—At Seamus's funeral she and I shook hands for the first time in years. We're getting on better now. She gave the rest of us some money a few years ago. She wanted that place. She always did. The mother wanted to see it gone years ago, but Una had her way. I couldn't give a fuck if I ever saw that place again. Then last year Una divorced the husband. I'm not sure they know that back there, so keep that one to yourself.

—Rarely do we talk, I said.

—She and the former husband own a few supermarkets in London. She looks after them. She's very good at it. She and him never had children. But I've no idea what she's doing building a house there. She couldn't wait to get the fuck away.

I asked how often he came up here. He said two or three weekends a month. He'd like to live only up here, but the upkeep of his buildings and handling tenants kept him very busy, and he had his eye on some more buildings up Route 9, in Beacon.

—The nineties were good to me, he then said. —And I married the right person, but we're glad not to be married anymore, but she's my best friend. She talks to my mother on the phone every few weeks. She's able to talk to them in a way I never could. Americans are good like that, the women are. I learned about this business from her, but I was good at it and I worked.

—You said in Boston she was a lawyer.

—She still practices, but buying those tenements in Dublin when I did was a good move, then selling them not too long ago was an even better one. You heard what's happening back there with real estate, so that's how I got this place. The first time I drove down the gravel road and over that bridge I opened the car window and saw and heard the stream. Then I looked up the yard at this porch and this tidy wooden house and the big window behind you and I knew I had found it.

He said his main place was about an hour south. A twenty-minute drive from the train and the river. He and the first wife had bought three broken-down buildings in the area a few years back and reno-vated them. She and their two children lived near Boston. He drove to see the children twice a month, or they visited him. He was dying to show all of them this place, but he wanted to get the wall built first, and there was a fire pit in the trees out the back that Anton was going to repair when he was done with the wall.

He said the second marriage didn't last a year. He still didn't know why he did it, but no children, so he didn't have to deal with her any-more. She was a lunatic, a fraud, the lowest sort of snob. None of this he found out until he married her. She was teaching some nonsense to do with writing fiction at a private school far upstate.

—But they must be all proud of you becoming a professor. I know I am, he said.

—Let's not go into that, I said.

—That's fine, Jimmy.

I looked up at the dusty boards on the porch ceiling. The rusted hooks for flowerpots and lights. He went to the railing and looked down across the yard.

—I remember your mother giving me a green apple, he said. —She peeled the skin off of it with a knife that had a handle covered in white tape like a bandage.

—Wonder what the fuck became of that knife, I said.

—She handed me the apple, but there was still strips of skin on it, and she took it back and peeled off the last of the skin and gutted out the core. Then she sliced the apple into small pieces and told me to hold my hands up. She sprinkled sugar on the pieces. The fathers were sitting at the range and talking away. She had fed them the tea.

I shook the empty beer bottle and bowed my head.

—I'll buy beer tomorrow, I said.

He turned from the railing. I looked up.

—You don't have to buy anything, he said. —And you're welcome to everything that's here.

I thanked him. He said he had to ring his foreman, and he walked around the corner, and when the sliding door opened I left the porch and stood at the deck railing. Anton's van was gone. I hadn't heard it because of the stream and the talking. At the edge of the path, the thick wall of trees. And the voice inside the house felt like it was years ago, but then it was at the sliding door. At my feet the deck floor was smeared with birdshit and littered with fat dead moths whose lime-green wings looked too big for their bodies. The sliding door opened and I turned.

—I think Walter's very upset, I said. —I thought I should tell you that.

—It's understandable that he would be, Jimmy.

—But he sort of worried me, Kevin—

—I can handle Walter, Jimmy. Don't worry about him. You're tired. Sleep for a bit. You've been doing all that traveling.

I turned and stared into the trees.

—He told me the truth about the woman, but I didn't believe him, I said.

—What woman, Jimmy.

—Nothing, Kevin. I liked talking to him. That's all. When I think about it now, I did.

—Jimmy, are you awake? Are you awake?

The room was dark. The air felt damp and cold. He was standing in the doorway. The stretched hand gripped the doorknob. Light in the hall made his body fully dark. He said he had made supper. I rolled off the bed and fumbled for my pants and shirt. I asked for a few minutes. He said to take my time and he quietly shut the door. Dark again and the smell of rotting trees and the sound of freezing water flowing over stones. Tess and Hannah were chatting and laughing. They were bringing buckets of clay to our mother's flower garden. The dark, rich clay from the foundation Michael dug to build the pump house. Then the scent of yellow dahlias. But I didn't know if dahlias smelled. Their yellow heads turned heavy then toppled. Their pointy petals littered the garden. But the mind was also in this other place. I was in a car with Zoë. She was driving through an American city. I didn't know the city. Poor people lining up outside liquor stores, and decrepit, neon-lit corner stores with bars on all the windows. Zoë and I were laughing. We passed a big clock. It was six in the evening. Sunlight cast on the red bricks of the tall buildings we drove past. Then it was night and Zoë was telling me a story. We were in the same city in the same car and Zoë had to be somewhere, but she had to leave me off first, and she had to finish telling me the story. She stopped the car in the middle of a dark and empty street with broken streetlights. She switched off the car lights and went on telling her story. I couldn't listen to it because I was anxious and I kept saying that she should turn the lights back on and keep driving because a car would crash into us. And I did not know what I was doing to make a living. And I didn't know how old I was. And I had no idea who I was in that empty American city with sunlight shining on red-brick buildings.

The day before, I'd driven Zoë to the airport. I had stayed at her place the night before that. During the forty-minute drive we listened to music. The airport drop-off was chockablock with traffic and people.

—Good-bye, dear James.

—Good-bye, dear Zoë.

We kissed. I watched her move gracefully through the crowd. Behind me the car horns beeped but I didn't stir till Zoë disappeared through the revolving airport door.

The kitchen was pitch dark. My fingers were moving in the grooves of the red-brick wall. Close to ten on the stove clock. I stood on the rug in the middle of the room and looked toward the large windows and the sliding glass door. Everything out there was in the dark. The charred smell of meat and charcoal. Then a light switched on behind me. I turned. He was sitting at the end of the couch, in the beam of the floor lamp. He had changed the t-shirt. The long feet were bare and the light shining on them made me see Saint Francis's feet in that picture. He looked up at me and said hello. I said hello back. On the coffee table before him were a beer bottle and a paper plate with a half-eaten hamburger and crushed potato chips.

—There's cheese on some of the hamburgers, he said.

—I'm very hungry, thank you, I said.

I walked over to the table and helped myself. Then I sat at the other end of the couch. He went to the fridge. He came back, put a beer before me, and sat back down. I said I'd had an odd sort of dream. I'd been having them the past few days. But I'd said it only to say something. And I added that a woman I was seeing and some other people were in the dream. I didn't say who the other people were. He asked did I want to tell about the woman. I said we were very fond of each other, but there was someone else on her side, but whatever she and I had was lovely, and I didn't want or need or expect anything more. He and I didn't talk then for a while. The stereo was playing a song that was popular during those years we lived in Dublin. Another song that his sister and I loved began to play. We used to dance like mad to it on

the paint-splotched tiles in her flat. I'd bought the single for her. One
Saturday afternoon I sat on the top deck of a 16 bus and clutched the
small square plastic bag. Before the song ended I was trying my best not
to see his brother lying dead on the cold steps of a London church. Then
a New Order song from the early nineties came on. When it ended I
asked would he mind playing it again. No problem. He loved the song
himself. And I took my sweet time eating the two cheeseburgers.

Save it for another day
It's the school exam and the kids have run away

When the song ended the second time, he turned the stereo off. He
adjusted the dial on the central air and went to the sliding door. He
held his hand above his eyes and pressed his face to the glass.

—Not a soul out there, he said.

—You're expecting someone, I said.

—Not a one, he said.

He sat back down.

—When Tommy rang from London with the news, it was late in the
day, he said. —I was down at the home place, and I called the mother
and we talked for a long time. She was more worried about me than
she was about herself. And then I got into the car and drove up here,
and I sat here with the light off all night. I brought a twelve-pack and
two packs of smokes, and I kept thinking about things that could have
been done to save him. Times I might have rung him, or tried to get
him help, but mostly I was thinking about him when he was this little
fella I saw every day. Fat, shy, but willful as fuck. He'd cry at the small-
est thing. And I hated him for that. He was too soft. And I hate him for
what he did to himself, and I hate him for what he did to me and to us.
You know what I mean.

—Go on, I said.

—The father used to say to me when I was young, Kick back at
them, Kevin, the priests and the teachers, kick back at every fucking

one of them and run away laughing as fast as your legs can carry you. There are some few things they have to tell you, he'd say, but don't ever let them tell you what to do, and don't ever let them fool you into thinking that you're one of them. The job they get paid to do is to make you one of them. Did your father ever say things to you like that?

—He cherished obedience, I said.

—So the mother would get mad at the father for saying those things. She'd say to him not to talk to me like that. What kind of life do you think he's going to have if that's the way he's to go about it? But my father would laugh at the mother and say, He'll have a great life, a great life he'll have. I could hear him saying it when I sat here that night, saying it with a smile on his face, after coming in from work—a great life, Nora, he'll have. The paper beside him resting against the milk jug and the sugar bowl. Cutting the food into small pieces. The pool of HP Sauce at the side of the plate. You're ready to see something, you are?

—Whatever you like, I said.

—You've had enough to eat?

—More than enough, thanks.

I stood on the other side of the counter. He wrapped the uneaten hamburgers and put them in the fridge. He came around the counter with two beers and opened the door next to us. He switched on the light. I walked behind him, down a short carpeted stair that wound around once. There was the smell of fresh paint. When we reached the landing, where the back door was, he stopped and raised his head.

—Listen to it, he said.

—Listen to what? I asked.

—You didn't hear the bird?

—I heard nothing, I said.

—Don't worry, you'll hear it, he said.

—I hope so, I said.

At the end of the short flight of stairs he turned on a light. We stood in a hall and faced two shut doors. To the far right another door led to the garage. The door to our right was his bedroom door. He said the stream sounded the sweetest from that room. The trees outside his window tempered it. He opened the room on the left and pulled a light string. He walked inside, stood aside, and asked me to come in. At first I thought it was your ordinary tool room, he being the sort to show you those, but the tools on the wall looked like they were from a museum—his father's tools, arranged on hooks, like his father had arranged them. Or the way I recalled them. The plywood desk built up on cement blocks. The old red bus seat. On the wall, the photograph of the hurling team. I'm not sure if it was the one I saw on his office wall in Boston.

—Everything like it was, I said.

—That was all I wanted from there, he said. —Nobody went near that shed with years. There was a hole in the roof. The dampness and the rain destroyed things.

I stepped closer to the tools.

—You remember the evening I was there with the father? I asked.

—I don't, he said. —My father let so few in there. Your father was let in.

—You were kicking a football against the back wall, I said.

—The father would never allow that sort of behavior, especially if he was in there. He'd send us running. But have a gawk in there.

He was pointing to a box on the desk. I walked over and lifted the flap.

—His notebooks, I said.

—Rain coming through that hole ruined most of them. That's what left.

—You read them, I said.

—No, but you will, he said.

—And what makes you think that? I asked.

—Because that's the sort you are. And they're your present for coming to see me.

I touched the notebook on top. Nothing was written on the cover. I took my hand away and stepped back.

—He wrote the dates on the wood, I said.

—I don't remember that at all.

—Either way, I can't take them.

—You have to take them.

—But they're none of my business.

—They're no one's fucking business anymore, he said. —I knew you would be into them. But I don't want to hear anything in them. Not one word. I loved him more than anyone else in the world, but I never once wanted to see what was inside his head.

—When did he write them?

—At night, he said. —A lousy sleeper. He'd wander around the house and check and recheck the front door and the back door and the windows when we went to bed.

—When my father got up from his knees that's what he did, I said.

—My father spent very little time on his knees, he said, but after he checked the door and the windows he'd take the flash lamp and slip quietly out the back door and down the path to the shed. I'd kneel on the bed and watch him from the bedroom window, the light of the lamp going back and forth on the path. And the light from his cigarette flaring up when he took a drag, and the low rattling noise of the chain when he pulled it quietly through the handles like not trying to make any noise. He only opened the shed door wide enough to slip in. Then the door closing and the light going on in the shed. The light shining in the cracks of the wooden door. Sitting at night in the shed he built for himself. I don't think anyone else did that where we grew up.

—That's for sure, I said.

—Odd fucking life, ha! But he's a long time gone from this world.

—He is, but I don't think I should take them.

—Jimmy, don't insult me.

—I must try my best not to do that, Kevin.

—Put them in your room. Read them in the morning. I'll be gone for a few hours. You'll meet my daughter tomorrow.

—From Boston, I said.

We were looking at each other. He at one end of the desk. Me at the other.

—Yes, from there, but another daughter. I met the mother in a night class at Bunker Hill Community. A class on real estate. I sat in the seat behind her.

He pressed his finger hard on the left side of his neck.

—She had this small black mole right there, he said. —She hated it. But when I sat behind her I used to stare at that mole till it put me in a trance.

I turned to a useless, battered mallet, then a useless, twisted awl.

—She's married, he said. —We're fair-enough friends. But I am very close to the daughter. She was the first one. So you're not into the college life anymore?

I walked over to the doorway and looked in at him.

—I'll get over it. I will. We go the fuck on, like always, I said. —But when I first started there was nothing like it. You stripped off this old coat that someone else made for you and made you wear for too long, and there was nothing like sitting in the classroom and talking about the life in books. I'd work jobs nights and weekends, I made friends, I had a wild time, but maybe the best part was the library. I'd walk up and down the shelves, pick out books at random, stack the books high on a desk, and sit there turning pages, stopping off in some places, not in others. It was all a chance. I knew that. I'd learned that much, but never before was I so content as when I sat there with no money, no fucking confidence, in a town and a country that was then so foreign to me. And all of them vanished. Every one of them. And that was what I wanted. It was like when I was a child and I'd do my best to hide from the work, and the father and mother never wanted to see you with a nose in a book before dark. Take your nose out of that book and find something useful to do! Can't you see all that's to be done! Are you that blind! And hiding from Anthony, who'd come along and box the book out of your hand—

—I've no idea what Anthony ended up doing.

—An auctioneer down in Cork. Doing brilliant in their boom.

—We were never friends like, but you know that, but the two of us did a job once. We lifted the twenty or twenty-five pallets of fertilizer from a creamery in north Kerry. Anthony drove one of the tractors. I drove the other one. It was a very long drive. There were a few of us involved. One long summer's evening and night. Big Johnny was the one who was behind it. He organized the tractors. And he paid us for it. We needed the money. None of us had any, but we hid the bags of fertilizer all over his farm. Hid them behind hay bales. One of the pallets broke and we'd to lift every bag by hand, like lifting bags of sand—

—I don't forget how heavy they were—

—But the sun was up. I was walking home across the fields and the Ryans were hunting in their cows, the other Ryans. I don't know if they were related to Big Johnny—

—They have to be—

—But I lay down in the ditch till I knew the cows were gone. The grass was long in the ditch. Ryan passed right by me but I was as still as a rock. If he saw me he'd wonder what the fuck I was doing lying in his ditch at dawn. I forget what I told the mother and father about why I was out all night. But Big Johnny had fertilizer enough for two or three years.

—Big Johnny had more land than anyone else.

—Big Johnny thought he was Robin Hood riding through the glen. He said he did it because of the creameries closing, but he was the one who profited from it. No jobs anymore on the miserable building sites in England, lads, he'd say. Are ye going to spend yer lives on the dole, lads. Look what the Tans did not so long ago, lads. Look at what they did to the men in Dublin, lads. Look at all who had to go abroad, lads.

—A fine history teacher lost in Big Johnny, I said. —I thought he was a saint. The rosary beads out at Mass. Waiting in line for Confession. You'd never think him—

—But you were always so naïve, Jimmy.

—I'm glad I traveled all this way to hear that from you.

—I had a small fling with Big Johnny's daughter. The nun. We met a few times before the two of us left.

—An adventure down in the glen for you, I said.

—But Jimmy, my daughter is at that age when she's mad asking what it was like when I was young and who was I friends with. I'm bringing her here tomorrow afternoon. I told her she was going to meet my very best friend from those days. It's only a joke but you might have to pretend a bit—

—So that's why you paid for me to come here, I said.

I took the stairs in a few steps. I crossed the big room and walked through the sliding door to the deck railing. A warm night. A wet wind rising. The full moon shining on darkened trees. Brilliant indifferent stars and the din of the stream. The sliding door opened. His footsteps came briskly toward me then stopped.

—I'm very sorry about Seamus, I turned and said. —But I'll head back tomorrow.

—What's the big deal, Jimmy?

—You're not deaf, I said.

—The notebooks are on the desk in your room, he said.

—I listened to people I shouldn't have.

—What people. I'm the person—

I shoved my hands in my pockets.

—You're the bastard. You always were, I said.

He stepped back.

—You've waited a long time to say that, he said.

—Yes, I have.

—And you live in your fucking head. You live in your dreams.

—And you're still a bastard, I said.

—I've been called worse, young Jimmy, he said.

—I bet you have.

He took a step forward.

—And I bet you don't know that your old man never paid mine for building that pump house.

I took a step toward him and laughed.

—Laugh, Jimmy. Go ahead.

He took a step back. I didn't budge.

—The morning he died, he and the mother were fighting about it, he said. —I was in bed and I don't know if this is before or after they kicked me out of their fucking school, but wanking in the bed was what I was doing. And the mother was shouting at him to ask your father for the money. That the money was badly needed. The father's heart was about to say adios and go fuck yourself and I was lying on the bed and laughing and wanking. And why hadn't he asked, the mother shouted! Why hadn't he paid! Then this big loud thump and then the silence that was broken by the mother screaming my name, but not a scream, it was the loudest fucking screech I've ever heard, and I landed in the kitchen and the father was facedown on the table. The hands hanging limp. His porridge bowl in pieces on the floor and the porridge spilled all over the table and the floor. The mother standing beside him. Her hands covering her face. She was crying his name and saying that she wanted to go back again, back to the day they met, the day she fell in love with him. Only a naïve dreaming fool like yourself could make that one up—

I took a step back.

—Lies, I muttered.

—The mother made me promise that I would never tell the others they were fighting, he said. —She wanted no one to think that the moment he gave up the fucking ghost that's what they were doing, but the truth is, Jimmy, that they fought all the time. He shuffled down his path to his cunt of a shed. And many nights I sneaked out and down that path and pressed my ear to that shut shed door and heard him inside. The chair creaking and him whispering a name that never once was Nora. A name I could never make out. And my mother washed her cups and plates and knives and spoons and snarled like a bitch and put up with him and us and cooked with a vengeance. So you think I'm dreaming that up too—

He turned and walked through the sliding door. I went back to my place at the railing. Moonlight on the gravel below. And then I heard it. Whip-poor-will. Whip-poor-will. It flew right above me. And then it was down by the stream and I heard it above the noise of the water. The sliding door opened. His feet came toward me. He put a glass of whiskey on the railing before me. His feet slapped back across the deck. A chair dragged. I lit a cigarette. Cicadas wailed in the trees. I turned but I didn't move. He was sitting before the big window. Sitting in the beam of his security light. Bugs crammed inside the beam. Mad things. Things delirious with life. He was staring down at his bare feet. He looked like a fighter between rounds. Catching his breath in his corner. And I've no idea what I looked like.

—I came because of Tess, I said.

I was standing in the middle of the deck with the whiskey glass.

—So how's Tess?

—Tess's painting pictures again.

—At times I'm living back there with Tess. And I'm this person I never was. A better one, to tell you the truth. But our trip to England put a full stop to Tess and me.

—Our trip to England, I said.

—We didn't go there for haircuts, young Jimmy.

—She never told me is what I meant.

—Sorry, Jimmy. That just slipped out. But at first we planned to go for good. She was in Cork. Me in Dublin. And we were going to go and not tell any one of you. Start all over again where no one knew us. I wanted that then more than I wanted anything else. And Tess was for it at first. Then she wasn't. Then she didn't want me at all. So we went and got it done and came back the day after—

—Christ, will you stop talking about it, I said.

The empty whiskey glass was at my feet.

—But Jimmy, we end up living in the sweetest land of the living.

He looked up. He blew smoke then smiled. On the windowpane the fat moths and the other insects twisted and turned and climbed and fell.

—She loved baking her apple cakes, like each one was a ceremony, I said.

—Your mother, he said.

—Yes. That summer the pump house was built she baked them for your father. I remember her saying he was fond of them. She'd take one down to him once a week. I'd walk before her on the path, down through her garden. She'd warn me to be careful and not damage her flowers growing over the path. But she asked me to walk before her so that I could open the red gate going into the paddock. She'd cover the cake with a clean tea towel. She didn't want the flies landing on it. It was like being at the head of Corpus Christi. Her head up. Pure grace. Grace that never existed in the world that I saw. And so I couldn't wait to get as far away as possible from that piety.

—My father was very fond of you, he said. —He'd say the second youngest of Tom's is very sound. I was thinking about the father saying that. And I wanted to think that's who you were.

—Well, I'm not, but your father was different than the other ones, I said.

—You're imagining that, Jimmy. He was the very same. All cut from the same cloth. But what Garfield film does he run down the stone steps to find the brother's body?

—*Force of Evil*. The last scene, I said. —I first saw it with the father. The Garfield character wants to think he is helping the brother out, but he does his brother harm. It takes him a long time to go down those steps. And the brother's body is lying at the edge of the river. It might even be the Hudson. "A man could spend the rest of his life trying to remember what he shouldn't have said."

—You'd remember that line.

—Yes, I would, wouldn't I.

—You would, he said. —But tomorrow morning I have to drive an hour and a half to pick the daughter up. The mother and I meet halfway. You'll like my daughter. And she'll like you.

—By the way, I heard it, I said.

—You heard what, young Jimmy, he said.

—The whippoorwill. A lovely sound, I said.

—A nuisance, if ever I heard one, he said. —But look up at that August moon.

—I've looked at it, I said.

—There she is, he said. —Shining above the river and the big city, and their massive forests and all their other mad cities, but there's no place in the world like up here. This place was meant for me. All those other places were only bus stops.

—It's going to rain tomorrow, I said.

—You think so, young Jimmy.

—It's on the breeze, I said.

—I forget I'm talking to the son of a farmer, he said.

2

Rain on the windows woke me. I pulled on my pants and went to the big room. Almost ten on the stove clock. A note on the counter: *Jimmy. Make yourself at home. I will see you later on.* The deck was invisible because of rainwater flowing over the roof ledge. I made coffee and took two bananas from the bowl and ate them. Then I headed out to the porch railing, where the rain looked like sand pouring down on the trees and the yard. The noise of the stream was muffled. Birds were silent. No work on the wall today. And I was staring into the trees when a dirty white goat wandered out. It crossed the path and began to nibble the long grass at the edge of the yard. Rainwater trickled from its ears and scraggly fur. I clapped my hands. The goat lifted its head. It had a beard like Anton's. The yellow-green eyes stared. The long ears twitched and the tail shook. It turned again to eating the grass. And I watched it until it wandered back into the trees.

In the bedroom I took from my bag the clock Tess posted to me. I wiped the clock's face with a towel, set it to the right time, and placed it on the empty mantelpiece above the fireplace. I tidied the bed and lay down on it. The rain had stopped. A bright and hot August day again. I got up from the bed and sat at the desk. I stared for a long time at the three shut notebooks. Then I stood and locked the door and when I sat again the notebooks were splashed with sunlight.

There were no dates. Two of the notebooks were filled with columns of building items. Prices in the old money, written in red ink, across from each item. The other notebook was a different story.

Cold sunshine this evening after five days of rain. Flood-
ing along the roads and down in the fields and meadows.
Went for a walk in the fields after supper. Una and seamus beside me. A quiet and thoughtful girl she will turn
out to be. Seamus got tired of the walking and I lifted
him up on my shoulders. Happy and laughing he was up
there pulling at leaves when we walked under the trees
along the ditch. Sky very blue and clear on the way back.
Stood on the ditch with the lads before going into the
house and saw the sun go below the flooded field beyond.
Sun sank down into the water like it was never going to
come back up.

Finished a small job indoors at hourigans. Hourigan
could have done it himself if he was of any use. Hourigan
standing there beside me all the time. And never once did
he shut his arse. Farts flying from his hole two a minute.
And he clueless. More than hinted at him a few times
that I needed to think about what I was doing. If he
wanted the job done any way right. His hands shoved
down in his pockets and making sounds in his throat.
Nora worried about some distress with kevin in school.
Told her to let him off. The teacher is a curse and kevin
can well look after himself. And nora says Im the only
one around here who thinks like that. And I said to nora
we are our own bosses in this life.

A few words with nell hogan after Sunday mass. Often see her on Sunday but this Sunday god knows what
came over her she came over to me in the porch and
shook hands with me. Said I looked grand. I smiled
away and said everything was grand. There's nothing
more I could ask for. She inquired about Nora and the
children. I said they were fine and if she wanted to ask
them herself she should stay right where she was be-

cause they'll be out now any minute. She said she had to rush off to the shops and the aunt was sick in the bed at home. Remember nell well from national school. Sat in the desk in front of me. Id tap her on the shoulder and ask for the loan of a pencil. Always forgot to bring the pencil. And mislaid so many of them for some reason. Nell bending over and rooting in her satchel and finding me the butt of one but it worked fine like a new one. Nell was a big strong girl then. A mighty smell of milk and the smell of sweat. But her sweat wasn't bad in any way. She milked the cows before coming to school. Youd know that then just by looking at her. The size of the arms and cowdung on her elbows. Her father was a hard man. Don't know so much about the mother but she must have been better than him because nell is a nice enough person.

A pleasure it is to sit here. The doors in the house all safe. Half after one in the morning already. A cold enough night it is. Should have put on them drawers that Nora left out for me. She said this evening when the lads were outside that whatever happens I want you coming in from that shed alive. I don't want you getting your death of cold and I don't want any of my lads going out there one morning and see you with your head on that plywood and that biro stuck in your mouth. The biro will be shoved up my arse Nora I said and she said what had she done in her life to end up with a person like me. I said we did nothing and that's what happened to us. She said I was a coarse person and I needed to keep my eyes open in the daytime along with the night. Things are going on in the daylight before your eyes she said and you don't see a thing. You cannot have it every way I said and asked if the lads were all right. She said the lads were all fine. The lads were as good as could be expected she said.

A minute ago it was half past eleven. Now its closer to two. All safe in bed. The cottage is dark. The doors are locked. The two older ones in a big fight this evening. Not at all sure what it was over. Told them to shut their traps and behave or they'd be sleeping out in the back yard. Or they can cross the ditch and spent the night with the neighbors cows. That put a stop to them quick enough. Theyre either the best of friends or the worst of enemies. Wish that they were more like the younger lads who are more quiet. Not a peep from the road. People going by on bicycles earlier. Didn't know the voices at all. Young people. A few cars went by and two tractors. Then the guards go on by. I know the sound of the squad. I think when they go by they'll stop and come up to the door and tell me theres something wrong I did and they'll cart me off to the jail in limerick city and Ill never get out of it again. I often think of Nora and the children looking at me through the bars and crying. But I think too they might look at me through the bars and have a good laugh. What would you like to see at your door. The tinkers the guards or a priest. Id take the tinkers about the rest of them. I wouldn't mind a nun standing there at all. They are gentle people and they do better work than them priests.

Finished the big job at scanlans. Have been hard at it for a few weeks. Dug out old wall and put in new wall in the back of their cowhouse. Foundation was not very sound but dug it up and put down new foundation stones. Wall will last for a lifetime of scanlans. Paid me and everything. Fed me well too. A long stroll with tom after the dinner. Talked about the races last Saturday and gave him money for the ones this Saturday. He said there was a few in the pool and Saturday would be the day I was lucky. Talked about last Sundays match. Went walking in the ryans big fields. Gave him the money at the bottom of the field but not all of it. Tom with the hand out saying ryans cattle look hungry. The cattle looked fine to me. A relief it is not to be a farmer.

Was up at grogans all week. Will get that job done as fast as I can. Hard being around them. The ten children come and stand at the door of the shed with their saucer eyes. Two of them redheaded. They look at me like I am in the zoo. I have never in my life been to the zoo. When I smile and make a face or say something funny they scurry like mice. Backward children by the looks of them. And grogan not a happy man with children. You can see that the way they scatter when he is about. Id say one child is even way too much for him. Rarely see the wife at all. Never see her at mass. Grogans don't have much in the way of land. Life would be tough enough for them. They would be getting something in the way of the children's allowance. I knew grogans brother in school. Sat two desks over from me. The right side of me. The younger one of them. Very fond of the girls and very fond of the drink. Got some girl in trouble but married her. It turned out all right I think. Lives up near emly. Had a job at the creamery up there. Grogans wife looks like she does not want anyone to look at her. Id say she has a tough life with him and all them children. A thin and worn looking woman. Will have trouble getting the money out of grogan. Know that much for a fact. Everyone says that. The sort he is. He will ask me to come down in the price. But Ill stand my ground with grogan. Owe tom some money from last weeks races. He says not to worry but you know the way people are. What people say and what people do are two very different things. I know that too well myself.

What sorrow to sit here. The tired clang of the shed door when I pulled it after me. The leaves of the birches clicking like the ticking kitchen clock. The leaves keeping time to my misery. In here is the only place I can get a bit of comfort or peace. All I can think about every second is that she is gone. All I can think about is that I will never again lay my eyes on her. Once a year in my life I have seen her since so many years ago. Looking forward to those summers so much. Knowing when june changes into july. The sound of the cuckoo goes from the hedges. The hay down and the voices of the farmers in the meadows. Knowing shed be around the second week. That way for years. Then only seeing her walk through the porch at mass. The eyes searching for me in the crowd. That's the way I always thought that. They are looking for me. Then the eyes meeting and us turning away. Going ahead with things. But I don't know if I was thinking in the right way. Them letters I wrote to her in my head only. The way I hid it all these years. But at times I think people could see right down into my soul. Everything exposed there like a yard light at the end of a barn in the middle of the night. Exposed and open in the end. Foolish and stupid and crippled for all the world to see. But then I would think that no one sees nothing.

The moment I walked in the door the evening before last Nora said did you hear that toms sister passed away in dublin. I said to Nora I ran into egan who ran out on the road and told me. Egan mad to be the one to tell me I said. Even though his cows were waiting to be milked but he likes to be first with the news for everyone I said.

Nora said she was crossing the street in dublin and got hit by a bus and the lord have mercy on her soul Nora said. Sure shes only our age Nora said. I said that was surely a fact. And she doing great work in that job Nora said. At the very top of it Nora said. Then Nora squints over at me and inquires if theres enough soap in the dish or should she put out a new bar. I said the soap will last another week. And then Nora says the supper will be on the table soon and then she squints at me again and says I look very pale and drawn like was I not feeling the best. Youre spending too much time out in that shed of yours she said. Youre driving yourself mad she said. Youre driving me and the lads mad she said. It looked like we are running a fine well run madhouse then I said. I had a hard day of it with the work and I might have a lie down after the dinner I said. She said the right thing to do might be to go and visit tom. I said ill see what ill do after I eat a bit and I asked how the lads were. Not a bother on them at all but the usual devilment she said. And when I bent to wash the hands and I was turned from Nora and I shut my eyes and thought what a cruel man I am. I squeezed the soap and it slipped through my fingers and I pushed my hands down into the water and brought the handfuls of water up to my face without opening my eyes. So very tired of all of it tonight and not much sleep since I heard the news. Have to go and see tom. Still owe him a few pounds from last weeks race. Building up a bit. He wont bring that up at all. And that thing I have kept from him all these years. And she being his sister. But he is not the sort you can tell a thing like that to. And they not even close to each other. The way a lot of families are it looks like. The way I am with my own brother when we pass on the road and don't salute. Looking over opposite ditches. Looking into different fields.

Went out behind the shed and stood in the docleaves that were damp. It was very quiet and I closed my eyes and whispered her name. I had to lean up against the trees and catch my breath that was tearing through me like wire or like glass. And I kept the eyes shut and said her name a few times again and I felt peace in whispering her name. But so little of it.

Such sorrow to sit here and try and put a few words down but the day went by fine. Buried in dublin twelve days ago now. But the passing days pass and don't get better. But was able to concentrate on the job I was doing for murphy. Had a few hours to myself. Its good being on my own doing the job. Its a bit easier. Nora asked again if I was all right that I looked especially pale last evening and my eyes were tired and sick looking. Una came and did her sums beside me at the kitchen table when I was eating the bit. Shes a pure topper at the sums. Did not talk but what a pleasure it was to have her sitting there. Her hair is like my mothers. I said that to her and she turned from doing the sums and smiled up at me. Then she goes back to doing the sums. I asked if I could be of any help but she said there was no need. I have to keep my place and its better when I don't look at Nora and the children in the eyes. But things are good around the house. Una did very well in the school. So did tommy who told me this evening he wanted to be a priest. I told him he might get over that but whatever he wants to be is fine by me. You know what you want to be better than I do I said. Last night I sat here. Did not write down one word. Just sat and didn't even turn the light on. There was some rooting at the door of the shed. A rat that was.

I put down the trap and the rat was in it in the morning. Picked him up with the spade. Flung that dead rat high beyond the docleaves before I went off to work in a dour mood.

Tom did not go up for the funeral. The moment I saw him I said the lord have mercy on your sisters soul. He blessed himself and said the years went by and she kept her life to herself. She stopped writing the letters home many years ago he said. Just came for the two weeks in july he said. What happens to all of the ones who go away I said. I suppose so tom said. But she was like that too when we were young he said. And then he immediately started talking about the races and the news. A very odd man at times but who am I to call anyone odd. The pot calling the kettle black. I was thinking all day about the first time I knew she was in the world. And she was not like everyone else to me. Not another everyday person. She was this person that took me away from being this everyday person. This person that put me in a torment. Thinking who I was before. How I got by. What the days were like. What I didn't notice the way I notice now. I would have seen her a few times before I knew what she was to me. Back when we were young. Before life got a hold on us. I would have noticed her before I fell because of her fine looks and manners but I only truly remember her the moment I fell and the long and bothering years that came after.

Give tom the money I owed to him but more is owed. He counted it quick and said nothing. Shoved the notes into his back pocket and talked about the fine evening. Having a bad streak of luck with the horses. But I never had much luck with them if I think about it. We walked for a long time but did not talk but a pleasant enough walk. He sighed to himself many times. I was going to ask him if things were all right but didn't think it was right to interfere. And I was afraid to say her name. What it might do to my face. The way I might act. The name would trip in my mouth. The children are young and don't understand much of who their father is. Nora keeps going the way she does. I keep the best side I can out.

It was the summer I dug the well up at clearys. Fifteen or sixteen years ago now. She was up at home with the older sister hannah. Clearys and them being neighbors. She was down from dublin for a few weeks. Tom was working abroad in england all that year. We were friends then but not great friends. But the dwyers are related to the clearys. The mothers were first cousins. But I was digging the well not too far from clearys house. The two cleary women lived there by themselves. There are a lot more in the family but they were dead or abroad or married. The clearys are gone with many years and the summer I am talking about they were well up in years. They had some few cows and a pony. That was a fierce hot summer and up on the hill there was not a drop of water. People carting water into the few small farms on the hill in tankards for the cows. I had someone working with me then who went off to england at the end of that summer. England it was I think but it could have been australia. A lazy worker you could not depend on to appear for work on time in the morning. Most of the mornings when he did he was late. But many of them mornings he didn't appear for work and I had to work by myself. I could work very hard then being younger and that first day Tess came out on her own with water and tea and a few tomato sandwiches. She was helping out the cleary women. Those old cleary women were very fond of her. I

well remember her telling me that first day she liked being at the clearys. Dwyers place was less than a mile
across the hill from clearys. Tess walked over to clearys
late in the morning. I was down in the hole digging the
well and the sun was beating down on me and then the
shadow came fully across me and I thought it was the pony
or one of the cows that had wandered over in a curious
way and I turned and looked up and she was smiling
down and saying that she had sandwiches and tea made
and I must be famished for water because did I see that
my water can was dry as a bone. I looked up at her and
squinted up at the sun. A slight person she was and she
would stay that way. I came up out of the hole and I
thought she would leave the things there and go about
her business but not at all. She spread the things out and
took the sandwiches from the towel and she sat down
with me and pulled her knees up and wrapped her arms
around the knees. She was playing with the hair. I remember that so well. Her lovely hair. Closer to bronze
than it was to black. Horse hair she told me her mother
called it. It did look that strong and thick. She said she
had brought a tea mug for herself. Did I mind sharing the
tea with her. I said to her that she had made the tea so
she was surely entitled to have a mug or two of it. She
said the cleary women were lovely but she was tired of
being in the house and listening to them bicker with one
another about nothing. She said she liked to drink the
tea out of doors. She said the taste of it was different. I
said I was fairly good friends with her brother in england
and she said she knew that. Hannah said that she said. I
asked how tom was faring out over there and she said he
writes to hannah and hannah says he was doing fine and
sending a little money home every week. Some of it to

save for himself and a bit of it that went to the house. I inquired if she missed home when she was away in the city and she said when she was back here she missed it frightfully and going back it was sad but she knew she would have to go back but she always cried on the train she said on the way back and when the train was near the city and the houses and the factories were up around her again she would think her heart would break. But in a day or two she would be back in the routine of the work and she was fine. We talked for a long time that first day. She told me about her mother and father who had passed a few years before that. Her mother she said was of no use after the father died of the flu and the mother did not last long after him. I should have been back down in that hole and I inquired if the cleary women would wonder where she was. They would not care a bit she said. They wanted her to be able to enjoy herself on her holidays. They are often too busy bickering to think of anything else she said. She said the older sister hannah was very bossy and she hoarded up the jobs for her. Kept the jobs until she came back from dublin. Sweeping from under the beds and washing the blankets in the tub and hanging them out on the line and spreading them out along the hedge and the gates. Taking out all the cups and the other things in the cupboard and washing them and scrubbing the shelves of the cupboard and putting the cups and the other things back on the shelves again. Scrubbing all the floor on her hands and knees with the scrubbing brush. She said Hannah says the knees are bad with her and she cant kneel down or reach up very high for things. That's frightfully handy for hannah I said and the two of us laughed. And she said that hannah never understood that this was her holiday and she did not want to work all the time. She didn't mind doing a bit of work she said. Sometimes she liked the mind and the hands to be occupied she said. We sat and talked and laughed. It was very easy to laugh with her. She likes the jokes. We poked fun at many people. She was as good as me at that and I enjoyed that. I could have done my dead best at making her laugh all day. I could have never stood up and went back down into that hole.

The next day I could not wait for her to come again. I wore a good shirt that day but I took the shirt off when I was going down into the hole like I always did anyway. But later in the morning it was hannah that was standing at the verge of the hole with her hands on the hips and she said that she had gone down to clearys yesterday and found out that tess was out with me for so long and was she causing me trouble and was she keeping me from my work. I said no trouble and the work was getting done fine. I could work even better with the bit of company. The man who was to be helping with the job I have not seen in a few days and I have no idea where he is I said. I was looking up at hannah with my hand shading my eyes and now her arms were folded and hannah leans over a bit and I moved into her shadow and took my hand down and she looked down at me dead in the eye and says that tess is a very mischievous girl. I was going to laugh but I was afraid that might give something away but I was very fond of that word mischievous. And I was thinking that my life was fine but it was not fine at all. And I was thinking why did I never see her like that before. And I was wondering then and I still wonder after all these years why did I go and bring that lifelong trouble on my-self like that. Everything was fine and I went looking for trouble. Or nothing at all was fine and is never fine and

that was why I went in search of it. That's what I did and
I don't know why I did it. Could I have not left well
enough alone. But some days I am very glad I lived my
life with that trouble. I say I am glad but I don't know
why. I am not and was never much of a husband for doing it. Feeling that way and keeping it to myself. But that
first day she stood and gathered up the things and I went
to the verge of the hole and looked down into the hole
and laughed and said here I go. And when I did I didn't
think anything had changed but I knew something had
happened. And I was a bit afraid but the fear made it
more intoxicating. The fine sunlight falling across the
hill. But it was in the night it happened. That was it.
When I went back home and the thought of her woke me
at an early hour of the morning. I woke and she was in
my mind. I didn't wonder why she was in my mind. It
seemed very natural that that is the place shed be. And I
think that was when the not being good at sleeping
started. And that well at clearys turned out to be a fine
well in the end but I had to go down a long ways to find
the stones and the spring gushing below the stones.

She wore a different dress for the three days. And
that first day she sat and pulled her knees up and put her
arms around the knees the dress was a shade of blue.
Know of late the color is azure. It happened then when
we drank the tea. No it happened the second her shadow
fell over me when I was down in that hole. I think the
first one of them cleary women died the next summer.
And the other one passed away very soon after. I missed
the two funerals. That summer the cleary woman died it
rained every day and I could do very little outside work.
I did a few jobs inside in a few places. But the jobs were
scarce and hard to come by. I didn't have a bob to my

name. Then I got the job in the copper mines and I stayed down in them for a few years. That november the second one of the cleary women died. I married Nora the last week of october.

But I forget to remember this part. When I went home that first day the house was empty. All outside with the cows and the father had an old dictionary. He kept it very near where he sat and at night you'd see him turning the pages. Turn the pages and call out words and say what the word meant. He called them out in a slow way because he could not pronounce them right and roger and me would laugh but only to ourselves. And that evening I came in and was very glad that the house was empty and I don't know what led me over there to open up the dictionary for whatever reason and run my eyes up and down the words and the word where I stopped was acquiesce. I said it to myself many times that evening in my head. I said it when I was milking the cows and the moon was rising about the trees behind the haybarn. acquiesce.

How sorrowful it is to sit here and write. That I will never ever see her again. No more Julys to look forward to. There is no heaven I mostly think. And if its the heaven they say it is I will never be let in. If there is a hell in the way they say there is that's the hole I will be thrown down into.

The second day she came out later. And she did bring the tea and the water and she brought me the few tomato sandwiches. I came up out of the hole and put on my shirt and she sat like she sat the day before. Pulled the legs up and put the arms around the legs. I ate away and said nothing at first. At some stage I said hannah was out this morning giving out about her and she laughed and said she was always trying to escape from her and if she knew she was out here now there would be ructions. She said the cleary women told her to take the tea and the sandwiches out to me and to not be worried about hannah. The cleary women said to her that I would be famished from the heat down in a hole. I said the hole wasn't too hot at all when you were in it was more on the cold side. And there was no sign of water yet. Asked her about her life in dublin and she said she had good friends in the hospital and shed go for walks and go to dances with them. I said to her the dances must be great fun and she said nothing to that but was I in the mood to go for a bit of a walk. I said a walk was the very thing I needed before going back down into that hole and she laughed and said I should stay out of the hole for as long as I can. Water or no water for the cleary women and their cows and the pony. We left that small field of clearys and went into their next small field. All were hilly fields. The grass parched brown in the sun. Only the furze and the ragworth and the thistles thriving. Strange how that goes. She said did I mind if she smoked. The cleary women did not mind her smoking at all but if hannah or tom caught her smoking there would be trouble. I said not at all I was having one myself. Her sister was far away and tom was even farther away. And it was when we walked through the second field of clearys and were going up the smooth stones going into coughlans field that I turned and put my hand down to her and she put her hand into mine and until we got back to clearys first field where I was digging that destitute hole we did not let go hands. We said only a few words to each other in coughlans field. Small remarks. My breath came heavy and so did hers. That was because of the hands and we knew that. I was listening to every breath in coughlans big field that went all the way up to the top of the hill. Up through the moss and the big white rocks and the furze bushes. And we looked up at the furze that always looked lovely from a distance. The yellow shine on them. Hearing her breath and trying to hide my own. Then after a while she said the sister would be very cracked at her. Today was the day she told the sister shed pull out the beds and sweep and scrub underneath them. I said I should be back down in the destitute hole. I should have been back down there more than an hour ago I said. She had to bring the curtains she had washed for the clearys in from the line and hang the curtains and that was going to take a good while but she said she had not once thought of curtains and scrubbing floors since we first came up the stones. I said I hadnt thought about being back down in that hole since I looked up and saw her standing at the verge of it more than two hours ago. Closer to three hours even. She lowered her head and said she had to go back to dublin soon. I said when exactly was that and she said it was the day after tomorrow. I remember her saying that still and turning her head away from me and when she turned the head the sunlight lit her hair up something fierce. That fine thick horse hair that I see and smell in my head still. And she squeezed my hand when she turned and I squeezed her hand and I brought it to my mouth. And I said will you come out again and see me tomorrow. And she said she most definitely will. And I said ill look forward to it so much. Ill spend all the seconds from now till then looking forward to it. And she said she will too. Then we walked toward the stone steps and we held hands again and she gathered up the tea things and I stood at the verge of the hole and watched her walk away

and she turned to me and smiled and pushed the hair
from her face and waved in a small way. Just the hand
shaking once before her forehead. That day it was a
pinkish dress that she wore. Or on the third day it was
the yellow dress I can't be fully sure anymore and that
day it was the white dress with small blue flowers on it
and she wore a white blouse. But that was when we went
down the stones into coughlans field.

   She did come the next day. Our last day. I tried to get
as much done down in the hole before she came because
I was not ready one bit to let her go so quickly. I wasnt
thinking that way. I don't know what it was I was exactly
thinking. And there she was on the verge of the hole. It
was a little after I heard the angelus bell strike in the
church steeple across the hill. I blessed myself when I
heard it and said a quick prayer for all of us. I knew
things had shifted and turned inside out and upside
down inside of me like everything in there was bubbling
and moving and going mad like a volcano or balls firing
across a pool table. I got out of the hole and put on the
shirt and we sat and we drank the tea and I was able to
eat something but not very much at all. A few bites and I
said I was sorry I did not feel so hungry this afternoon. It
must be because of the heat I said. She said she had not
had a bite to eat since yesterday. The appetite was gone
out of her. The heat I said and she nodded. She said the
cleary women were happy the way the curtains turned
out all right. But it took her a frightfully long time to get
them back up and the cleary women were not much help
because they were so feeble and what they were mostly
good at was bickering with one another. And hannah
was very mad at her because she had let her jobs pile up
at home and she did not get back there till late in the

evening. She did not pull out the beds and sweep the clouds of dust and balls of fluff and she did not know if she would have time to do it now. She had told the sister that she was going to mend a dress and put a patch in an apron because she was handy with the singer but she did not have the time to do all that now. Then she asked of me would I make her laugh. I made a stupid face. I poked right good fun at people and I poked right good fun at hannah and I am not going to write down here what I said about those people or about her sister but the truth is anyway that I forget. She was laughing and I was laughing and I said we should go for a walk in coughlans field. And we stood and when we walked through the gap into the next small field of clearys we held hands and I could smell exactly who she was and it was a lovely smell. She had lipstick on and that was the only day she wore it and it was very becoming on her but she would be equally very fine without it. And we walked together up the smooth stones into coughlans field. I went up first. She said we should walk by the ditch up toward the furze. And I said I was having a hard time thinking that this was our last day. And she said she felt the same way. And she was not going to leave her sister tomorrow in the best of form but it would give her sister and her brother something to complain about. Hannah would write to tom in england all about it. It would give hannah something to write about apart from the awful heat and that there was no water. And it was cooled down in the shade of the trees. We walked into the tall cow parsley and the hedge parsley and she stopped and touched the wild carrot with the blood red flower in the center. And I pulled her into me. And I put my hands down around her and kissed the side of her face. And down we fell. And we were laughing when we landed in the weeds and I ran my fingers through the horse hair and pulled her skirt up. My fingers went under her elastic band. And her fingers fumbled with my belt and I got the knickers down to her knees. And our tongues were in our mouths and her hands and my fingers did fine work and I forgot all about the time and the hole and then our panting breaths. We have to stop michael she said and she sat up and fixed her clothing back into place and I sat up and said yes we have to and fixed myself but I am not going to say sorry I said and she said neither was she and when we were going back up the smooth stones at coughlans she turned around and pushed the fringe out of my eyes and she leaned into me and kissed me and the powder from the weeds was stuck to her lips. And it was that that put the stamp on it. That was the very beginning and very end of it. And when we walked back to where the hole was my breath and other parts of me were going mad and I felt my heart was the biggest now it will ever be. Every day after this the heart will shrink and shrink and turn into one of those punctured and wrinkled footballs that the young fellows fling into the ditch because its of no use to anyone. A punctured and wrinkled thing that an old sheepdog will come and chew on and dribble on and piss on. That the centipedes will lay their eggs in. That will harden like a rock and be frozen by ice in the months of winter. That will be smothered in spring and summer with the sharp grass and the thistles and the docleaves. That the wasps will build in and raise wasps in.

She gathered up the tea things and I could still hear her tears. And my heart was still swollen. And I clenched my fists to my sides and kept looking at her. And she had all the things gathered up and she stood there staring at me and her eyes still wet and I was about to go over to her but she put her hand out. I don't know what to do I said. I don't want to go back down this hole. You have to go she said. We have other people to think about she said. And I had nicely forgotten it. The other people to think about. Like you can't ever shut them out like when I shut the shed door behind me at night. I have someone in dublin she said. Im great with him for a while she said. Im engaged to Nora madden I said. Engaged with a while I said. I know she said. Hannah told me she said. She told me a million times she said. I don't think Im too happy anymore Tess but I have never been so happy in my life and I will never forget you as long as I live I said. I wont forget you michael she said but I have to go in and finish a few things at clearys and face hannah again and I have to pack my bags for the train tomorrow. And I have to go back down this hole and now that I know what it is and what I might have done I hope I will never come back out of it I said. You will come back up out of it she said.

Thirty five days since she died. More than a touch of autumn in the breeze this evening. I clanged the shed door shut. Tom was by this evening and we went for a walk. Kevin and some other few young lads out of the road kicking the football and I told them to be careful with the cars coming around the bend getting faster every year it looks like. Nora shouted out at him to put on his jumper or hed get his death of cold. Listen to your mother I said to him and he went in immediately. Nora came out then and asked tom if he wanted a cup of tea and he said they were just after it at home. Decided we would walk the road and not go into the fields. A few showers of rain earlier and the fields would have been wet. Had to leave the job I was doing early. Was hoping to be finished with it this week but that will not happen. Was walking the road for a bit and who did we run into but daly on his bicycle. He was on his way back from the junction and was in a very good mood as he always is. He shoved his hand down his pocket and counted out the money and handed it to tom. Then went on about people he saw over at the junction. Some holdup with the dublin train being late. A tree fell down on the tracks. He said to tom he remembers his young sister getting off the morning train on the Monday of the second week of July. The lord have mercy on her soul he said. Daly said another few words. He was looking at me and I was looking at him and then away from him. I remember him down in the mines talking about her. Making remarks about how grand she was but hes not the sort to do no more than talk. All talk with him. And I was not in the mood to be listening to him at all but you have to pass people off around here or god knows the things they'll make up about you that might alltold be true. About ten minutes after he left and we back to the walking. Tom says to me out of the blue it was not an accident at all. The young sister he said. Not an accident he said. She was in a bad way for a while he said. The nerves mad at her he said. Eating away at her he said. Didn't I think when she was here this summer that she was odder than usual he said. She spent nearly the full week in the sitting room where the mrs put up the bed for her. It was in the telegram he said. We dont know who posted it at all he said. But whoever did wanted the truth to be aired he said. They had their mission and they didn't keep their mission to themselves he said. Bringing trouble on people is what they were up to if you ask me he said. I don't want to know anything about them he said. Wanted her buried there and everything he said. Said they would look after all of it he said. Said there was her real home and not here he said. Said she wanted to rest there he said. God forgive all of us he said. God forgive me he said. I said nothing because there was a choking inside of him and we went on walking. God forgive me he said one more time. And the choking still in him. And we went on walking. He took out a hanky and ran it about his mouth and his eyes. We went on walking. When I have the job done at walshes ill have the rest of the money I said. Tom nodded and we walked the rest of journey to the cross without saying anything more. He kept the hanky out and he kept swiping it at his face. Sure what can you do he said at the cross. I didn't say a word. I did not look at him. I could hardly wait for him to go away so that I could be with myself. He went his way without saying another word and not looking at me at all and I stood for a while and watched after him before I turned toward home. But I didn't go home immediately. I walked into cahills big field that at one time was owned by the lennons. It runs by the roadside and around the cross. I sat underneath one of the big elms. It was cold enough and the cows were out in the grass. The grass was dying. No more of it would grow again till the spring. The ground was getting cold. The ground was getting ready to go to sleep for the winter. I heard voices far away. Farmers talking in a haybarn or a cowshed. The voices died away after a few minutes and I was more than thankful. Thankful to be on my own. And the night was falling down on top of me like time falls down on top of you and I squeezed my eyes shut and for the first time I could see her walking down a Dublin street. I could see her stepping up steps with the umbrella open. Shaking

the raindrops from the umbrella. I could hear the click of
her fine sharp heels. On top of my thighs and my belly
and across my back and my fat hairy arse. And I could
see her buttoning up a raincoat. Turning a key and pushing in the tired out door of the house she lived in. I could
see all that like the gift was given to me there and then.
And I could see her having a chat with her friends. That
she liked it when people liked her. That she thrived. That
she might live. That she might live. That the people you
love might live. That you might love the people you live
with. That it all might be different. That the world might
not be the way you fashioned it. That she and me might
be like we once was. That you could have those three
days back. That we might be like that first time we was
when I found there was someone else in the world apart
from myself. I could see that smile at the corner of her
mouth. A smudge of lipstick on fine teeth. I could see
her picking up the post from a table when she got inside
her door. I could see her waiting for a bus to take her to
someplace I don't know and will never be to. She holding
the purse in front of her. Her head bowed and the horse
hair falling over her face. I could see her taking her shoes
off at night and sitting before a mirror and brushing her
hair. I could see her standing at the sink washing under
her arms with a sponge. I could smell the sour armpits.
The smell I first smelled in coughlans field. Washing the
tits until the nipples were pebbles. Streams of water running down her thick sides and onto the floor. And she
rubbing the sponge up and down over her lumpy navel
and the sponge going around and down the crack of her
arse to her lovely hole. I could see all that. The gift was
in me. And I stood up from the tree and crossed the ditch
and walked down the road home and the young lads

were still playing football and when kevin saw me coming he waved. He was running and laughing along the
road. He was dancing in the air around him. It was very
close to dark and his hand going into the air and he
called me and I held my hand up to him and did my best
to smile but he would have seen no smile anyway me being far away and it being close to dark.

And that night no word would come to me. The next
night no word would come to me. The night after that no
word came. The night after that one no word came to me
and I walked out to the docleaves behind the leanto and
relieved myself and when I came back in I pushed the
chair back and put my head on the desk. Fell sound
asleep squeezing the biro for dear life in my hand. It was
so long since I slept and she came to me. She was there
like when she stood at the verge of that hole the summer
I dug the well up at clearys. And the heart so big then.
She was wearing a new dress. The color of it was gray
but it was a light gray and not a sad gray and she did not
look sad at all. And she says to me sorry michael it took
me so long to come to visit you. And I said what did all
that time and all those years matter as long as you are
here now. My life was shorter than a minute she said. I
cant believe how fast it all went by she said. You were
looking after people I said. You looked after so many
people I said. I kept myself very busy she said. You never
nursed the sickest of all I said but my life is still going
and the children are getting older I said. I never met them
at all but I saw them at the distance at mass she said. The
eldest girl and the eldest boy look like you in the face she
said. They can face the world she said. So they all say to
me I said and I have no idea how the children are going
to turn out or where they will end up but like so many

born around here they will end up not here. Life is the
devil I said. A pigs house I said. Only sometimes it is she
said. You would know better than I would I said. In spite
of all my misery I look at the children sometimes and
have this blow of happiness I said. Like a bony fist to the
jaw I said. I look at Nora and think what a devil ive been
and how little room I kept for her in my heart and how
to be truthful I blamed her for things that were my own
doing. I am a coward I said. I am and I know it I said.
And there is no other word for it I said. How was your
life I said. I enjoyed much of it she said. But things got to
me in a bad way at times she said. I saw some few men
and I enjoyed them. But I worked very hard in the hospital she said. You looked after all them sick people and I
was always very proud of you I said. In the end I put everything I had into the work she said. Work was the only
thing that worked for me she said. I found no other way
to manage it she said. It was always hard coming back
here but I looked forward to it so much she said. Summers toward the end I didn't want to come at all she said.
But Id see you Michael for those two Sundays in the
church porch she said. I was fine then she said. It was
great to see that you were still in the world she said. I
could stand this world if you were in it she said. I looked
forward to it much I said. That's all life is michael she
said. Most of it so easily forgotten. Most of it we are not
there at all but I was so glad to see how fine you looked
she said. That would keep me going for a long time she
said. That would feed my life she said. Feed the heart
and feed the soul she said. My friends would say I was a
fool and my life is a dream but I would say to them that
the dream is fine with me she said. A dream might be all
it is she said. Would we have been different if we married

I said. Would we have been happy I said. Would you and me have been different people than the people we turned out to be I said. You can never know she said. How could you know she said. I could never imagine us making each other miserable in any way or shape or form I said. It might have all turned out unbearable she said. It might have been dreadful she said. Don't say that I said. You know theres no truth to that I said. How can you say that I said. We got to live it the best way of all she said. I want you to think about it that way from now on she said. You and I were the luckiest people of all she said. I want you to remember I told you that she said.

I woke up after that. The bulb had gone out in the shed and it was pitch dark. The gift was gone from me. Gone for good and the air in the shed was damp and dead and freezing cold like the air was when I was down in the copper mines. And this terrible shivering all over my skin like there was fingers touching it. And outside the dark shed the leaves on the birches ticked in the most mysterious way. A way Id never heard them ticking before.

If I wrote to her then I would write that the day I stood at the altar and married she was the one on my mind. The day my daughter was born she was on my mind. The day my son was born she was on my mind. The day the twins came screaming into the world she was on my mind. That's all Id need to write.

3

I lay on the bed and listened to the stream. That evening years back on the cobblestone path, the two men in the shed looked like phantoms conjured up out of the Sweet Afton smoke. That smell of new wood was mixed with the cement dust. I stood there ever so obediently. Ever so innocuously. Staring through the smoke and trying to hear the men against the thumps of the ball. Nora's shadow appearing then disappearing on the windowpane. He at the back of the shed. Me at the front. The Nissan lorry with the black stripes along the sides was parked in the driveway. A red wheelbarrow crusted with concrete lay upside down in the truck bed. Shovel handles sticking out. The moon rose above the silver birches. And the air turned chilly in the fading daylight.

I sat in the backseat of my father's car. Golden ribs of straw were stuck to the stained and torn seats. The head of Hannah's doll was on the floor. I kicked the head under my father's seat and it kept rolling back and I kept on kicking it as the car rolled along. My aunt was sitting silently in the passenger seat. We had picked her up at the Junction. My father drove like time had stopped. He didn't like driving the main road. But to me then that journey was like going to another country. Houses brightly painted in the passing villages. People I didn't know glanced at through the car window. And Aunt Tess kept touching her radiant horse hair. She touched it the way I sometimes long to touch the glass of a painting in a museum. Her nails were this brilliant red. Before the month was over she would fling herself under a Dublin bus. But that day she would have been thrilled. Being so close to seeing him again after the year's wait. On Sunday he would wear the hat with the feather. Una or Nora would have brushed the hat for him.

Kevin was back with a while. He'd come to the door and knocked. He'd turned the knob and pushed. I was standing behind the door. I held my breath.

—Jimmy, are you in there? There's someone out here who can't wait to see you.

Then he was talking loudly in the big room. I went and lay on the bed.

—Jimmy must be out walking in the trees. He locked the door before he went, darling . . . Yes, we will eat out on the deck . . . Anton put the picnic table there especially for you. He put a nice tablecloth on it. I told him you liked the white and red squares . . . Did you put on the bug spray? Your mother warned me that you put it on, darling. She warned more than once . . . I will so start the grill if you help me. I'm grilling chicken because I know my darling likes it. Anton will bring the corn he grows himself . . . That's the plan. We'll stick to that . . . Yes, there's soda in the fridge. Okay, you can have one. But you should have orange juice, darling. But have a soda if it's what you want . . . Daddy has everything his darling wants.

I got up from the bed and went to the window. The grass was sparse because of the trees. The Lenape Indians made their paths through those trees before they were either butchered or banished to Ohio. A bird flew across. I thought it was a blackbird. And I left Tess out of the story I told him about the apple pie. Tess was the one who opened the red gate. Tess ran ahead. I walked beside my mother. I carried the plates and the forks.

Right up until the day before you left, you and Tess made up stories about the things your parents said in the kitchen. Their remarks about neighbors with more land and money. *Sure their money is killing them. Never brought them a day's luck.* And their remarks regarding the moods of hens and ducks. *She only laid three times this week. I don't know what's come over her at all.* And me and Tess acted out things about the National school teacher. We lay on the girls' bed. Our heads were at the bottom and our bare feet were propped on the pillows. I had opened the window and the wind blew at Aunt Tess's red curtains and the smell of cow manure spread through the room. Our faces were very close and Tess was telling you how to do it to yourself. Doing it to yourself was what Tess called it. *I can't believe you don't know that yet, Jimmy. You don't need other people at all, Jimmy. Never once do you need them, Jimmy*—but my mother on the path with her covered pie was telling Tess to behave herself. My mother's box of letters abandoned on the wardrobe floor of that flat on Botanic Avenue. That shoebox was what was in your head when the plane wheels touched a runway at Logan Airport. A feckless and cowardly act it was. Though maybe you did actually forget. And your mother demanding that Tess go inside this second and wipe that muck from her eyes.

—Don't you dare go down the paddock in front of the men looking that way! Is it Queen Maeve you think you are!

But Tess ran on and pretended not to hear our mother's words. Tess skipped into the paddock. She was wearing her pink dress and her red hair was down and her arms were spinning like the spokes of a windmill. The two dogs ran alongside her. Their tongues were out and very long in their shadows. They used to wait on the hall doorsteps for her and when she appeared they barked and wagged their tails. Crows circled the poplars. In one of Tess's paintings the crows were bright red splashes of blood on a white wrinkled sheet pegged upon a sagging country clothesline. Kevin stepped down from his father's ladder the moment Tess opened the gate. He and his father dropped their tools. Dropped them like they would rocks. With sighs of relief. Michael messed with his John Garfield fringe. He was smiling at the three of us. Love for my dead aunt might not have been killing him in that moment. He put it away in the daylight then let it roam free at night in his shed. Tess pranced around Kevin, who was lighting a cigarette and smiling. Michael wiped dust from an upturned cement block. He sat down on it and was chatting with my mother, who knelt before him and cut the cake with the knife with the bandaged handle. I handed Michael a plate and fork first and then I handed the others plates and forks. The dogs stuck their noses into everything.

The questions Tess will ask: Did you get on all right with him, Jimmy? Tell me, what does he look like now? Did he put on weight? How is he handling Seamus? What did he say and what did you say? Where does he live and what's it like?

He put on a small bit of weight, Tess. And the hair has a few light streaks of gray and is shorter than back then. He's very upset about Seamus. What's to be expected. But he's doing all right. He has a wooden house in the woods not too far north of New York City. Another place not so far from there. I visited the house in the woods. A loud stream at the end of a grassy yard surrounded by very tall trees. A stone wall going up at the end of the yard. A wide deck on one side of the house and a porch at the front. The windows are huge and bare and the house and the trees are one. He has children by more than one woman. And I told him he was a bastard and that he always was. And he told me I was the naïve one. And that I lived in my fucking head. But what do I care anymore what he thinks. The brave teenager who pushed you into the river and ran away. He called you a filthy useless cunt that evening. Stephen and Hannah never heard it. They were too busy fishing. Too busy minding their own business. And sorry to have to tell you this one, Tess, but your father was an illegal bookie. He kept his receipts in the biscuits tins our mother's friend posted every Christmas from London. He burned the receipts on the range. Burned them when his best friend and his wife were dead. He felt guilt then. Yes. Useless guilt. Hannah saw him. She walked into the kitchen and there your father the bookie was standing over the range with his biscuit tins lined up. But if I asked Hannah now she'd say she never saw that. That never happened. But I wonder, Tess, if he admitted it in Confession. And it would have troubled him on all those nights he spent on his knees. I tried so many times to listen to him in the confession box. I'd slide my arse down to the end of the pew and cock my head. But not once did I hear a word. All I heard were mumbles and grunts—but I wonder did he admit it, Tess. Bless me, Father, for I am a secret bookie for the parish. And on top of that I never paid the man who dug my well and built my pump house. The man who piped hot water into my kitchen sink and cold water up the fields for my fourteen cows. That man was my best friend, Father. But Father, he owed me money on a few horse races. And, Father, we all must pay our debts. Don't we, Father. But you won't tell Tess any of that. Won't tell her he told about their day trip to England. Nor the notebooks. Or the unpaid pump house. No. Won't tell Tess.

That goat was in the window frame, watching me, standing in a patch of sunlight that had made its way through the thick branches. Blades of grass hung from its mouth. My eyes followed the sunlight up and when I looked down the goat had vanished.

I quietly unlocked the door, opened it an inch or so. Out on the deck Kevin and Anton were talking with the girl. And like a thief in a cartoon I sneaked across the hall and into the bathroom. Before I quietly shut the door Kevin's loud laughter rang through the big room. I locked the door. A long piss. I brushed my teeth. A quick shower. I dried myself and put on antiperspirant. That smell that Zoë liked. Back in the room I changed my underpants and took a shirt from the bag. An ironing board was hanging on the back of the wardrobe door. I ironed the shirt and put the ironing board and the iron back. And I went back into the bathroom again and checked my face one more time in the mirror.

4

—We thought you were lost in the trees, Kevin said.

—I was out walking earlier. I came back and fell asleep, I said.

I shut the sliding door behind me. He was standing over the grill with a long two-prong fork. Mesquite-scented flames licked the blackened grill bars and the chicken pieces. His t-shirt and the shorts were new. His feet were bare.

—There's a girl here who's been waiting to talk to you.

She was sitting on the other side of the picnic table. Anton sat opposite her. She had the large dark eyes and the dark hair, which was parted in the middle and behind her ears. Her long-sleeved dress was the shade of sunflower petals, and around her neck was a seashell necklace. I said hello to Anton. He smiled and raised a beer can. He wore a white t-shirt, shorts, flip-flops.

—Jimmy, say hello to Deirdre, Kevin said.

Deirdre stood. She was touching the necklace. I stepped forward, bowed a little, and shook her hand. She was almost as tall as I was.

—Nice to meet you, Deirdre.

—Hi, Jimmy.

—I'll get you a beer, Jimmy.

—Thank you, Kevin.

He leaned over and opened a cooler next to the grill. The icy can touched my bare arm.

—Grilled chicken, Anton's corn, and Anton's going to make a salad, Kevin said.

—Daddy's favorite, Deirdre said.

She tucked her dress underneath her and sat down.

—Mine, too, sweetie, Anton said.

He moved up the bench. I sat myself across from Deirdre. Anton put a bowl of chips before me. I took a handful and looked over Deirdre's head at the wall of trees and the blue and empty sky. Kevin and Anton were talking. Anton said that the wall might be done by the end of the week if there was no more rain.

—How old are you, Deirdre? I asked.

I put the bowl of chips before her.

—I'll be eleven in November, Jimmy.

She broke a chip into small pieces. The ridges on the chips were like the ones on the shells.

—Deirdre wants us to have a big party up here for her birthday, Kevin said. —Her two sisters and her brother will come. Jimmy, you're welcome to come, too.

—I'm sure your birthday will be great fun, I said.

—It wouldn't be the same without Jimmy, Kevin said.

—You must, Jimmy, Deirdre said. —You will meet my half brother and sisters. Anton will be here.

—With bells on, sweetie. Snow everywhere then, Anton said.

—I love snow, Deirdre said.

—Me, too, sweetie, Anton said.

—You're enjoying the summer, Deirdre, I said.

—I go to the pool and the library every day.

And with both hands she lifted the necklace around her head and laid it in a heap in the middle of the picnic table.

—That's a lovely necklace, I said.

—Daddy gave it to me this morning, Deirdre said.

—No pool up here, but we have that smashing stream, darling, Kevin said.

The phone kept ringing in the big room. The answering machine was off.

—I can't swim in the stream, Daddy.

—But the stream is pretty, darling. You said so yourself.

—I saw something today, I said.

—Well, Jimmy, so what's the story? Kevin said.

—Who knows what you might see. West Point's not so far, Anton said, and laughed.

—I only saw a goat, I said.

The phone stopped ringing.

—Daddy, you never told me about the goat, Deirdre said.

—A goat, Anton said.

—Am I hearing Jimmy rightly?

—You heard Jimmy, Daddy.

—I saw the goat twice, I said.

—Jimmy's joking, darling. There's no goat up here.

—There is one, I said.

—Jimmy always acted the clown on the school bus, darling.

The grill hissed. The phone was ringing again.

—Never can escape that bloody phone, Kevin said.

—I could turn it off, I said.

—Best to leave it, Jimmy.

—I've never seen a goat up here, Anton said.

—I love goats, Deirdre said.

The phone stopped ringing.

—Me, too, I said.

—I knew a woman once who raised them, Anton said. —She lived in a cabin not far from here. A New York City girl. Went to Vassar. She sold the goats' milk. It tasted bad but it's healthy. I still have a coffee mug she made me. My favorite mug.

—My father kept goats once, I said.

—I never remember goats over at your place, Jimmy.

—I don't know what happened to them. I was very young, I said.

—I must watch out for the goat, Anton said.

—I'd like to milk a goat, Deirdre said.

—That woman showed me how, Anton said.

—But Jimmy's having us on, Kevin said. —I've walked for miles into the trees and climbed the rocks and I have never once seen a goat. Maybe it was a small deer. I've seen many of those.

—I know the difference, Kevin.

—You do, sorry, Jimmy.

He opened the cooler and passed me two cans of beer. I handed one to Anton.

—But you couldn't beat Jimmy for the jokes back then.

—Daddy and you took the bus to school together.

—A red double-decker, Deirdre, I said.

—And Daddy and you did your homework together after school.

—Never did we miss an evening of homework, Deirdre.

—Jimmy played tricks, darling. Jimmy was the joker.

—I danced and sang up and down the bus aisle, I said.

Kevin began to whistle loudly. So did I. Deirdre laughed.

—Singing and dancing in the bus, I said.

—What songs, Jimmy?

—You name it, darling. Jimmy sang it.

—I had my repertoire, Deirdre.

—Buses like the English buses, Anton said.

—Exactly, I said.

—I studied abroad for a semester in London, Anton said.

—None of your wild stories in front of my daughter and my oldest best friend, Kevin said.

—Whatever you say, boss.

Anton laughed and dropped his hand into the chip bowl.

—Daddy said I did meet my uncle who died in London, Deirdre said. —My uncle visited once when I was a baby.

Kevin put the fork down. He turned to his daughter.

—Your mother and I have talked to you about this, darling, he said.

—And we agreed in the car not to talk about it up here.

He turned back to the grill. Deirdre looked glum. Anton gulped at the can. Flames flared up.

—Now she's cooking, he said.

The flames whooshed. He stepped back. We all laughed. The slanting light along the deck was golden. Someone had swept up the bodies of the dead bugs and the moths. Probably Anton.

—Jimmy, did that bloody bird wake you last night?

He was wiping his furrowed brow with a paper napkin.

—I didn't hear a thing, I said.

—How could any human being sleep through it?

—Well, I did.

—Jimmy sleeps soundly, he said.

—Another can, boss, Anton said.

I passed the can to Anton. Insects circled the chip bowl. Anton stood to light the candles. Deirdre asked if she might light one. Anton placed the candle before her and handed her the lighter. Her father turned to watch. He was smiling. He turned back to the grill when she was done.

—Did they call you Deirdre after Deirdre of the Sorrows? I asked.

—Her mother's grandmother, Kevin said.

—Daddy, I can answer for myself.

—You sure can, sweetie, Anton said.

—My darling has been telling me that a lot lately, Kevin said.

—Daddy, can Jimmy and I go to the stream!

—I don't know if Jimmy's in the mood for it.

I said I was fine with it.

—Well, let's wait a few minutes, darling. I like us all together.

—Maybe the goat is at the stream, Jimmy, Deirdre said.

—Hiding in the trees, I said.

—There's no goat. Jimmy's joking, Kevin said.

—There might be one, Anton said.

—I know there's one, Deirdre said.

—Jimmy's pulling our leg. That's Jimmy for you.

He took a swig from his can and picked up the napkin.

—Some things never change, darling.

—I knew Jimmy and I would be friends, Deirdre said.

—I thought so too, darling.

—Jimmy, will you write me when you go back?

—I will, Deirdre, if you write me first, I said.

—This chicken's looking good, Kevin said.

—Daddy, when can Jimmy and I go to the stream?

—In a few minutes, darling.

I asked Anton if his family was from around here.

—They are, he said. —Settled here when it was native land. I left here once. I lived on a beach in California. One March I was out there. We went to the beach every day, but I'd look out and feel bluer than the ocean.

—Anton gets morose when he's had more than one beer, Kevin said. —He might think about boiling the corn and making the salad.

—I like Anton, Deirdre said.

—I do, too, darling, but not when he's morose.

—I knew I had to live back here, Anton said.

—Jimmy, tell my favorite daughter more about your clowning ways on the bus.

—I'll tell you everything, Deirdre, I said.

—I got some stories, Anton said, and laughed.

—Anton took to the road when he was a teenager, Kevin said.

—College wasn't for me, Anton said.

—Another beer, Jimmy, Kevin said.

—I'll have one, thanks, I said.

—Daddy, come and sit with me.

—I have to keep an eye on the chicken, child.

—Daddy, I have told you not to call me child anymore.

—I keep forgetting, darling.

—Jimmy, you are really going to tell me about you and Daddy, Deirdre said.

—Every single thing, Deirdre.

She clapped her hands. I smiled then sipped the beer.

—Anton, you put that clock on the mantelpiece?

He turned from the grill. I dropped my hand into the chip bowl.

—Not me, boss, Anton said.

—The goat did it, Deirdre said, and laughed.

—My favorite daughter needs to pipe down.

I raised my hand and looked up at him.

—You recognize it, I said.

—It's a few years old.

—It was my father's. Yours had one exactly like it.

—I don't remember that, he said.

—Daddy, can I have the clock? Deirdre said.

—No, your mother or Bob will not like that—

—Daddy. Why can't I!

—Stop it, darling! Right now.

He turned and picked up the fork and stabbed the chicken.

—I got my granddad's grandfather clock, Anton said.

—Anton, you're working hard on the corn and the salad, Kevin said.

—Yes, boss.

Anton laughed loudly going through the sliding door.

—But Daddy, I want the clock!

He turned to his daughter. He wasn't smiling.

—No, darling. And that's the end of it.

—I don't really want it, Deirdre said.

She shrugged. Then she laughed. The phone started to ring.

—Let's not say any more about the bloody clock, Kevin said.

—Goats and clocks are not kosher, I said.

—Daddy, Mommy says you're not to curse in front of me, but I won't tell.

She slapped her hands on the picnic table.

—It's the whippoorwill's fault, Deirdre, I said.

She clapped her hands.

—I'll put you to bed early, darling. That's what I'll do. Or I might make you sleep out in the trees.

—I'm sleeping in Daddy's room, in my new bed, Deirdre said.

—Your new bed is going under the trees where the whippoorwill will get you, Kevin said.

The phone stopped ringing.

—Darling, run down in the yard. Jimmy and you can go to the stream in a while.

Deirdre was already standing. Smiling and pushing her hair behind her ears.

—Put on your shoes, child. The gravel will cut your feet. Spray on bug spray.

She rolled her eyes.

—Darling, you're going to wear the necklace I got for you.

—I don't really like it, Daddy.

She skipped across the deck. She gazed down the steps then giggled and hopped down. I was standing.

—She's the very best, he said.

—She is, I said.

She was singing on the lawn. He picked up the fork and turned to the grill. The phone started to ring.

—That might be Walter, he said. —He is supposed to call around now. Trouble with tenants not paying. He's not handling it at all. So the foreman tells me. I should have asked someone else to do it.

—I'll take Deirdre to the stream, I said.

—Stay with me, Jimmy. He'll ring me back. He always does. He needs the money.

He shut the lid of the grill, wiped his forehead with the crushed napkin, and took two cans from the cooler. He handed me one. We left the deck and stood at the porch railing. Deirdre was lying in the middle of the yard. She was lying in the shadows of the treetops. A butterfly passed above her. She reached her open hand up but the butterfly went higher. The sunlight was thickened with flower dust. He had propped his elbows on the railing and was watching his daughter. The phone had stopped ringing.

—I didn't tell the truth, Jimmy. He did ring me.

—Who, Walter? I asked.

He straightened up and took a long slug.

—No. Not him.

He placed the can back on the railing. We lit cigarettes. Deirdre had dozed off. Our smoke flowed into the sunlight and the flower dust. Things looked and felt and sounded fine.

—Seamus rang me, but I wish he never did.

Seamus left four messages in one hour. "I need to talk to you. You're the eldest. Here's my number. Ring me back."

At lunchtime Kevin rang the number. A woman with a Donegal accent told him it was a homeless shelter in Camden Town. She did know Seamus Lyons. He came and went. And she saw him a quarter of an hour ago. She was organizing clothes for him. Not looking the best, to say the least. And she gave Kevin the number of a public phone in the hall and told him to ring it in twenty minutes. She'd find Seamus. Kevin ate his lunch and made two quick business calls. He checked his watch. On the fifth ring, Seamus picked up. Kevin asked his brother how he was. Seamus said he didn't want to talk about that. That's not why he'd rung.

—I did him in. I did our uncle Rodger in, Seamus told his brother.

Rat poison. Nora had made enough beef stew to last for the week. Roger was turning hay and said he was way too busy to come in and eat. Seamus offered to take the stew out to Roger, and each lunchtime Seamus left the house with the bowl of stew and the bread and went to the lean-to at the back of the shed and stirred the rat poison into the bowl. Then he added salt. Roger loved the stew. And Roger loved salt. He'd clean the bowl in no time. Sop the gravy up with bread. Didn't even bother getting down from the tractor. Seamus handed the bowl and the bread up to him then stood and waited. But on the fourth day

Roger told Seamus to tell his mother to go handy on the salt. Still Roger wiped the bowl clean and shoved the bread into his mouth and handed the bowl down to Seamus. Hours later, Roger drove the tractor into the ditch. A local teenager found him. Roger was paying the teenager to help him out with the hay.

—He told me this in about five minutes, Jimmy. And then he hung up on me.

Kevin called the number again. No answer. He called the other number and talked to the Donegal woman. She said Seamus walked out the door a few minutes ago. When she saw him again she'd let him know his brother rang. A day later, Tommy rang Kevin to say that Seamus was dead.

—So that's what the bold Seamus says he did, Jimmy.

He drained the can and went back to the grill. I followed him. He picked up the fork and lifted the lid. He poked the chicken pieces. His shoulders were hunched, like those of an old man, and I watched that hollow place between a man's shoulder blades.

All the time in the world, Miss Una. All the time in the world.

He shut the lid then took another can from the cooler. He opened it and turned to me.

—But, Jimmy, the drugs made him mad.

—That's what it was, Kevin.

—Drugs and vodka. We know what they do to the head, Jimmy.

—We do, Kevin, that's what happened.

—So you agree with me, Jimmy.

—Of course, Kevin.

—Take Deirdre to the stream. I need to find out what Walter is up to. Mind her, won't you.

—I promise you I will, I said.

I headed toward the stairs. He said my name. I turned back to him.

—Sorry about the clock, he said.

—I thought it might bring some comfort—

—You keep it, Jimmy. It's your father's. That one's yours.

—Fine, Kevin.

—You're the one I could tell it to, Jimmy. We ended up here.

—We did, Kevin, was all I said.

He opened the sliding door. Anton was singing a Neil Young song and running the water. Washing lettuce and tomatoes. Slicing cucumbers. He slid the door shut and stared at me through the glass. I stared back. Faces that revealed nothing. And then a glare of sunlight on the glass caused him to vanish. But I knew he was still there and looking and I kept looking. And my mind went to him crying in his car. Tess was telling him to go away. Go away for good. If you took away all that other stuff, pity was all you had left. Pity that made us equal. Pity that made him braver than I ever let myself admit. Pity because of the weight of them. Shame in myself.

5

I rolled my pants legs up. We each sat on one of the big rocks. We were facing the bridge. The sunlight was low in the trees whose shadows trembled in the rolling water. On the count of three we dropped our feet in. Deirdre laughed and screamed then pulled her feet back out. She hugged her knees. Water splashed onto the stones. I kept my feet in. The hem of the sunflower dress was soaking wet.

—On summer evenings, Deirdre, when I was your age I went to the river with my younger brother and two sisters.

—Was Daddy ever there?

—Sometimes your daddy was.

—Was it like this, Jimmy?

—The water was not fast, Deirdre. There were a few rocks on the bank. The river divided a hay meadow. It drained the water. The cows drank from the river when the grass grew back. This was after the hay was cut. And there were no big trees. Just a few bushes.

A cracking noise came from inside the trees near the bridge.

—Jimmy, that might be the goat.

—Should we go and have a look?

—Let's stay here for now, Jimmy.

—Here is fine, Deirdre.

—Daddy and you were never best friends.

I looked into the water. The shadow of a hawk appeared. I looked up. The hawk sailed high above the trees.

—Did your daddy tell you that?

—I just know. I have friends.

Anton laughed loudly. Then her father laughed.

—Your daddy and Anton are having great fun up on the deck. Is your dress dry?

—It's almost dry, Jimmy.

—Your daddy and I were never friends.

—I'm right, Jimmy.

—Indeed, Deirdre.

A noise again from inside the trees. It was closer this time. Deirdre gripped my shirtsleeve.

—Someone's there, Jimmy.

—A deer, Deirdre. Maybe the goat.

She let my sleeve go.

—Your daddy is going through a very hard time right now.

—That's what Mommy says.

She grabbed the shirtsleeve again and pointed into the trees across from her.

—Did you hear it, Jimmy?

I shaded my eyes and stared. Things buzzed. Birds were singing. Insects skated above the water. I asked Deirdre to change places with me. I said it was my turn to sit next to the trees. And so we did, and I told her to put her feet into the stream one more time. She laughed and shivered. Finally, she said the water was awesome. I asked if her dress was dry. She said it almost was. And then we heard it.

—The whippoorwill, wow, Jimmy.

—It's early this evening, Deirdre.

It sounded again. Up near the bridge. We looked there. And I pointed to the hawk and told Deirdre to look up. The hawk moved in wide circles and we watched it until it vanished over the treetops on the far side of the bridge.

—Daddy said he dated your sister.

—He told you that.

—In the car this afternoon. Do you miss her, Jimmy?

—More than anyone else.

And a noise in the trees again, like rotten branches being stepped on.

—There's someone in there, I'm sure of it, Jimmy.

—The deer or the goat, Deirdre. No need to worry.

I watched up and down. I listened.

—We should go back to the deck, Deirdre. The midges are getting bad.

—Let's stay a few minutes more.

—Whatever you like, Deirdre.

—I want to visit where Daddy grew up.

—You will someday.

—Will you be there?

—Probably not.

—But you must write me.

—Promise you I will.

Then a loud crash inside the trees.

—The deer. That's all, Deirdre. They come down here in the evening for water.

—It's not deer, Jimmy. I know it.

—Only a deer, Deirdre, but your dad is expecting us.

—Let's go, then, Jimmy.

—I'm very hungry, Deirdre.

—Me, too, Jimmy.

—Don't tell your daddy about the noises in the trees.

—I won't. I was just scared. I know it was only a deer.

—That's all. Or the goat. But we don't want to worry your daddy.

—I understand, Jimmy.

—I know you do, Deirdre.

—I don't want to go back in the morning, Jimmy, but I told Mom I would.

—Then you must go back, Deirdre.

—You're right, Jimmy. I must.

I said we should walk through the yard. I threw our shoes over the unfinished wall and stepped over it. Deirdre stepped onto it and held out her hand. I held it and she jumped down. I picked up our shoes. Sunlight bloomed red on the long porch window. We walked in the dappled light. Walked in the shadows of the treetops. And we laughed in the pillar of midges. The grass was warm and soft. Smoke from the grill poured out over the deck. Like smoke on a battlefield when the battle is over. The chicken smelled delicious. He appeared at the corner of the deck. He called his daughter's name, and when we walked into his shadow he waved and Deirdre skipped ahead. She called, Daddy! Daddy! He laughed and called her name again. And he called mine. I waved and called his then looked down at the grass. Zoë was going through the airport gate. Tess was walking her dog along the riverbank in a midland town. Una's shadow darkened her single bed in that flat on Drumcondra Road. I would have seen her shadow on that bed many times. But the first is the one that stayed. And my mother was watering her yellow flowers with a plastic green can that my father bought in the Market Yard in Tipperary town the same day he and Michael bought the clocks. I used to fill that can at the yard spigot and bring it to her in her garden. And then I looked up because he was telling us to hurry on. The chicken was well ready. Anton had made a smashing salad. And when he waved again he looked like someone on the deck of a ship that was slipping out of the harbor, and his daughter and I were in that crowd on the shore. Weeping and waving back.

6

Kevin had dropped Deirdre off, and was back at the house with over an hour. Pizzas were delivered from Cold Spring. Kevin paid. We ate them at the picnic table. Anton ate with us, and when he went back to the wall Kevin picked up the seashell necklace Deirdre had forgotten.

—How careless of her, how selfish.

He spoke those words in a glum way, but then he put the necklace down and said he was so excited about the two-hour hike we were about to take. He'd taken it a few times on his own. The morning after he'd heard about Seamus, he got up at seven and did it. Uphill and downhill on a winding path through the trees. Then a shady, boggy laurel grove. After the grove, a broad dry riverbed that led to hilly meadows where a herd of Friesians grazed.

—Sounds like home, I said.

—Strawberry Fields, I call them, Jimmy.

—And nothing to get hung about, I said.

He reached across the picnic table and patted me on the shoulder then said we'd head out when Walter rang, though he wasn't waiting all day to hear from him, but he was terribly pissed at him for not ringing back last evening. Kevin had rung his foreman that morning. He did before he and Deirdre got into the car. The foreman said Walter hadn't shown up for work. Kevin rang the foreman again when he arrived back, right before he ordered the pizzas. Still no Walter. The foreman also said Walter hadn't done the job he was supposed to do, but then Kevin stopped talking about Walter and began to laugh about something Deirdre had said in the car. I forget what that thing was. And I forget one other thing about that afternoon, but in the seven years that have passed since then I've asked Deirdre on the phone many times, So you don't remember the thing you told your father in the car that made him laugh? But Deirdre doesn't, and she also forgets what she and her father talked about on the two-hour drive back, but she knows they had a great time, they stopped in Danbury and ate burgers and fries and drank Cokes under an umbrella, but Deirdre says she wishes she remembered the last thing her father said to her at the rest stop outside Hartford, when she got out of the car—her mother's car was pulling in a few spaces up—but Deirdre never forgets the noises in the trees when we sat on the rocks in the stream, and she says those noises came and went in her head when we were eating supper on the deck, and everyone was in high spirits, we were waiting to hear the whippoorwill, her father and I even took bets as to what time we might hear it—when he went inside and came back out with the whiskey bottle, we did—except that none of us heard the whippoorwill again, and Deirdre never forgets taking off the necklace and leaving it on the picnic table. But I had the necklace. I mailed it to her. Six days after that afternoon, I did, after she and I had talked on the phone for a long time, but her father's laughter drowned out Walter's feet on the gravel path and the deck stairs, though Walter was always so quiet. And it was me who saw him first. I did the moment he stepped off the top step. I happened to be facing that way. My face changed. Kevin was looking at me, still laughing then, still talking then. He saw the change and turned to look where I was looking.

—Well, speak of the devil, Kevin said.

The tattered backpack was strapped high on Walter's back. He wore the good shoes he'd worn on our drive with Zoë, and one of the shirts that Una gave me. Which shirt it was is the second thing I forget. Kevin stood up from the picnic table. Then I did. Kevin took a few steps toward Walter, stopped a few feet from him, and asked Walter if he'd like a slice of pizza, he'd heat one up in the microwave for him. Walter said he was grateful, but he wasn't hungry, and then he pushed up the bill of the Indians cap. He pushed it up high so that his forehead was exposed.

—So you didn't bother going to work today, Kevin said.

—I'm at work, man, Walter said.

He took off the backpack and laid it on the deck floor. He unzipped it a few inches, reached in, and took out a wrinkled brown paper bag. The sort you put your lunch in. He left the bag there at his feet, straightened up, and put the backpack back on.

—Killed your bird, man, he said.

—You killed what? Kevin said.

—You asked me to deal with the bird.

—I didn't say to kill it.

—What other way do you think there is, man?

—Well, there must be more than one of them.

—Get them others for you some other time.

—So what's the story about that other job?

—What about it?

—I talked to my foreman. That's your what about it.

—Won't do it, man.

—You get paid to do it. So you have to do it. Don't get on your high horse with me.

—Two kids. A woman. Didn't understand her, man. Don't know Spanish. Woman was crying, man. A kid in the crib. Kid was crying. She said the kid was sick. Couldn't work 'cause of the kid. Could say the word *sick*—

—We've a work order next week to install a new kitchen and bathroom in that apartment. Not a penny rent paid in three months. I looked after you. Didn't I? Don't I? And who do you think you are that you don't have to do your job? What fucking country do you think you're living in?

—Ain't doing it, man.

—There ain't no ain't about it. And I ain't asking you, I'm telling you.

—Ain't. And you're the devil, too.

—A figure of speech, Walter. A joke. Not an insult.

Kevin lowered his head. He shoved his hands into the khaki pockets and began to pace back and forth between Walter and me. He paced like a caged dog. Walter's eyes followed his. Then Kevin stopped directly in front of Walter, so that I couldn't see his face, and Kevin raised his head, turned sideways, and with his left hand pushed his hair back from his forehead, the way his father pushed his John Garfield fringe, pushed it back, but he didn't have his father's fringe. Didn't really have a fringe at all, his hair being short, but pushed it madly a few times, then shoved that hand back into his pocket, shrugged, and, in a cheerful way, he asked Walter if they might finish this conversation inside the house.

—Okay with me, man.

Kevin turned to me.

—Why don't you go for a walk, Jimmy. None of this business is yours. It won't take me long. I'll give you a shout when it's over. We'll go on that hike.

—I can bury the whippoorwill, I said.

He said nothing, having already turned. He was opening the sliding door. He stepped inside. Walter walked in front of me and stepped inside. Neither a look nor a word. Like I was not there on that deck. His sunburned face, the high forehead, and the noble nose I've never mentioned. Kevin slid the door to, without looking out. I heard him tell Walter to sit on the couch. And I heard him ask Walter if he'd like some coffee. He was making some for himself. I never heard Walter's reply, but the truth is that I wanted to get off that deck. And I was trying terribly hard not to think about the wrong and the right. And you still don't talk about the wrong and the right. You don't to Tess, Deirdre, Stephen, or Hannah, but what you did when you headed toward the deck stairs was tell yourself it wasn't about wrong and right. It was really and only about what people wanted, and people believed they deserved whatever the fuck it was they wanted. Americans did. Americans like me and Kevin Lyons—but you told Zoë. You did because Zoe didn't know any of them. And Zoë would understand. And so you and Zoë sat on her deck on weekend evenings that subsequent fall, and the maple leaves dropped slowly around you and turned red and yellow on the deck floor and you both smoked pot and drank whiskey. And one night after too much of those you confessed to Zoë that you didn't know anymore which part of it was the hardest for you to bear. The part when Walter took a gun out of his backpack in that front room and killed Kevin with one bullet to the head and then killed himself with one to his own. Or the part that you will never tell the others. Their row on the deck. What Walter the lunatic refused to do. And Zoë leaned over you and put her arms tightly around you and kissed your head and said, James, Walter was crazy. He'd lost everything, James. Crazy and violent, James. You were never really a part of it, my dear, you just so happened to be standing on that deck. And I admit I'm just happy you weren't in the room, my dear.

In so many words that's what Zoë said.

Zoë. Sweet Zoë. A name I then used to say quietly to myself. And I still conjure up Zoë. In the secret life, I do. Zoë, who at the end of that fall semester quit her English studies at the university, broke up with her boyfriend in Austin, and moved back east to live closer to her mother and father. Zoë enrolled at Fordham Law School. Zoë fights now for those on Death Row. And you quit the studies soon after Zoë did, but you stayed on in that town. You became an English teacher at the best local high school. A professor at the university who liked your work put in a good word for you. He and the high school principal were racquetball friends. And the week after you were offered the job, you met Emma on a Sunday afternoon at a book sale in the public library. She was holding four fat English novels that were written before 1900. You had three books on gardening. Emma looks a bit like Zoë in the face. But otherwise they are not alike. And not too long after you and she met, you left that flat on West Washington Street and moved in with Emma, who teaches math at a high school outside the town. And two years later you and Emma bought a house in the town. A blue two-story with three bedrooms, an unfinished basement, a roof and a driveway that need repairs, though there are lovely old shutters on the windows, a wide deck out back, a backyard that you both wish were bigger, but on all sides the maples shade it. And in what feels like the most contented of times you stand at the deck railing and stare into the splendid maples. And what you see then are glimpses of what you never did see. Seamus Lyons is prying open a tin of rat poison with a soup spoon in the lean-to at the back of his father's shed. His hands shake when he sprinkles the poison onto the stew. Tess and Kevin are sitting on a bench on the deck of the Holyhead ferry. A cold wind blows stinging seawater onto them. Their arms are around each other. And Walter unzips the backpack, reaches his steady hand in, stands calmly up from the couch, and levels the gun at Kevin. Kevin laughs. You must be fucking joking me, he says. And those words you imagine to be his last. And you bite your lip and turn from the deck railing, walk into the house, and stand next to Emma, kiss her, wipe down the countertop. Whistle while you unload the dishwasher. Add a little water to the rice cooker. Set place mats and silverware on the table. Change the music. And while doing all this you and Emma are talking. Though you are never talking about what you see when you stare into the maples. No. Friends are coming over for dinner. And that house wasn't blue when you bought it. You painted it a light blue before you moved in, and after you moved in you dug and planted a flower garden in the far corner of the yard. You never mentioned to Emma why you did any of that. Either way, Emma was delighted with it, but on that warm August afternoon I picked up Deirdre's necklace from the picnic table and dropped it into my pocket. Then I crossed the deck and picked up the brown paper bag and headed down the deck stairs. It was on my mind to walk down to the wall and ask Anton how the work was going. No. What was on your mind was to go down and tell Anton there was aggro between the two men in the house, and it was making you a bit nervous. I had paused on the middle step, was staring down at the sunny gravel. The reason I paused was because I wanted to go back and tell Kevin that the shirt Walter was wearing was a present from Una on my seventeenth or eighteenth birthday. But then you imagined Kevin looking at you like you were bonkers. Interfering.

—Why don't you go for a walk, Jimmy.

I stood on the gravel path. Sunlight through the trees made patches of the yard grass a vivid green. The grass was still flattened from where you and Deirdre had walked from the stream the evening before. Anton was lightly tapping a stone with a small hammer. His shirt was off. His back was to me. Lines of sweat ran down it. And I felt it wrong to disturb him. And so I turned to the miles of trees behind the house. The goat was grazing at the edge of them. It raised its head and stared at you. Then it bounded into the trees. And so I headed toward them.

I was standing in the fire pit when I heard the first shot—a big fire pit, perfectly round, with crumbling walls—and I was lifting out rocks that had fallen off the wall. The shot didn't sound the way I thought a shot might. It sounded like a beer can when you tear the ring back. Though I knew immediately what it was. And I was running toward the house when the second shot was fired. But then I stopped. Stopped, panted, swatted at the insects, stared into the quiet trees, and then went back to the fire pit. When I finished flinging out the rocks I gathered up armfuls of withered leaves and flung them out. The goat stood a few feet away. It chewed and stared. Anton's voice had echoed by then. My name shouted three times. But I kept at what I was doing, and for a minute or so I allowed myself the luxury of thinking that Walter and Kevin had stepped back out onto the deck. The whole thing was sorted out. Beers were opened. Cigarettes were lit. But there I was, on my knees, digging a grave with a flat sharp stone. The fire pit had no floor, and I dug through the layers of ashes from fires lit in the past. It took about fifteen minutes. It wasn't hard. I had this fierce energy for it. A square hole. Ten by ten. Twelve inches deep. I pared the walls with the stone until I was satisfied that they were straight. I wished I had a spirit level with me. And when I was done I stepped out of the fire pit and plucked a few maple leaves and the goat was still there and still looking at me when I knelt again in the fire pit and layered the grave with the leaves. I opened the lunch bag to the sound of the sirens. I took out the whippoorwill's body. It was about half of a body. No head or neck or shoulders. He'd blown those right off. Blown them off the evening before by the stream—but you go back and forth on that. Some days you think him, not the deer. Not so on other days. And when and if Deirdre brings it up you always say the deer—nevertheless, dried black blood on dull brown feathers. The body fitted the grave perfectly. I scraped the clay back in with the stone. I stamped the clay with my hand and put some more maple leaves on top and put the digging stone on top of them. Sirens still wailed. Then up from my knees and out of the fire pit. I said part of a prayer. One my father recited on his knees. I might have said more of it but I recalled only a part. The goat was gone. I headed into the trees. Away from the house. Hearing only the birds and the insects. Sunlight flashing through the branches like it did on the first day. I was thirsty. I might have drunk a beer. And I'd forgotten the cigarettes. Then the trees were behind me and I was standing near the edge of a wide ravine. I had no idea how long I had walked. I stepped right up to the edge and stared in. Sharp rocks, roots, bushes, and, far below, the thick treetops. I felt dizzy but kept on staring. The goat appeared a few feet away. It planted its hooves on the edge and looked out. It had no fear. My mother is walking through the field behind the house where I grew up. My father is at the top of the field. He is mending a fence next to the sycamore tree. We played in that tree when we were children. My father built a swing on it. Tess asked him to. My mother is taking my father a mug. The handle of the mug is broken off. She walks in a hurry. She forever does. The mug holds a raw egg and a corkful of whiskey. My mother took this to my father every day when he was working. My father is wearing his woolen pants with the suspenders. His shirtsleeves are rolled up. There is tangled white hair where his shirt is open at the neck. My mother is wearing an apron. Her hair is up in pins. It's August. And they talk about whether the rain will or won't hold off. My father looks at the sky and turns to my mother and says there's no fear of rain— there's no fear of rain, there's fear of rain, was the way he used to put it—and he drinks the contents of the mug in one swig and hands it back to my mother and puts his hand into his pocket and takes out a box of matches and his Sweet Aftons. He lights one. They talk about hay needing to be brought home from the meadow where the river is. She has jobs waiting in the kitchen. It's close to milking time. And she looks down at me and asks me kindly to go and turn the cows in. I can't remember what her face looked liked. Can't remember, but I stepped back from the edge of the ravine. Stepped back, unzipped my pants, and pissed over the edge, this long and lovely piss into nothing, while thinking about those who turned away from people and places. Dreamers. Recluses. Fools. Artists. Saints. Queers. Misfits. Lawbreakers. The goat was gone, for the last time. I turned back. I told myself to not forget the clock and the notebooks. And I didn't. I stopped for a while at the fire pit and looked down at the grave. When I came out of the trees a heavyset blue-eyed policeman walked quickly toward me and abruptly held his hand up. Three or four more policemen were standing on the deck, which was wrapped in the yellow tape. Police cars parked around the house like boats at a marina. Spinning sirens making no sound. I told the policeman I was visiting the guy who owned the house, and that I knew Anton. The policeman shook my hand. He was Anton's first cousin. Anton was at the morgue. He'd told his cousin about me. Said I must have gone hiking right after lunch. Then the policeman looked down, kicked at the grass with his right foot, rested his hand on his gun, looked up, and said that the body of the guy who owned the house was found on the large rug in the middle of the room and the other guy's body blocked the sliding door. They had to cut the glass out of the sliding door to get in. Gun was in the other guy's hand. And I turned from the policeman's flashing blue eyes to the deck and said that it was the most beautiful house I'd ever been inside.

Part Three

A month ago, around the middle of July, Una sent a brief e-mail. She was visiting Chicago for a few days in August. She gave the dates and the name of her hotel. Might I come and see her? I wrote back that I would, and wrote no more. Over dinner that evening I told Emma an old neighbor from home was visiting Chicago in early August, and I'd like to visit him. Emma said the timing was perfect. She'd visit old college friends in Pittsburgh.

Friday morning. August fifth. Emma dropped me off at the train station. We kissed and said we'd see each other on Sunday evening. I boarded the train. Emma drove on to Pittsburgh. A little over five hours later I walked out of Union Station, headed across the bridge then down past the shops on the Miracle Mile. Una's hotel was a few blocks northeast of there. The man at the desk rang her room. He put down the phone, told me the room number and the floor. I scribbled them on an index card. When I looked up he smiled and said she'd been expecting me to arrive sooner.

I walked along corridors of fat carpet, past flowers in vases on small round tables before oval mirrors. I knocked on the door. No answer. Knocked again. I pulled the index card out of my pocket. The right door, but the wrong floor. Three more up.

The door was ajar. A breakfast tray on a stand in the hall. A bagel on a plate. A folded white napkin. I tapped the door with my knuckles. She said to come in. I pushed the door in, stepped across the threshold, but did not shut the door. A large room. A stalwart bed, with all sorts of pillows piled high. She was standing at the window, next to a floor lamp and a leather armchair. Her back was to me. The light inner curtain was drawn. The heavy outer one was pulled back. Her shadow was on the inner curtain. The blurred outline of the tall buildings surrounded her. She was as tall as they were.

—I expected you sooner, Jim.

She did not turn. Her arms were folded.

—The train was late, Una. And I walked from the station.

—You know this city, Jim.

—I've brought students on day trips to one of the museums. So few of them see what's so beautiful about Cézanne's apples.

—I heard about you being a secondary school teacher, Jim. Do you like it?

—I do, Una. But how are you?

—Fine, Jim. I spent a few days in Boston with Kevin's ex and his two girls.

—I guessed you were there, I said.

—The two girls look like him, Jim. One is a bit mad. She was caught with hash or grass in school, but they're doing all right. His ex is very gracious. And I was treated like a terrorist at the airports. I could not abide living in this country, Jim, but Kevin's ex asked about you. I told her I was going to see you. She wishes you well. She thinks of you fondly.

—I met her the day after it happened, Una. She told me her plans for the cremation. She said that's the way Kevin would have wanted it, but she would hold off on the ceremony to give all of you a chance to fly over. She invited me to fly back for the ceremony. Offered to pay for the flight, but I told her it was best left within the family—

—We understood that, Jim. She and I drove down last week with the two girls to where we dropped my brother's ashes high above the wide river. Seven years ago this week, Jim, if you can believe it. The train went by like it did on that day. A mile-long train from end to end. The ex and I knelt on the rock and said prayers. So did the two girls. I left flowers there. Wildflowers I went and picked.

—You met Deirdre.

—I did, Jim. The ex arranged it. Deirdre is so fond of you.

—We keep in touch.

—She said you help her out with college.

—Deirdre needs no help from me.

—She says how lucky she was to meet you.

—We hit it off. Deirdre is the best.

—Oh, Jim, Tommy keeps telling me that Kevin and I brought all this trouble on the family and everyone else has to pay the price. He says we're the fault of Seamus—

She pressed her right hand flat against the window. I thought she was crying. I was about to go over. She took her hand away. She wasn't. I stayed where I was. She folded her arms.

—I'm sorry about it all, Una. I don't know what else to say.

—I know you are, Jim, but Tommy says Kevin and I could never get enough. He says we wanted what we didn't have, what others had that we didn't need, and we just went and helped ourselves to it. But Tommy would have become a priest, only our father made so much fun of him over it. I think Tommy's still bitter over it.

She undid her arms and turned from the curtains and switched on the floor lamp. I put my hands in my pockets and looked down when the light came on. Then I looked back up and pulled my hands back out. She was looking over at me. The father's eyes. No lipstick. The face lovely, but bonier. The hair straight, tightly cut, neatly parted to the left. A tight black suit and white blouse.

—How is your family, Jim? Sorry I haven't asked.

—Where should I start, Una?

—Your sisters, Jim. I remember them, and the younger brother who's away.

—Australia fits Stephen. It's like he was born there. Hannah rang two weeks ago to tell me Coleman Daly had died.

—The man at the Junction, Jim. My father never liked him.

—Hannah says he was dead in the house for a few days before anyone found him, but his funeral was the biggest she'd attended in a long time. And Tess is living with an English painter she met at art classes a few years ago. He was her teacher. They've moved to the Galway coast. Tess paints and works part-time in a restaurant. She's having an exhibition next summer. Emma wants to go over for it. I haven't made up my mind yet. But you're still in London, Una . . .

—For now, Jim, but I'm moving to Berlin in a month. I've bought a place there. It's a big loft. Very nice. But I can't sell the house I built at home. You can't sell anything there now. We're back down in the doldrums again, but I never even finished building the house, Jim. I only saw the plans. I thought it might be a lovely surprise not to see it till it was finished. I've no idea what I was thinking.

—Una's mansion of many rooms, I said.

—Is that what they call it there, Jim?

—So Hannah says.

—But I sold off some of the shops in London, Jim, so I'm fine in that regard, but remember that night in Dublin?

—Which night?

—Which one do you think? The last one, Jim.

—I'm sorry about that night. It came into my mind in the train.

—You don't need people that much, Jim, and I used to think back then that you were always living your life someplace else, but that night I followed you, Jim. You don't know that.

—I didn't.

—I tried to find you, and sometimes I think that if I'd found you that night it might all have all turned out in a different way.

—It doesn't matter, Una. You know it doesn't. And it wouldn't.

—You're right, Jim. Doesn't. Wouldn't. But you ran down the stairs. I put on my coat and followed you down. You banged the hall door and vanished so fast. Like into thin air. But I walked up as far as the North Circular, I don't know why I went that way, I must have looked up there and thought I saw you, but then I came back down and I ended up walking all the way up to Griffith Avenue. I pressed your bell for a long time, and I came back up Drumcondra Road and walked down the bank of the dark canal. I stayed out walking all night . . .

—But how's the mother, Una?

—She's strong, Jim. Tommy and her go to Mass every morning. But I've offered you nothing to eat or drink.

—I'm fine. I ate breakfast. And I'd a few doughnuts on the train.

—So are you going to come away from the door or not?

—I'll come away from the door if you come away from that window.

I turned and shut the door. We sat on opposite sides of the bed. The quilt was covered with drawings of red, yellow, and green leaves of all shapes and sizes. She reached her hand down and gently stroked the leaves.

—It's so lovely where Kevin's ashes were flung, Jim. There's a laurel grove close by. We walked through it. I took photos, and I took one of that long train. And boats going up and down the lovely river. My brother was such a brave man.

—He was, Una.

—No one could best him, Jim. He stood up to things. Stood up to people.

—That he did, Una.

—That man murdered him because he was jealous, Jim. Jealousy was the reason.

—That was the reason, Una.

—So you're in love with this woman, Jim.

—I've never been happier, Una.

—Live with me in Berlin, Jim. You and me. No one else. You don't need to live here anymore. This is a heartless country. I'm seeing someone in London, but we're not suited.

The hand stopped stroking the quilt. I reached my hand across and laid it lightly on hers. I didn't even think twice.

—I'll go with you, Una.

—We'll be very happy together, Jim.

—I know we will, Una.

—I miss you terribly, Jim.

—And I you, Una. I've never once stopped thinking about you.

We flung some of the pillows onto the floor.

Later we ordered up ribeyes, desserts, a bottle of champagne, and bottles of red wine. We never left the room.

I woke around ten the next morning. Woke to this old ache. One never too far away. One you never put a name to, but connected to there, and to them. And I dressed, packed, straightened Una's shoes, and did a mediocre job of tidying the room. My hand was on the doorknob when she spoke.

—You're leaving me, Jim.

—I have to, Una.

—I know you do, Jim.

I looked at my watch.

—A train leaves after twelve, Una.

—Won't you turn and look at me, Jim?

I shut my eyes and squeezed down hard on the doorknob.

—I want to very badly, Una, but I won't. I can't.

—I understand, Jim. We'll see each other again.

I opened my eyes and turned the doorknob.

—You never know what might happen, Una.

I saw him the moment I stepped out of the cab across from Union Station. He was leaning against one of the pillars. His back was to the street. People moved around him the way a rock diverts water. The worn and soiled backpack. The height, the build, and the stubborn gray hair. I crossed the street, went up the steps, and laid my hand flat on the backpack, like to surprise an old friend. He turned quickly. He was no more than thirty-five. I didn't know what to say. And so I asked if he needed money. Blurted not asked.

—Fuck you, mister. You're not from here.

He spat on the pillar then turned and vanished into the station. I went down to the footpath and smoked two or three cigarettes before I went inside. Then inside I discovered that the train to Michigan was gone, and there wouldn't be another for some time. But a train to New Orleans was leaving shortly. I eyed the stops. I'd been to Memphis, though not the other places. I wanted to visit Centralia, Illinois. I knew it from the Woody Guthrie song about the mining disaster that happened there in the forties.

My fingers are weak
and I cannot write,
Good-bye, Centralia, good-bye.

What was August like in Centralia? There were monuments to the dead miners to see. Was there a nice river? I'd walk around the town for a few days then get back on the train and head south to New Orleans. Such a shame I'd never visited there. And so I headed to the City of New Orleans platform, but I lost my way and found myself on the California Zephyr platform. This train went through the Rockies and ended up in San Francisco. I'd seen the Rockies once at night from a car window. Sarah was at the wheel, but I'd never seen the Sierra Nevada, Donner Lake, or San Pablo Bay. Those names sounded magical among the rushing strangers, like each one came at me like a javelin. But I somehow managed to purchase a ticket to San Francisco. When I returned from the ticket window, the train was boarding. I joined the line. I remember being eight people away from the man in the uniform punching the tickets. I remember when I was five. And when I was four. And when I was three. At two I slipped out of the line. This big dude behind me muttered something about some folks never being able to make up their darn minds. I looked him in the eye and said that immigrants were like that. Then I went and boarded the train back to that town in Michigan.

A NOTE ON THE AUTHOR

Patrick O'Keeffe was born and grew up in Co. Limerick, and moved to the United States in his twenties. His first work, a collection of novellas called *The Hill Road*, was published by Bloomsbury in 2005; in the US it won the prestigious Story Prize, in competition with such authors as William Boyd, T. C. Boyle, James Salter and Robert Coover. He currently teaches in the graduate creative writing program at Ohio University. He lives in Athens, Ohio.

A NOTE ON THE TYPE

The text of this book is set in Linotype Sabon, named after the type founder, Jacques Sabon. It was designed by Jan Tschichold and jointly developed by Linotype, Monotype and Stempel, in response to a need for a typeface to be available in identical form for mechanical hot metal composition and hand composition using foundry type.

Tschichold based his design for Sabon roman on a font engraved by Garamond, and Sabon italic on a font by Granjon. It was first used in 1966 and has proved an enduring modern classic.